"All this and Montana, too. Talk about treasure."   —*Kirkus Reviews*

"The best [Cassie Dewell novel] yet."   —*Booklist* (starred review)

"Excellent . . . Box has rarely been better in his plotting. . . . The story culminates with one of Box's most satisfying payoffs."
    —*Publishers Weekly* (starred review)

"Readers needn't be familiar with the series to appreciate this fast-paced mystery that pits betrayal, anger, and hate against hope and longing as it examines the lasting effect of a community used and abandoned after making a fortune for the titans of the copper mining industry."   —*Library Journal*

The Bitterroots

"Box's characters are well developed, his writing is vivid, the tension runs high, and the plot unfolds at a rapid pace."   —Associated Press

"C. J. Box has never lacked in talent for writing rugged frontier-type heroes, like Joe Pickett and Nate Romanowski, who've helped define the postmodern Western. His Cassie Dewell character is all that and more. . . . A tour de force."   —*The Providence Journal*

"One of Box's best."   —*Kirkus Reviews*

Paradise Valley

"Excellent . . . Box keeps *Paradise Valley* taut, with twists that are as suspenseful as they are believable."   —*The Washington Post*

"[Box has] crafted fascinating characters and put them in riveting, challenging circumstances that test their mettle and threaten their worlds."   —*The Durango Herald*

Badlands

"Absorbing . . . strong and compelling."   —*Star Tribune*

"Suspenseful—you can't put it down." —*Library Journal* (starred review)

"The unrelenting cold makes this the perfect beach read."
                                                             —*Kirkus Reviews*

The Highway

"A violent, tension-packed, well-written thriller spiced with Box's vivid portrayal of the Western landscape."   —Associated Press

"Be warned: This is one scary novel."   —*The Globe and Mail*

"*The Highway* is the summer's most terrifying novel. . . . Prepare to be scared."   —*South Florida Sun Sentinel*

"Get off the genre interstate and take *The Highway*."
                                                             —*Billings Gazette*

Back of Beyond

"A roller coaster ride of unexpected twists and turns . . . Box's characters are so real that you want to reach out and shake their hands or flee from them as fast as you can."   —Associated Press

"One of the best mysteries of [the year]."   —*The Seattle Times*

"Once again, Box provides the complete suspense package."
                                                             —*Kirkus Reviews*

"Terrifically entertaining stuff that comes together with a bang in the end."   —*Booklist*

TREASURE STATE

A CASSIE DEWELL NOVEL

C. J. BOX

MINOTAUR BOOKS
NEW YORK

Published in the United States by Minotaur Books, an imprint of St. Martin's Publishing Group

TREASURE STATE. Copyright © 2022 by C. J. Box. All rights reserved. Printed in the United States of America. For information, address St. Martin's Publishing Group, 120 Broadway, New York, NY 10271.

www.minotaurbooks.com

Designed by Meryl Sussman Levavi

The Library of Congress has cataloged the hardcover edition as follows:

Names: Box, C. J., author.
Title: Treasure state : a Cassie Dewell novel / C. J. Box.
Description: First edition. | New York : Minotaur Books, 2022. | Series: Cody Hoyt / Cassie Dewell novels |
Identifiers: LCCN 2022016380 | ISBN 9781250766960 (hardcover) | ISBN 9781250768032 (ebook)
Subjects: LCGFT: Novels.
Classification: LCC PS3552.O87658 T74 2022 | DDC 813/.54—dc23/eng/20220407
LC record available at https://lccn.loc.gov/2022016380

ISBN 978-1-250-88955-3 (trade paperback)

Our books may be purchased in bulk for promotional, educational, or business use. Please contact your local bookseller or the Macmillan Corporate and Premium Sales Department at 1-800-221-7945, extension 5442, or by email at MacmillanSpecialMarkets@macmillan.com.

First Minotaur Books Trade Paperback Edition: 2023

10 9 8 7 6 5 4 3 2

For the good people of Anaconda and Butte, Montana.
And for Laurie. Always.

For where your treasure is, there will your heart be also.

Matthew 6:21

I am in love with Montana. For other states I have admiration, respect, recognition, even some affection, but with Montana it is love, and it's difficult to analyze love when you're in it.

John Steinbeck, *Travels with Charley*

There is a smile of love,
And there is a smile of deceit,
And there is a smile of smiles
In which the two smiles meet

William Blake, *The Pickering Manuscript*

one

EIGHTEEN DAYS BEFORE

Private Investigator J. D. Spengler of Tampa Bay, Florida, was taking the highway exit from I-90 West onto Montana State Highway 1 when he was blinded by the setting sun and he ran over something big enough on the road that he nearly lost control of his rental car.

Thump-thump.

It happened in the late spring evening just as the fireball of a sun started to slip behind the mountains. The sun ballooned as it did so and he'd reached up and lowered the visor so he wouldn't have to stare right into it. That's when he glimpsed something dark and bulbous appear right in front of him on the asphalt.

Thump-thump.

Spengler eased off to the shoulder of the highway while applying the brake. Delineator posts shot by the passenger window as he decelerated and one clipped the outside mirror but not hard enough to break the glass.

He came to a stop and took a deep gulp of air. He felt a wave of prickly sweat wash through his scalp and crotch. His heart raced and his breath was shallow.

A quick glance at the rearview mirror revealed the dark lump behind him on the road. It was too small to be human, for which he was immediately grateful. It was some kind of animal. He hoped it was wild and wasn't a loose dog that belonged to a local. Whatever it was, it wasn't moving.

There were crumbs from on-the-go fast-food meals on his lap and J. D. Spengler brushed them off with his hand before he released the seat-belt latch. He didn't like living in a car but it was too often part of the job. Because of that, he was careful to keep the car as clean as he could and not clutter it up. The rental guys appreciated that but he didn't do it for them. He did it for himself because he didn't like to think of himself as a pig. He wished he didn't look so much like one with his huge belly, thick limbs, round face, and upturned nose.

He knew what people thought when they met him. He'd heard it all his life. He'd once heard a client describe him as having "porcine features." That stung.

Spengler grunted aloud as he pushed the door open. He was stiff from being behind the wheel the entire day. He was too fat, he knew that, and he was uncomfortable. Every movement seemed to hurt these days. The car was cramped as well. He'd need to talk to his employer, yet again, about springing for a roomier SUV if she was going to continue to send him to places like this.

As it was, Spengler drove a shadow-gray 2021 Chevrolet Malibu four-door with Idaho plates. It was the most boring car on the highway, he thought. The only advantage to the rental was its absolute anonymity. He wished the rental had local Montana plates with their "The Treasure State" nickname so he would be able to blend in even further. Instead, he was stuck with "Famous Potatoes."

He got out and stretched. The heat was palpable, but the air was dry. It smelled of spring, something he recalled from his youth in Pennsylvania.

First, he walked to the front of the car to see if there was any damage. There wasn't, aside from the nick on the mirror, but he would have to see if the left front tire was out of alignment from the collision. It was likely, he thought. Then he noticed the long needle-like projectiles that bristled from the rubber side of the tire. He squatted down and touched them. He'd buy a set of pliers at a hardware store and pull them out later, he thought.

He walked around the car and slowly back along the highway. The fields on both sides of the car hummed with insects. The air was thin and he breathed in deeply to get more of it. Spengler guessed that one of the reasons he was sweating was because of the lack of oxygen at this altitude. He hoped he didn't overwork his lungs or have a heart attack so far from home.

The dead porcupine was still. Its quills glistened in the hard light of the late afternoon. Black blood snaked out from beneath it to form rivulets on the surface of the road. He could see dull open eyes, yellow teeth, and yellow claws. Fleas teemed through its coat.

He sighed. Porcupines were his granddaughter's favorite animal. Spengler didn't know why. She called them "porky-pines" and had dressed up as one the previous Halloween. Her mom, Spengler's only daughter, had attached a dozen brush-heads to the back of her costume using Velcro. It wasn't very imaginative but he'd said nothing at the time. His heart broke when his granddaughter cried and told him people thought she was a space alien, not a porcupine.

He thought about taking a photo of the dead animal and sending it to his granddaughter but he couldn't find an angle where it didn't look dead. So he gave up on that idea and lumbered back to his car and got in.

It was beautiful country if you liked mountains, a huge blue sky, poor food, and too much distance between towns, he thought. He was not a mountain person. He was not a wild animal person, or an *outdoor* person. He liked his sun to sizzle into the ocean while he had his first cocktail rather than have it hide behind a mountain and create dramatic shadows on the contours of the terrain.

Although it had been hot and dry the entire day, he was startled by how quickly the temperature dropped on the digital display when the sun vanished. He attributed that to the elevation as well: five thousand, three hundred feet above sea level. His condo back home was at *eight feet* above sea level. This was ridiculous.

He checked for traffic. Seeing none, he pulled back onto the highway.

As the interstate receded in his rearview mirror, Spengler realized how suddenly alone he was on the two-lane. There were no oncoming cars and none behind him. The only thing on the road was the dead porcupine. The fields on both sides were covered in grass—hay, he supposed—and mountains dominated the horizon on all four sides. As wide open as it was, he felt oddly hemmed in.

A towering smokestack reached up into the heavens to his left. That was all there was, just a smokestack high upon a tawny hill. No buildings, no plant, not even an obvious road that led up to it. There was no smoke coming out of it. It looked like it was a thousand feet high, a middle finger extended straight up into the sky.

Then, as he drove, he noticed a sign on his right for a turnoff to the small burg of Opportunity. A few miles later, on his left, was a turnoff for Wisdom, Montana.

"Fuckin' A," he said aloud to himself with a bitter smile. "I passed both Wisdom *and* Opportunity. I just whizzed on by. Is this some kind of a joke?"

As he neared the town he noted the massive mountain of coal-black debris on his left. What was it? It was bigger than several city blocks and the surface of it glistened in the waning sun.

The smokestack was even with him now, high above the black mountain. It was so high he couldn't see the top of it from the driver's side window. He imagined that with a low cloud cover the top of it couldn't be seen at all during the winter months.

He drove on.

The town came into view in front of Spengler. It was nestled into a valley, packed in there ahead with tall vertical hills on both sides as if to keep it in place.

Before he entered the town limits he eased to the side of the highway onto a small pullout. Spengler dug his phone out of his shirt pocket and opened the text app.

As she insisted, he'd kept his client apprised of his movements and progress over the last five weeks. He did it via text because then she didn't have the chance to clutter up his time with asking questions. He kept his messages terse and pithy.

Their method of communication had evolved since the early days of the case.

With his thumbs, he typed out:

Still in Big Sky Country. Got some good intel and I'm closing in. I think I'll locate him tomorrow. Will keep you posted.

The attractive little WELCOME TO ANACONDA display passed by on his right and Spengler felt a kind of melancholy relief. He was close, all right. He could feel it in his bones. He snapped a photo of the sign on his phone and forwarded it to his client.

The journey had been much longer than he'd anticipated, and it had certainly been more harrowing. What he'd uncovered still astonished him.

Miami, Boston, New York City, DC, Chicago, Seattle, LA, Santa Monica, Sun Valley. And he doubted he'd discovered all of the victims.

Only his client wasn't surprised. She urged him to keep going and she'd paid his three-thousand-dollar retainer and his ninety-dollar-per-hour rate once he blew through it, plus travel and mileage expenses. She'd turned into his cash cow and although it was lucrative, Spengler was tired of travel. He wanted to go home.

Tomorrow, it should all be over.

First on his agenda, though, was to find a motel, then a bar, then a restaurant. He doubted there would be women available in a town this size, but he could check a few websites and maybe ask around. Spengler was perfectly okay paying for companionship. He was away from home, after all. Plus it was cleaner all around without built-in deceit or obligations afterward. But the smaller the town, the less opportunity there was. This place was probably too dinky for working girls to flourish, he thought. Meaning another night in a strange bed watching YouPorn on his iPad.

He drove by Smelter City Skate Pit. There were some kids out there, zooming around.

The town itself was, he thought, equal parts charming, homey, and appalling. It didn't *look* like the Montana of his imagination with cowboys, cowgirls, hikers, and fly fishermen resembling Brad Pitt in *A River Runs Through It*.

Instead, Anaconda looked like a western Pennsylvania steel town picked up and dropped into the vast mountains of Montana. The streets were lined with tightly packed single-dwelling houses; solid little bungalows sometimes no more than a foot apart. Most were in good repair, but some appeared ready to collapse into a heap.

A scrum of high school kids stood around outside a Dairy Queen and he saw a sign that read: ANACONDA—HOME OF THE COPPERHEADS.

The downtown was mostly composed of aged brick buildings that must have been something back in the day, he thought. Most of them now looked repurposed into something else. Or boarded up entirely.

Many of the homes and small businesses had ANACONDA STRONG posters in their windows. He wondered what *that* was about.

He drove through the community until he realized he was out of it already. Then he made a U-turn and went back in.

The smokestack dominated the southeastern view. It glowed like a beacon as the last of the sun climbed up its bricks.

Anaconda, Montana. Population nine thousand, one hundred and forty.

J. D. Spengler had no idea he'd never leave this place alive.

two

⊷⊶◉⊷⊶

Two weeks later, on June 2, a hundred and eighteen miles to the east, Cassie Dewell cruised through Bozeman Pass on I-90 toward town. The sharp timbered canyon walls prevented the evening sun from reaching the surface of the road, and she kept her eyes out ahead of her as she took sweeping turn after turn. She knew from growing up in Montana that this was the magic time of dusk when deer, elk, and sometimes black bears appeared on the highway in the canyon. In her thirty-eight years on earth she'd dodged them all at one time or another.

Since her Jeep Grand Cherokee was barely six months old, she wanted to preserve it the best she could. Hitting an animal would be bad news all around. Plus, she'd promised to be home in time to cook dinner for her sixteen-year-old son, Ben. And for her mother, Isabel, who would probably not want to eat whatever she prepared.

Cassie had spent the entire day doing surveillance on a narrow leafy street in the north part of Livingston, twenty miles away on the other side of the Bridger Range. Her client was Great Northern Insurance, and the man she'd been hired to observe was named Rupert Skeeze.

From the internet research her agency had done on him, Cassie had learned Rupert Skeeze was a longtime local who'd bounced between Livingston, Gardiner, Belgrade, Big Timber, and Belfry picking up jobs on highway construction crews. He wasn't a skilled heavy-equipment operator. Instead, he worked as a flagman. He never seemed to last very long with any particular company and he languished through most winters drawing unemployment.

The summer before, Skeeze had been working for Beartooth Construction on a stretch of two-lane state highway along the Clark's Fork near Belfry ("Home of the Belfry Bats!") when he claimed he'd been injured by a careless pilot car driver who'd made a sloppy three-point turn after leading a caravan of motorists through the work zone. Skeeze maintained that the young pilot car driver, who was also the son of the owner, had clipped him as he stood on the shoulder with his flag and handheld radio. The accident had hurt his back, he said, and he'd sued for damages as well as lifelong disability payments. After the incident, Skeeze said, he could no longer work at his chosen profession.

The owner of Beartooth Construction disputed the claim not only because there were no witnesses and the driver was his son, but also out of principle. It was a clear-cut case of insurance fraud, he claimed. Beartooth's insurance company hired Dewell Investigations in Bozeman to observe Rupert Skeeze in his native environment to prove or disprove the severity of his injury.

Skeeze lived in a modest three-bedroom home set back from the street. Since his Dodge Ram pickup was in the driveway, Cassie assumed he was inside. She'd parked her Jeep a half block from Skeeze's home on the same side of the street in front of a home with an overgrown lawn and a FOR SALE sign in its front yard. She'd chosen that place to park because it was vacant. In a small town like Livingston, one didn't park in front of an occupied house and therefore draw suspicion from the occupants.

She'd spent the day observing his residence in her rearview and side mirrors instead of straight on. If Skeeze was wary about observers—as he *should* be—he'd look for strange vehicles with a clear view of his residence from where they parked. Meaning through the windshield or side window. Skeeze likely wouldn't pick up on a parked car facing the wrong way down the block. And if he did see her car, he'd see that the person behind the wheel was an overweight woman pushing forty and dismiss her. That's what Cassie had hoped, anyway.

She turned out to be right.

This kind of surveillance was usually long, boring, and tedious. She spent the day listening to true-crime and history podcasts and chastising herself for finishing an entire package of chocolate chip cookies. Cassie was constantly opening and closing the windows in her Jeep in a quest for a cooling cross breeze. She got a headache from watching Skeeze's home through the slightly distorted mirrors of her car.

Then, at four thirty in the afternoon, just as she was calculating how much longer she'd stay before heading home to cook dinner, Rupert Skeeze appeared. Not out the front door as she'd anticipated, but out the back. He was tall and rangy and dark, and it looked like he hadn't bathed or shaved for a few weeks. He wore a dingy wife-beater and stained cargo shorts and he was carrying a can of beer.

His outfit alone made Cassie dislike him. When he wheeled a lawn mower out of a shed in the back and vigorously yanked on the cord to start it, she affixed a zoom lens to her digital camera and clicked it into place. Then she turned on her seat and rested the barrel of the long lens on the top of the headrest so she could shoot photos out the back window.

Skeeze finally got the mower started with a cloud of blue smoke. The whine of the engine cut through the still silence of the afternoon.

She watched and snapped photos as Skeeze cut his lawn. He did so with power and grace, and he showed some athletic ability on each corner when he deftly turned the mower and practically danced behind it. At one point, the blades hit a rock or some other kind of hazard and he jumped back as if bitten by a snake.

Click-click-click-click.

When he was done with the back lawn, Skeeze paused and drained his beer. Then, as if adding the coup de grace to her assignment, he went into the shed, came out with a basketball, and shot a series of jump shots on a backyard hoop. She got a particularly good action photo of him lunging for his own rebound.

Click-click-click-click.

Before leaving, Cassie reviewed dozens of photos in her camera to make sure they'd turned out well. She wasn't disappointed.

Great Northern Insurance and Beartooth Construction should be pleased, she thought. Rupert Skeeze would soon be in a world of well-deserved trouble. He'd be exposed as the cargo-short wearing deadbeat that he was.

She'd certainly earned her fee. And she'd be home on time. For once.

Cassie took the Main Street exit into Bozeman from the interstate when she cleared the canyon. It was a sultry evening and after the long winter she powered her windows down to drink in the air.

Locals and tourists were out downtown, and the bars and restaurants had taken their tables and chairs out from storage and set them up outside. Cassie had recently relocated Dewell Investigations from a small dumpy two-room rental house to a larger upstairs suite of offices at 28 W. Main Street, directly above the Country Bookshelf. Downtown Bozeman had a kind of carnival atmosphere in the summer, something she wasn't yet used to. Parking was an issue, but since there were so few walk-ins in her business it wasn't a problem for clients.

As she passed her building—it was next to the Lovelace Building with Wild Joe*'s Coffee located conveniently next door, she glanced up and was surprised to see that the lights were still on at Dewell

Investigations. Had the last to leave forgotten to turn them off? Or was somebody—either her mother or her new intern—working late?

Then she saw a shadow pass by the shaded window of her office near the corner of the building. Someone was in her office after hours. Which, for the most part, ruled out Isabel or the intern. There was no good reason for either to be in her space.

Cassie drew her phone out of her bag and speed-dialed Ben at home.

"Hey," he said. She still was surprised how deep his voice had become.

"Is Isabel there?" Her mother was the only person she knew who refused to use a cell phone. Isabel was suspicious of technology in general and she worried that phones transmitted electromagnetic pulses that would make her become ill.

"Yeah, she's here."

"Okay, just checking."

"That's why you called?"

"Yes."

"That's weird, Mom."

"Yes, it is," she said and punched off.

Could it be her intern? Cassie doubted it. She'd yet to give her new employee a key. She looked at her phone contacts and realized she hadn't yet entered the intern's number.

She decided not to call the police. It would be embarrassing if the intruder turned out to be a janitor or building maintenance worker. They hadn't occupied the floor space long enough for her to know what evening cleaning was done.

Plus, Cassie had an uncomfortable relationship with local law enforcement. Both the Bozeman police and the Gallatin County Sheriff's Office would rather she wasn't around. They distrusted private investigators in general and perhaps Cassie in particular. She'd felt the same way toward PIs when she worked for law enforcement in Lewis and Clark County and also in North Dakota.

PIs, in her opinion at one time, were shifty and dedicated mostly to discrediting the work of dedicated cops. Now she was on the other side of the fence.

Like everywhere she'd been, cops talked, and cops stuck together. It wasn't any different in Montana. The fact that she'd brought down the local sheriff in Lochsa County two years before was well-known. So was the fact that she'd shot and killed a Montana highway patrolman in self-defense.

Her past exploits, especially bringing down the Lizard King, had turbocharged her reputation when she applied for and received Montana PI license number #7775. Business was good but the police were wary.

No, before calling law enforcement, she'd check out who was in her office first. If it was a break-in, she could hold the perpetrator until the cops arrived.

Cassie drove around the block and turned into the alley and parked in an alcove directly behind the building. Her office suite came with two assigned spots. There wasn't a vehicle in the other one. Instead, there were two scruffy slackers in outdoor-themed clothing getting high. They beat it when she pulled in.

Before climbing out, she retrieved a gear bag from the passenger-side floor. In it were her standard tools of the trade: handguns, Taser, canister of pepper spray, Vipertek mini stun gun, zip ties, flashlight, binoculars, and digital recorder. She selected the subcompact ten-round .40 Glock 27 in its holster and clipped it on her belt.

Cassie was dressed as she always was when working in the field. Jeans, tooled cowboy boots, a flowing light jacket over a cotton V-neck top. The jacket helped to conceal the firearm on her hip.

She climbed out of her Jeep and shut the door and looked up at the rear windows of her office suite. There was no one up there looking back at her.

The building itself was halved by two sets of stairs, one from the front entrance and one from the back. They met on the landing of the third floor. On the third floor, Dewell Investigations was to the left and an accounting firm was to the right. Both outside doors locked automatically at 6 P.M., but anyone inside the building could exit at any time.

Cassie fished her key out of her pocket and entered the back of the building. She activated the audio recording app on her cell phone so she could document anything she said—or the intruder said.

As the door wheezed closed behind her she heard the muffled thundering of footfalls on the stairs going to the front door. Someone was in a hurry to leave the building but she couldn't see who it was.

She ran up the stairs as quickly as she could to try to catch a glimpse of the intruder, but she wasn't fast enough. Cassie paused and stood on the landing breathing hard. She looked down the other set of stairs. All she saw was the door closing and she heard an audible *click*. The door to Dewell Investigations still hung open a few inches, confirming that someone had been inside.

Cassie raced down the stairs to the front entrance and nearly crashed headfirst when her right boot heel caught on the edge of a step. She kept herself upright by reaching out and bracing herself against the wall and she felt a sharp pain shooting through her right wrist.

Then, gathering herself, she descended the rest of the way and pushed the door open, almost hitting a hipster who was strolling down the sidewalk looking at her phone.

Cassie looked both ways on the sidewalk while the hipster glared at her and made an exaggerated loop around her. There were people in every direction, some looking into the open door of the bookstore, others sipping coffee and window-shopping. No one obviously hurrying to get away.

She scanned the street to see if anyone was climbing into a vehicle to drive away. Every parking space was occupied but the cars
were empty.

She sighed loudly. Whoever had run from her building had either ducked around the corner before she got there or had melded
seamlessly into the crowd.

Wearily, Cassie again climbed the stairs. Her wrist throbbed with
pain. She was grateful she hadn't been forced to draw her weapon
because she wasn't sure she could have gripped it with confidence.

She pushed the door all the way open and stepped inside. Dewell
Investigations had a simple floor plan: a couch in the waiting area
just inside the door, two desks in the main room, and her office in
the back. Like the entrance door, it wasn't closed all the way. She
knew she'd shut it that morning as she left for Livingston.

There was no obvious damage inside but there was no doubt
someone had been there looking for something. File drawers were
open and desk drawers gaped.

Cassie carefully circled the two desks out front before entering
her office. If anything had been stolen she couldn't determine what
it had been. The files in the cabinet looked like they'd been rifled but
it was impossible to know if any had been taken. Would Isabel know?

Cassie guessed she wouldn't. Isabel wasn't known for her attention to detail when it came to filing. Or anything else, really. The
intern was too new and unfamiliar enough with procedures that
she would likely not shed any light, either.

How had the intruder gotten in? Cassie examined the lock and
she could see no signs of forced entry. Meaning they were expert in
the art of picking locks or they had a key.

Cassie guessed the latter. There had been many tenants of the
suite before Cassie found it. There had been lawyers, accountants,
and others. She had not thought about changing the locks when

she rented the space. How many keys were out there, she wondered? She knew that the first thing she'd do the next morning was to contact the building supervisor and get all the locks changed. And install closed-circuit cameras.

She drew her weapon and held it out in front of her with both hands, then used her hip to nudge her door completely open. There was no one inside but her computer monitor glowed. They'd obviously tried to access her digital files but they'd been unsuccessful because the password screen was still up.

She holstered her Glock and sat behind her desk and keyed her password into the computer. It had not been accessed since that morning before she left for Livingston. All of her files were there that she'd left open, including all of her current cases. She was grateful her password wasn't "password."

The intruder *may* have found what he was looking for, she knew. He or she could have removed documents but left the files intact, or photographed them so they wouldn't have to carry anything away.

The intruder must have seen her pull in the back, she thought. She'd interrupted the search and they'd run out of there in a hurry.

She tried to guess what the intruder was looking for. There was a lot of incriminating information on individuals they'd investigated, as well as files, field notes, and reports for scores of past cases. If someone was looking for dirt on her clients or past targets they could find it.

There were several open cases at the moment that might be of interest to the intruder, she thought. One in particular had turned out to be quite high profile. That case might be big enough and include enough valuable privileged information that it might be worth breaking into her office to obtain.

Cassie slid open her bottom right desk drawer and found the manila folder file titled "Sir Scott's Treasure."

She rifled through it but could find nothing missing. But she couldn't be sure unless she checked the documents against the log sheet.

Because she was rattled by the intrusion and already running late, Cassie gathered up the Treasure files to take home. She could access the digital log sheet from her laptop later.

It seemed almost silly to close and lock the door to her office, she thought. It was obvious someone out there knew how to get in. But she turned off the lights and locked it anyway. She stretched a thin strip of clear adhesive tape from the bottom corner of the door to the doorframe. If someone opened the door using a spare key, the tape would break.

She speed-dialed the Bozeman PD on her way down the stairs to her car.

Cassie explained to the dispatcher what had happened and the dispatcher asked if she should send over an officer.

"That's not necessary," Cassie said. "I've locked up the place and I won't know until tomorrow if anything is actually missing."

"Do you have a description of the intruder?"

"I didn't actually see him—or her," Cassie said. "All I know is that they're faster than I am."

"What would you like us to do in the meanwhile?" the dispatcher asked. She sounded slightly annoyed, Cassie thought.

"Just keep an eye on our floor during the night," Cassie said. "If there are any lights on up there it means the intruder has come back."

three

✦═◈═✦

Still rattled from the break-in and an hour later than she'd planned to be home, Cassie entered her house from the garage with a bucket of fried chicken, containers of coleslaw, and a bag of biscuits from KFC. Her mother, Isabel, looked up from where she was reading the *Bozeman Daily Chronicle* at the dining-room table. When she saw the large plastic bag of fast food she cringed.

"Don't say it," Cassie said. "I'm not in the mood."

Isabel had long gray-white hair parted in the middle and she wore flowing caftans and sandals. She hadn't applied makeup in forty years. The style she'd adopted so long ago had come back into fashion, especially in the new Bozeman.

Isabel lowered the paper. "Not only is the food you brought home processed, those chickens lived the cruelest lives possible at their factory farms. They're trapped inside cages and force-fed until they're taken away to get slaughtered. Many arrive at the slaughter-house with broken bones from being picked up by their legs by workers and jammed into containers. Their little throats are cut by machines and they're dipped into scalding water while they're still conscious."

"So you've told me, Isabel."

"I think I'll make myself a salad."

"Please do."

"I thought you were cooking tonight."

"I'm late because someone broke into the office."

That took a second to register. "What? Why?"

"I don't know the answer to either question," Cassie said. "Did you notice anyone suspicious hanging around the building when you left tonight?"

Isabel creased her brow and thought it over. "No." Then: "Maybe it was that new intern."

Cassie rolled her eyes. Her mother and the new hire had clashed almost immediately. It was amazing how quickly her mother could irritate people. But she was good on the phone as a receptionist and Cassie didn't know what she would have done without her to be with Ben when Cassie was working late or out of town. Plus, Isabel *was* her mother. They were stuck together.

"I doubt that," Cassie said in response. "We're installing new locks and cameras tomorrow, that's for sure."

"Was anything taken? *Did they take my plants*?"

"Why would anyone want your plants, Mom? And no, I couldn't determine if anything is missing. We'll need to do a complete inventory tomorrow."

"Do you think it was someone trying to find food or shelter?"

Cassie wasn't surprised her mother went there so quickly. In Isabel's worldview, 99 percent of the US population struggled from hunger, homelessness, poverty, racism, and the greed and humiliation of heartless megacorporations. If someone broke into Dewell Investigations it was probably because they had a good reason, in other words.

"I doubt the intruder was looking for food in our filing cabinets," Cassie said.

"Oh dear."

Ben entered the dining room from the hallway. "I thought I smelled fried chicken." He grinned.

Ben had grown six inches taller in the last year and he was already a head taller than Cassie. He was a strapping boy with dark hair and an open face and he looked more and more like his father, US Army Sergeant Jim Dewell. Cassie's husband and Ben's father had been killed in combat in Afghanistan. Ben had his father's facial expressions and loping gait and it gave Cassie a slight chill because Ben had never even met his dad.

Ben was a junior at Bozeman High School, where he wrestled, ran track, and worked as a sports reporter for the high school paper. He ran with a good crowd, Cassie thought, and she had no reason not to be proud of him. Her biggest fear over the years was that Ben would suffer from growing up in a household with no men in it to serve as a role model.

Cassie had had men in her life, but she never brought them home. She had vowed to herself never to do it until she was sure the man was, in fact, the one.

But Ben had turned out fine, she thought. Ben was gentle, empathetic, and thoughtful. Those were qualities he *hadn't* inherited from his father, but Cassie never told him that. Ben wanted to think his dad was a hero in every regard, and she'd never hinted otherwise.

The three of them talked about the break-in while eating dinner.

"Do you need some help going through everything tomorrow?" Ben asked. "You know—trying to figure out if anything you were working on was compromised?"

"What about school?" Cassie said.

Ben shrugged. "Those teachers made me wear a mask for two years. I don't owe them anything."

"That's a bad attitude," Isabel interjected. "It was for your safety and for their own health."

Isabel had reveled during the pandemic and Cassie suspected

that she missed it: the masks, the social distancing, the judging of others.

Cassie winked sympathetically at Ben and said, "Are you sure you don't have an ulterior motive for coming to the office?"

Meaning the new intern from Wyoming. The girl was older than Ben by five years and she was a recent graduate from a community college in her home state. She was a brash cowgirl and rough around the edges, but there was no doubt she was attractive: blond, green-eyed, outdoorsy. Cassie had been charmed by her when she gave the reason she'd applied for the paid internship as wanting to "get garbage off the street." Her new intern reminded Cassie of herself at around the same age.

When Ben dropped by the office he was instantly smitten. Now, his face flushed red at Cassie's question.

"Geeze, Mom," he said.

"You can do better," Isabel said to him in a huff. "*Much* better."

"I'll let you know if we need any help," Cassie said.

After dinner, Ben went to his room to do homework and Isabel sat in front of the television watching MSNBC.

Cassie placed the "Sir Scott's Treasure" file on the table and opened it. The very first item was an eight-by-ten digital photo taken of a poem scrawled onto a whiteboard at an old-school lounge and steak house called Sir Scott's Oasis in Manhattan, Montana. Apparently, the "poet" had entered the closed establishment after hours through an unlocked rear door and left the poem. The perpetrator, according to restaurant staff, had erased the specials of the day and substituted the poem itself. It was written with a dry-erase marker and the handwriting was elegant.

Before diving in, Cassie grumbled and reached for a pair of readers and put them on. It was a concession to age she hated to admit, and she was constantly misplacing reading glasses and buying new ones. Readers within constant reach was just one more thing that complicated her life.

The poem read:

Sir Scott's Treasure

In the twilight of my being
I've filled the chest with gold,
And placed it in a special place,
That fate and time foretold.
Begin where the rivers marry
And take the hidden trail,
It's not obscure or buried,
Stay in the shadows and you will prevail.
From there you'll have to summon strength
The walls are closing in;
Depending on the season,
You may have to wade or swim.
If you've been smart and found the burn,
Look west to spy the treasure,
Then pick it up and take it home,
And be wealthy beyond measure.
Many will ask why I won't say more,
And why I hid my riches,
The answer is I've done my time on earth,
And taxmen are sons of bitches.
So listen hard and dream my dream,
And begin your quest with muscle,
If you are wise and full of grit
My fortune is your puzzle.

The Treasure case was easily one of the strangest assignments Cassie had ever taken on. It had begun a month and a half before when a call was placed to her office. Isabel fielded it and announced over the intercom: "The man wants to talk only to you. He has a very strange voice and he won't give me his name."

Cassie had frowned while she connected the call on her handset. She noted that the caller ID read UNKNOWN.

"Cassie Dewell," she said. "Who is calling, please?"

He laughed and said, "If I told you that there would be no point in hiring you." His voice was odd and tinny and she guessed he was using software that altered it.

"Excuse me?"

"Miss Dewell, I've been following your career from afar and I've done some discreet inquiries in Montana and North Dakota where you've been. My inquiries confirmed my thesis that you're the best around."

"Thank you for the compliment. What can I help you with?"

"I'd like to hire you in the hope that you *don't* solve the case. In fact, I want you to fail." Then he chuckled.

"What's this all about?" Cassie had asked. "You're wasting my time. I ask because if you don't provide more information—*like your name*—I'll hang up this phone."

"First let me ask you a question," he said. "Have you heard of Sir Scott's Treasure?"

She was obviously thinking along the same track but she didn't reveal it. "Of course. But I have no interest in finding it. I doubt it even exists. So with that I'll say goodbye. There are plenty of other PIs out there so I'd suggest you call them."

Again, the annoying chuckle. He said, "Don't hang up until you at least hear me out."

"You're on the clock," she said.

"What is your rate?"

"We charge a hundred and fifty dollars an hour with a thousand-dollar retainer. That doesn't include expenses."

Cassie was purposefully increasing her actual rate by fifty dollars an hour to put him off.

"I'll have two thousand dollars sent to your office this afternoon to get you started. You accept cash, I assume."

"For what?" Cassie asked.

"I don't want you to look for the treasure," he said. "There are too many people on that quest as it is. What I want to hire you for is to try to find out who hid the treasure and wrote the poem. It's my thesis that if one of the treasure hunters finds out the identity of who hid it they'll be able to figure out where it's located much more easily."

Cassie was suddenly intrigued. Since the poem had appeared two years before at Sir Scott's Oasis, thousands of people—no one knew how many—had been in search of the gold. It had become a big thing in the mountain west primarily but also in locations around the country and overseas. People quit their jobs to look for it and some spent their entire vacations scouring the countryside.

Sites on the internet were devoted to "Sir Scott's Treasure" and every word of the poem had been analyzed for true and hidden meanings. Cassie had overheard treasure hunters talking about the poem and speculating on every line. Because the poem appeared in Manhattan and contained lines including "Begin where the rivers marry" and "Look west to spy the treasure," most of the hunters thought the treasure was located in Montana. Others thought that conclusion was based on red herrings and that the gold was actually hidden in Wyoming, Idaho, Utah, or Colorado. Rumors circulated that the poem itself was bogus and there was no treasure at all.

That's when a post appeared on a popular treasure website from someone claiming to be the person who had hidden the gold and written the poem. The poster urged that the hunt should continue and it included a tightly cropped photograph of an open chest filled with gold coins. Internet sleuths determined that the post had been sent from a public computer located in a library in Billings, Montana. The user couldn't be identified.

"Are you one of the treasure hunters?" Cassie had asked the caller.

He laughed again and said, "No. Not at all. I'm the man who hid the gold and wrote the poem. I'm hiring you to try and find me."

She sat up and raised her voice so that Isabel turned around in her chair. "*What*?"

"It's true," he said. "I got this whole thing started. I think it's wonderful. I think I've covered my tracks well enough that none of the treasure hunters will be able to figure out who I am. My fear is that if one of them does they'll look into my history and know where the gold is hidden. I don't want it to be found that way because it isn't fair to the others. I want them to find the gold by parsing the clues in the poem. I want it found legitimately, not because they know who I am and have therefore traced my history and writings."

Cassie noted the word "writings" and tucked it away without comment.

She said, "Let me get this straight. You're hiring me to try and find you but you hope I fail. Do I have that right?"

"You have that perfectly correct," he said. "If you're able to find me then it's very possible a treasure hunter can do the same. But if you're unsuccessful, which I hope you will be, the hunt for my treasure will remain pristine."

"Your treasure hunt has caused the death of at least five people," she said. "It should stop."

People had perished by plummeting down canyon walls or drowning while swimming across rivers. State and federal authorities had put out pleas urging the end of the treasure hunt.

"Ah," he said, "every one of those deaths is a tragedy. I mourn for their families. But frankly, the individuals who died were wildly off base in their search. They were reckless. I'm not saying they deserved to die, not at all. But the careful, thoughtful treasure hunters shouldn't get cheated by me calling off the search. Many dedicated people have put weeks and months into this treasure hunt. One of them will find it. I'm sure of that. And whoever does find it the right way will deserve every penny."

"How much is the gold worth?" Cassie asked.

"Three and a half million dollars, give or take," he said. "The value fluctuates based on the price of gold, of course. Right now it's quite pricy."

"Are you really telling me you could afford to hide three and a half million in gold?"

"It's worth it to me just for the fun and adventure of the thing," he said. "Who doesn't love an actual treasure hunt? It reminds me of pirate treasure and sunken ships. This is the stuff of boyhood dreams, really. I can't wait to shake the hand of the person who finds it."

"How will they contact you?" she asked.

"Now I'd consider that a question from a clever private investigator on the job," he said with a laugh. "Don't worry about that. If the treasure is found and I authenticate it, I'll contact the lucky person and congratulate them myself. I don't mind going public at that point, but not before. And if the lucky person asks me to keep it all confidential for tax purposes or some other reason, I'll honor that request as well."

"How do I know that you're who you say you are?" Cassie asked.

"Oh, you don't. You either trust your instincts or you don't. Either way, I'm paying you your exorbitant hourly fee. I'll even add a bonus of twenty-five thousand dollars if you show up at my location and we shake hands. It's worth it to me to find out where I might have slipped up."

"This is insane," Cassie said. "This isn't what I do. I do skip tracing, asset searches, background checks, fraud, criminal defense investigations, domestic cases, and surveillance. I don't try to learn the secret identities of my clients."

"See," he said. "You're already thinking of me as a client. So I think we're getting somewhere."

"How do I contact you?"

"I'll send you details."

He terminated the call and left her flummoxed.

That afternoon, a manila envelope marked "Dewell Investigations" arrived at her office. Inside was two thousand dollars in hundred-dollar bills. The person who delivered it worked at the coffee shop next door and she said she found it taped on the door of Cassie's building with "Cassie Dewell, Esq." written on the outside. The barista didn't see who had left it there.

Also inside the envelope was a scrap of paper with a website address for the Alberta Beekeepers Commission. Under the address, in the same elegant handwriting she recognized from the whiteboard poem, were the instructions: "Use the name Cassie Buzz-Buzz and be vague and discreet. I'll respond as King Bee."

She'd called up the site and registered using the Cassie Buzz-Buzz handle. No further information was required. It appeared to be a very legitimate chat forum dedicated to amateur and professional beekeepers throughout the province of Alberta, Canada. There were questions about how to maintain hives in winter, parasites, honey extraction, and other bee-related topics.

Cassie typed a very simple message as Cassie Buzz-Buzz: "I'm so glad I found this forum."

The next day, among the responses welcoming her to the community, was one from King Bee. It read simply, "Welcome to the mysterious world of bees."

Cassie had done very little further on the Treasure case since the envelope arrived except to think about it. Thinking, in her profession, was working.

She'd placed the money in a dedicated escrow account and had not drawn a penny against it in case she decided to return it in full.

She'd decided that she needed more verification on her "client" before proceeding full bore. She had plenty of work on her docket as it was.

She also concluded that it was good strategy on her part to lay low and wait for the man to get impatient enough to contact her again. She'd ignore the beekeepers forum and wait for him to call. When and if he did she'd be ready this time and she'd be prepared to try to smoke out his location or at least get more personal information like "in my writings."

Cassie would also see if she could obtain authorization from a friendly judge and local law enforcement to trace the origin of the next call when it came. Although the first contact was likely made from a disposable burner phone that was discarded after the initial call, it would be extremely helpful to find out where the next one was placed to her even if the client got rid of the burner afterward.

During ongoing weeks of the waiting game, Cassie saw an item on the internet that mentioned that a second post had appeared on the Sir Scott's Treasure hunters forum allegedly by the man who had claimed to have hidden the treasure and written the poem. She called up the site to read it.

The post was addressing persistent rumors that the gold didn't exist and that both the poem and the treasure were frauds.

The post read:

Listen hard and dream my dream, people.

The treasure is real and it's waiting to be found. It is not a hoax. That is why I posted a photo of it in this forum. You will find the gold by parsing the clues. No other methods will work. I know this because I've hired the best professional investigators in the country to prove me wrong and so far they can't. The hunt for the treasure should be pristine. Have fun with it. Who doesn't love an actual treasure hunt?

Cassie instantly noted the similar phrases in the post to those used by the man who had called her. "Parsing the clues," "pristine," "Who doesn't love an actual treasure hunt?"

It was the same person, she was sure. The man who hid the gold and wrote the poem was the same man who had called her office. Either that, or he was the perpetrator of an enormous and cruel hoax that involved keeping the fraud alive for years while people died trying to find the nonexistent treasure. He'd also paid her two thousand dollars to try to find him. If it was indeed a hoax, he didn't mind throwing cash at it to keep it alive. Cassie thought that was unlikely.

Had he actually engaged the services of other "professional investigators" as well as Cassie? If so, she found it annoying. Her waiting game strategy was hatched when she thought she was the only PI involved. He might not become as impatient if he had, in fact, employed others. Also, she didn't like the fact that he revealed publicly that he'd done it because it might result in calling attention to her firm.

Which might have been the reason someone had broken into her office. If she later learned that was true, she thought, she'd charge the client expenses for installing cameras and changing the locks.

While she opened a bottle of wine and thought it over, she came to a couple of working theories that seemed to fit the facts as she knew them.

One, the man who called her office was more than likely the same man who wrote the poem, sent her a retainer and the note, and posted to the treasure hunters forum.

Two, an obsessive treasure hunter might very well have read the second post by the perpetrator and decided to break into Cassie's files and find out what she knew about the identity of the client. Thus the break-in.

Three, her client was much more patient than she'd thought he'd be. Since she'd accepted the retainer and gone silent he hadn't reached out to her again.

Four, although there was no way to be sure, her client was likely from Montana. There were several facts pointing to that. Sir Scott's Oasis was locally recognized as an old-school out-of-town steak house (Manhattan was twenty miles away from Bozeman and a much smaller town), it wasn't a tourist stop or known much outside the area. The restaurant would be an odd choice to post the poem to someone who wasn't already aware of it.

That he said he'd done research on her was significant as well, she thought. Her name was fairly well-known in the state and somewhat in North Dakota for the high-profile cases she'd cracked in both places. But beyond those locations? Not likely. She'd been chosen for a reason, and she surmised it was because she was Montanan.

The retainer had been taped to her door. That meant he had physical access to her location. Although he could have been passing by later in the day that he first called her, it suggested he didn't have to travel far. An accomplice could have delivered it, sure. But would a man this secretive about his identity have an accomplice?

Then there were the clues in the poem itself. Although Cassie hadn't become obsessive about the clues in the poem as so many treasure seekers had, there were indications in it that the treasure was hidden in a state with mountains, canyons, and seasonal rivers or creeks. Montana had them all in spades.

Fifth, Cassie Buzz-Buzz was no closer to finding out the identity or location of her "client" than she was when she started.

four

Cassie arrived at her office early the next morning and breathed a sigh of relief when she found the door still locked. She checked the strip of tape. It was still attached. There were no additional indications of intrusion.

She went inside, got a cup of coffee from the Keurig machine, and went into her office. She'd come to treasure the first hours of her day. It was quiet and she could get her head together before Isabel arrived and the downtown block woke up.

She opened her window to the cool mountain smells of pine. With Yellowstone to the south, the Bridger Range to the northeast, and the Tobacco Root Mountains to the west, there were lots of trees. The air was thin and sweet and it reminded her of growing up in a much more rural Montana.

It was early summer and there weren't any forest fires yet. Considering how dry the season had started out, there was no doubt they would come. Soon. Sometimes she wondered if the fires would run out of timber to burn.

Cassie located her readers in the bottom of her purse and wrote a quick email to Great Northern Insurance about her surveillance of Rupert Skeeze the day before. She was attaching the most representative action photos of him when she heard rapid footfalls coming up the stairs. April entered wearing her backpack and she stopped short in the lobby. Her eyes were opened wide.

"What happened here last night? Why are the drawers all open?"

"We had a break-in," Cassie replied. "Give me a second to finish this and I'll catch you up."

Cassie sent the email and got up from her desk. April had been given a small desk on the east wall in the lobby. Cassie had purchased the desk, the chair, and the computer secondhand. She'd learned how expensive it was to employ even a low-paid intern.

"Let me ask you something," Cassie said to April. "Did you see anyone suspicious hanging around the building when you left last night? Maybe somebody who looked out of place?"

April laughed. "Half the people out on the street in Bozeman look suspicious to me. This is quite the crazy place, but I think I like it. But no, I don't remember seeing anyone odder than usual."

Cassie nodded. April came from a small mountain town in north-central Wyoming called Saddlestring. She found the name charming.

April was dressed in cowgirl-chic style: tight bejeweled jeans, boots, a tight tank top beneath an open yoked shirt. She had an impressive belt buckle for winning All-Around Cowgirl at the Central Wyoming College Rodeo.

"I wanted to ask you about that last night," Cassie said. "I realized I didn't have your cell phone number in my phone."

April whipped her phone out of her back pocket and sent a message to Cassie's phone. Cassie heard it *ding* on her desk.

"Now you do," April said.

"I'd like you to spend some time right off going through your desk and especially everything you've got on your computer," Cassie said. "Make sure nothing is missing. Check to see if any files were accessed last night after you left. If you find anything, let me know right away."

"I don't have much to access," April said with a grin. "I just got started."

"You've got all those past case files I asked you to review."

April smacked herself on the forehead with the heel of her hand.

"Oh yeah, right. I didn't think of those. I was reading up on the Lizard King yesterday afternoon. That's an *amazing* story. Good God!"

Cassie nodded.

"Do you have any idea who broke in or why?" April asked.

"I've got my suspicions but no facts to back it up yet."

"Who is the perp?"

Cassie stifled a smile. "I'll let you know when I can confirm it. In the meantime, I've got a couple of assignments for you."

April swelled up with obvious excitement. This was the first time she'd been given a specific task since she'd started the week before. Her time had been spent reviewing case files and doing clerical work for Isabel.

"Won't that piss off Isabel?" April asked.

"Probably, but don't worry about that. I'll deal with her."

"Thank you. I don't think she likes me very much as it is."

"You two have different worldviews, I'm afraid."

"I'm fine with her, by the way," April said. "She's just an old hippie. I learned to live with them at college. I had teachers like Isabel. It's best just to put your head down and let them spout their nonsense. If you argue with them they'll give you a D or worse."

Cassie said, "I'd like to put you in charge of locating the best locksmith in the county and getting them here as soon as possible. Also, contact a few security companies and ask them to come by and give us a bid for closed-circuit cameras. Make sure to check their references."

"I can do that," she said, nodding. "In the meantime, do you want me to rig up something that might stop the next guy?"

Cassie frowned. "Like what?"

"I was thinking we could set up a trip wire about six inches high on the floor just inside the door. We could wire it to the trigger of a double-barreled shotgun aimed chest high."

To demonstrate where the blast would hit, April placed both of her hands on her chest. "That'd stop him."

"That would get us put in the women's prison in Billings," Cassie said. "Let's concentrate on the locksmith and the security company, okay?"

"Yes, ma'am. I'll get right on it. Was there another assignment?"

Cassie nodded. "I'll need a list of writers who live in Montana."

"Writers?"

"Authors, I should say. Fiction, nonfiction, technical. Male only. Include screenwriters, I suppose. It'll be a long list."

Cassie once overheard a well-known mystery writer pontificate from his corner bar stool in Missoula, attempting to woo a young female grad student. The author, who looked like a cross between a buffalo and a walrus, said, "In Missoula if you throw a stick you'll hit a goddam writer. I wish more people would throw sticks."

"Where will I find this list?" April asked.

"Start with the Montana Arts Council in Helena, the state capital. They might have a list. If they don't, someone there might be able to help you find one."

"I'll get to work," April said.

The call from Candyce Fly of Boca Grande, Florida, came two minutes later. Cassie took it directly because Isabel, whose job it was to act as receptionist, was late to show up as usual. Cassie liked the optics of having a receptionist fielding calls because it suggested her firm was more established than a one-woman show.

"I'm sorry to call so early," she said. "It's what, three hours earlier than Florida time?"

"Two hours," Cassie said. "We're on mountain time. It's the forgotten time zone. A lot of folks don't know it exists."

"Oh my. So it's eight there?"

"Yes."

"It's ten here."

"Okay."

"I'm calling to speak to Cassie Dewell, please."

"I'm Cassie Dewell."

"Oh. I guess I didn't expect you to answer your own phone."

Cassie scowled and said, "As you mentioned, it's early here. Our receptionist isn't in yet."

"Oh, that makes sense. Tell me, do you Zoom?"

"Of course," Cassie said. "We can do that even in Montana."

"Tell me your email address and I'll send you a link," the woman said. "I like to see who I'm hiring. My name is Candyce Fly, by the way."

That's presumptuous, Cassie thought but didn't say. She gave the woman her email address and hung up. The link showed up ten minutes later in her in-box.

Candyce Fly was blond and willowy, with a deep tan and a face so taut from skin-tightening procedures that it was almost masklike. Cassie guessed her age at late fifties, early sixties, but it was hard to be certain. Fly was obviously a stylish woman who kept herself fit and she could afford cosmetic fixes that preserved her in a vague kind of amber. Only her green eyes were animated.

She wore a pink sleeveless golf top and behind her was a well-appointed home office with framed photos on the wall. No books. Visible on the top of the screen was the bottom slice of a gold and crystal chandelier. When Fly spoke there were rat-a-tat flashes of perfect big white teeth. Candyce Fly had obviously set up the angle of her webcamera and had positioned interior lighting so it looked like she was speaking from the set of a television studio.

Despite Fly's inability to display emotion, Cassie thought she saw a hint of disappointment in her eyes when she first viewed Cassie on *her* screen. Cassie's background was a flat white wall with her framed PI license on it. The direct morning sunlight from the window made every wrinkle in her face stand out. She wished there was a webcam filter that would make her look twenty pounds lighter.

"Miss Dewell, I'm interested in hiring you to locate a con man named Marc Daly. That's Marc with a *C*. I believe he's in your state of Montana."

Cassie jotted down the name on a pad to indicate she was listening.

"Marc Daly is a grifter and a charlatan and he *must* be stopped," Fly said.

"How about we start at the beginning," Cassie said. "When did you meet him and what do you allege that he did?"

"There's no alleging about it," Fly said. "He stole millions of dollars from me and then he vanished from the face of the earth."

"I'm not trying to argue with you. I just need the facts as you know them, please."

That seemed to satisfy Candyce Fly. She sighed deeply and began. Cassie surreptitiously reached over and slid her digital recorder across her desk and placed it beneath the monitor of her computer. She wanted an audio record of the conversation in case she missed something in her notes. Since Fly had initiated the Zoom session, Cassie was unable to record it herself.

"What were your questions again?" Fly asked.

"When did you meet Marc Daly."

"Last February. The end of February. I don't know the date. Is that important?"

"I don't think so but go on."

"I met Marc the first time at the Lemon Bay Golf Club. I try to play a round every morning before it gets too warm or too many people show up. Ask anyone around here. If you want to find Candyce Fly, go to Lemon Bay early in the morning."

"Okay," Cassie said.

"Have you ever been to Boca Grande, Miss Dewell?" Fly asked as she tried to arch her eyebrows.

"No, ma'am."

"It's an interesting place. Boca Grande is a cute little island with a lot of wealthy residents and truly spectacular homes where people drive around in golf carts. It's a small town, really. Everybody knows everybody and what lots are available rise in value every year. What I'm saying is that not just anyone can show up and get a tee time at Lemon Bay."

"I'm not sure I understand your point," Cassie said.

Fly started to explain, but apparently couldn't find the right phrasing. Instead, she said, "Let's just say Marc didn't look out of place at Lemon Bay. He didn't look like a tourist who just walked in from the street. He looked like he belonged."

"Gotcha. So what happened?"

"I hit a good drive on the third fairway—one of the long holes—and I couldn't find my ball at first. All I knew is that it landed near a pond but not in it. I didn't see a splash. So I was walking along the edge of the pond when I saw my ball sitting there in the weeds about *three feet from a great big alligator!*"

"Goodness," Cassie said.

"Yes, I know. That's a very real hazard here that I'd say you don't have to worry about in Montana."

"No," Cassie said. "We have grizzly bears, rattlesnakes, and mountain lions. But go on."

"Well, I was standing there trying to figure out what to do when a cart drove up. The man driving it was alone as well, and I thought he was going to ask if he could play through. But when he saw my predicament he laughed and he said, 'If you'd like me to, I'll wrestle that alligator to get your ball back.' He was quite ... charming, I must admit."

"This was Marc Daly?"

"Yes, but I didn't know his name at the time."

"Did he get your ball back?"

"He did. But he used one of those telescoping pole-like things you use to get balls out of the water. He didn't wrestle the alligator or anything."

Cassie thought, *If this were a movie this would be called a meet-cute.*

Instead, she asked, "What happened next?"

"He drove off."

Cassie paused. "He didn't introduce himself or ask your name? He just drove off?"

"Yes."

In her peripheral vision, Cassie noted the flowing robes of Isabel as she came in the door. Isabel placed both of her hands on her cheeks as she surveyed the open filing cabinet and desk drawers. Cassie got up and eased her door closed.

"Where did you go?" Fly asked.

"Just closing the door so I can concentrate. Please go on. When did you see him next?"

"Two nights later. I was waiting for a table in the bar of Gasparilla Inn. He walked through the lobby and saw me and stopped. He asked if I had any more alligators that needed wrestling."

"So he remembered you."

"He certainly did. And I remembered *him*," she said. Cassie thought she saw Fly almost blush.

"Describe him, please."

"He's a quite good-looking man," Fly said. Her description of him was so precise and so detailed that Cassie almost stopped listening. On her pad, she wrote: "Sandy hair, great jawline, mustache, blue eyes, six foot two, well-built, muscular, wonderful smile. Good dresser."

"Do you have any photos of him?" Cassie asked.

"That's a very strange thing," Fly said. "He always seemed to avoid being in photos, like when we were in a group and someone wanted a shot. He'd be in the bathroom or something and miss it. I did have a few of the two of us on my phone, I'm sure of it. But he must have somehow gotten my phone when I wasn't looking and deleted them. I have a couple of blurry shots my friend Trixie took but they aren't very good. We were kind of far away on the dance floor when Trixie took them. I sent them to the last private investigator."

"Excuse me," Cassie said. "The last private investigator?"

"Yes, I probably should have mentioned that. You're the *second* private investigator I've hired to locate this snake. The first one, like Marc, seems to have vanished as well. He was in daily contact and closing in—or so he claimed—when all of the sudden he stopped communicating. No texts, no calls. And he hasn't sent me any invoices for expenses, either. That leads me to believe that something happened to him or he's too embarrassed to admit that he failed."

"Hmm," Cassie said. "First, you haven't hired me yet because I haven't accepted the case. Second, it sounds pretty suspicious that your first guy in is the wind. When did you last hear from him?"

"Two weeks ago," Fly said. She picked up her cell phone. "I can read you the last text he sent me on May nineteenth."

She did.

"Still in Big Sky Country. Got some good intel and I'm closing in. I think I'll locate him tomorrow. Will keep you posted.

"He sent me this photo," she said. "Here, I'll forward it to you."

A second later Cassie's in-box chimed and she opened up the graphic.

"Anaconda?" Cassie said. "He was headed into Anaconda?"

"That's as much as I know," Fly said. "I didn't know it was a real place until I looked it up. It sounds kind of . . . snakey to me."

"It's a real place," Cassie said. "It's off the beaten path but I've been by there many times. It's a little less than two hours away from me."

When Cassie thought of Anaconda the first thing that came to mind was the lone standing smokestack off in the distance from the interstate. The first time she'd seen it was on a high school basketball trip many years before. One of her friends giggled and said it looked phallic. She could never quite shake that description in her mind.

The second was Anaconda's colorful and tragic history. It had once been one of the state's most important locations and had been in the running to be named state capital. Anaconda's past was filled with labor strife, copper mining tragedies, federal occupation, and violence. She'd heard Anaconda—and Butte, just a few miles from it—had defined Montana's hardwired anticorporate heritage in both good and bad ways. It was known as an extremely tight-knit and insular community that was still hanging on years after the copper smelter was shut down.

"Have you contacted the authorities in Anaconda to look for your guy?" Cassie asked.

"I didn't but his office did," Fly said. "The sheriff's office there took down the missing person report but never called back. As for me, I kept waiting to hear from him. Now it seems kind of stupid since it's been so long."

"What's his name?"

"J. D. Spengler. He's out of Tampa. He came highly recommended."

"Have you followed up with his office since?"

"Yes, about a week ago. The girl there said she hadn't heard anything from him, either. But she also said it wasn't that unusual when he was in the field."

"It sounds suspicious to me," Cassie said. She circled the name J. D. Spengler on her pad several times.

"I don't know what to think," Fly said. "But that's not why I'm hiring you—to find an overweight private investigator from Tampa. I want you to find Marc Daly."

"Got it, I understand. Why was Spengler going to Anaconda?"

"I don't know for certain. He didn't fill me in on any details other than he thought he was closing in on Marc, like I said. Spengler was in Montana for three or four days doing interviews before he vanished."

"Interviews with whom?"

"I don't have any names."

"Can you please send me the transcript of the texts he sent you?"

"Does that mean you're taking the case?"

Cassie had gotten ahead of herself and she regretted it. She was really more interested in the disappearance of a fellow PI than in Marc Daly. But she didn't want to say that to Candyce Fly.

"We can circle back to Mr. Spengler later," Cassie said. "Let's go back to your relationship with Marc Daly. What happened after you encountered him at the hotel?"

"I was dining alone, you see. Since I lost my husband to cancer four years ago I do that quite a lot now. We were close. We were partners in the largest real estate company on the island as well as in life. It took me ages to summon the courage to go out by myself after I lost Dick. But now I'm more comfortable going to dinner or to a movie—or to play golf. So it wasn't unusual."

Cassie tried not to be distracted by the fact that Candyce was married to a man named "Dick Fly."

"Did Daly ask to join you?"

Fly hesitated a moment. Then: "I asked him to join *me*."

Cassie found that interesting but refrained from saying it.

"We had a lovely dinner together," Fly said. "Maybe too much wine, but very lovely. He passed himself off as a very interesting man and I admit I was quite taken with him. Later, when I look back at it, there were red flags all around me. But I didn't see them at the time."

"What do you mean by red flags?"

"Look, I've had quite a few men hit on me over the years, especially since Dick passed. And, honestly, some when he was still alive. It's no secret around here that I've done very well for myself and there are plenty of predators targeting rich and lonely women on an island like Boca Grande. But I'm sure you know how most men are when they meet you. They can't stop trying to impress you by talking about themselves. Marc didn't talk about himself at all. He asked me about *me*. And he listened."

"That is unusual," Cassie agreed. It was one of the primary reasons she rarely, if ever, went out by herself when she wasn't on a case. But she guessed Candyce Fly had many more such encounters.

"When it came to Marc's history, I literally had to pry it out of him," Fly said. "He'd make little self-deprecating jokes about how it was better to be lucky than good, that kind of thing."

"What did you find out?"

"Only what he finally told me," Fly said. "He made several passing references to being the principal of a hedge fund. He said he was tired of traveling so much between New York, Atlanta, and San Francisco and that he really enjoyed the slower pace of life here in Boca Grande. When he learned about my background in real estate he asked if he could impose on me when it came to buying a place here. I readily agreed."

"Did he buy a home?"

"No. I think that was all for show. It was a way of indicating to me that he had the means to buy one."

"Were there other red flags?"

"Yes. He always paid cash for everything he bought. I thought it was quirky at the time but I now realize he was probably doing it so there'd be no credit card receipts. I mean, who pays with cash these days?

"Also, Marc never looked at his phone. You know how people are these days, especially wealthy financial-services types. You can't even get them to look up. But not Marc. I don't know if I ever even saw him use his phone."

"Did you call and text each other?"

She hesitated again. "Yes, we did."

"So he had a phone."

"Yes."

"Did you send each other photos?"

This time, Fly did blush. She said, "A couple. But the ones he sent me . . . wouldn't really identify him, if you know what I mean."

"He sent you explicit photos?"

"Yes."

"Was that another of your red flags?"

"No," she said. "I asked him to."

"Oh."

"Look, Miss Dewell," Fly said. "I'm not stupid. I'm not naïve. I feel like an incredible idiot even telling you all of this. I know I sound like a love-struck teenager when I talk about Marc. I know that.

"But it had been decades since someone made me feel the way Marc made me feel. *Decades.* Dick and I had a very convivial relationship but there hadn't been passion like this for years and years. In the end, we were more like siblings or good friends than husband and wife. Marc made me feel giddy when I was around him. I said and did things that make me cringe when I think of them now. Like the photos. Look, I'm not hiring you to put me on trial."

Suddenly, Candyce Fly's expression contorted and she looked as though she'd swallowed something sharp and bitter. Tears, like snail tracks, coursed down over her cheeks and she looked away from the camera lens and brutally wiped at them with the back of her hand. It was as if something had just snapped inside her and the mask she'd so carefully maintained had dropped.

"Are you okay?" Cassie asked.

"I'm fine," Fly insisted. "I'm just fine."

You don't seem fine, Cassie thought.

"Can we please just get on with this?" Fly asked, turning back to her camera. Her mask was again firmly in place, and Cassie had no idea what had just happened.

"As I said, I don't want you to put me on trial here."

"I'm not trying to do that," Cassie said. "I'm just trying to get as many facts and pieces of evidence as I can so I can do my job. Did he tell you the name of the hedge fund he managed?"

"He said it was called Empire Capital. I Googled it and it looked legitimate. He was listed as the president."

With that, Fly deftly brushed her hair back in place and reassumed command. Cassie let it go.

"But he wasn't?" Cassie asked.

"Like everything, he was lying about that. But I just didn't know it at the time."

"What do you accuse him of doing exactly?" Cassie asked.

Fly sighed. "Well, I told you he rarely said much about himself, so it was really odd one night when we were in bed that he seemed distracted. That was out of character because—and I'll ask you to hear this in complete confidence—Marc was a magnificent lover. Warm, sharing, *very* skilled in bed. He made me feel like no one has ever made me feel. But on that night it was obvious there was something on his mind."

Cassie nodded for her to go on.

"Finally, he said something at work was driving him crazy. He'd identified a start-up in Silicon Valley that he was sure was going to be the next Uber or Airbnb, but his partners didn't agree with him. It was something about a new way of manufacturing batteries for electric cars. He said there was some kind of agreement among the partners that they all had to be unanimous when making a large investment, so the money Marc had available in his venture capital account wasn't enough to make the deal by himself. He said he'd never been so sure of an opportunity before and it was upsetting to him that he couldn't pull the trigger on his own."

Cassie saw where this was headed. "How much did you offer to go in with him?"

"Seven million," she said. "I actually offered ten but he said seven would be enough. I realize now that by trimming it down he'd seem more credible. And he tried several times to talk me out of it. He said he didn't want to risk our relationship if something went wrong. That meant everything to me at the time."

"You paid him how?"

"He gave me the details to an offshore account in the Caymans. I wired the money. He said we had to do it that way so his partners wouldn't know."

"Did you do any due diligence?"

Fly shook her head sadly. "I was so wrapped up in Marc the details were secondary," she said. "I thought at the time it would bring us closer being business partners as well as a couple. I was *such* a complete fool.

"Marc said he needed to fly out to California to close the deal and that's the last I saw or heard from him," she said.

"Before he vanished, Spengler did quite a bit of research on Marc Daly and Empire Capital," Fly continued. "In a nutshell, neither one actually exists."

"Can you send me his reports?" Cassie asked. "I'd like to see them."

"Of course, but only if you agree to take the case and we have a contract in place. I hope you understand."

"I do. But you can tell me what he found out."

Fly sighed. "The website for Empire Capital turned out to be a complete sham. According to Spengler, it was put up the month before I met Marc. The account in the Caymans was closed the day after my money arrived there. Even the cell phone number Marc gave me was bogus as it turned out."

"He used a burner, I suspect," Cassie said. "That's why he never let you see his cheap phone."

"Exactly."

"Spengler found a few hits when he searched his name using some kind of special people-finder database," Fly said.

Cassie was familiar with the methodology. Her firm subscribed to several such database services. They were expensive but essential to her job.

Fly continued, "He said Marc had sprinkled his name around in financial news articles that turned out to be bogus. They were designed to be located with a casual Google search, but when Spengler tried to verify them he found out the sources were phony. If you didn't know they were fake news, you'd be taken in. Like I was."

Cassie said, "You're suggesting Marc Daly did quite a bit of prep work before you met him. Do you think he was specifically targeting you?"

"Yes. He knew where to find me on the golf course. But I wouldn't be a bit surprised that he's done this before," Fly said. "Conning women who should know better."

Cassie shared Fly's outrage now that she knew more.

"I'm intrigued," Cassie said. "But before I officially take the case, I've got a few other questions for you first. And a lot more later depending on how you answer."

Fly peered with concern at her webcam. "What?"

"I need a better idea of what you hope I can achieve," Cassie said. "If I find him do you want him arrested for fraud and a half-dozen other crimes? Do you want him put in jail here and extradited to Florida to stand trial?"

"I want revenge," Fly said. "I want him to be humiliated like he humiliated me. If I can get my money back, all the better. But most of all, I want him brought down so he can't do this to another woman in the future."

Cassie doubted her sincerity on the last one, but it sounded good and she withheld comment. She said, "I'm not a cop or a journalist. PIs can only do so much, you know. If I can find him I can build a case against him and turn it over to law enforcement. I won't leak it to the press because that's not what I do. What you do with the information is up to you, however.

"But let's say I find him and build an airtight case," Cassie said. "Then what?"

Fly paused. "Find him first. I'll decide what course to take after he's positively identified. How is that?"

"Okay, I guess. We'll play that part by ear. And why me?" Cassie asked. "And why Montana? Is it because Spengler went missing here?"

"Partly," Fly said. "But it's also because Marc mentioned once that he'd grown up there. He didn't say where, and when I questioned him about it he just deflected with jokes like he always did. I told him my grandfather and great-grandfather lived in Montana for a while and he seemed interested but it was one of the few things I ever said he didn't ask me more about. I find that curious in retrospect. I think it might have been a slip on his part and maybe the only true thing he told me.

"It makes sense to me that if Marc grew up in Montana that maybe he still lives there. And when Spengler said he was going to Anaconda, well . . ."

"I get it," Cassie said. "Why me?"

Fly smiled widely and it looked painful to Cassie. "You're the only private investigator I could find there."

Cassie sat back. "Well, that's a ringing endorsement . . ."

"I did some online research as well," Fly said. "You've been in the news, it seems."

"I try to stay out of the news."

"So will you take the case?"

Cassie outlined her terms and cost per hour. She didn't inflate them as she had with the Sir Scott's Treasure client.

"I've got quite a few things on my plate right now," Cassie said. "I can't devote my full time to this."

"That's disappointing," Fly said. She said it like a woman who was used to getting what she wanted when she wanted it.

"I'll send you our standard contract via scan," Cassie said.

"Thank you. I hope you don't mind if I have my lawyer look at it before I sign. I'm a little gun-shy about trusting people right now, as you can imagine."

"That's fine," Cassie said. She knew the contract she used was absolutely airtight. It had been written by Rachel Mitchell of Mitchell-Estrada. Cassie was often retained by the firm to do their investigative work.

"Once you return the contract, please forward Spengler's reports and the photos you have of Marc Daly, even if they're lousy. And I can get started."

"I really hope you're successful," Fly said. "This man needs to be stopped."

"I'll do my best," Cassie said. "I have a good track record."

"If you shoot him in the head like you did that Montana state trooper it would be fine with me as well," Fly said before signing off. "Just get my money back first."

"Quick question," Cassie said. "Is he likely armed?"

"I never saw him carry a weapon when I first met him," Fly said. "But one night I peeked into the side table near his bed at the hotel. There was a gun there in a holster within easy reach. I never told him I found it and I wasn't all that surprised. Everybody here has guns and Marc probably grew up in Montana, after all."

"Good info to have," Cassie said.

Cassie took a moment to digest the call with Candyce Fly before getting another cup of coffee. Although she planned to look into Marc Daly, there was a niggling caveat in her mind. She had the suspicion Fly herself might not be totally on the level and that she was withholding something. Cassie was also a little shaken by Fly's surprising loss of her cool façade.

What if Fly was simply a bitter, scorned woman out for revenge on the man who rejected her? She wouldn't be the first.

What if Marc Daly could be found but he had a completely different version of events? Cassie could imagine a scenario where Daly felt pursued and smothered by a woman who would never give up—and he fled. Men took action with their feet more often than their words, especially when up against strong women. Cassie knew this from experience.

Perhaps the truth would be a version of both of their stories?

Maybe Fly *did* invest with Daly but the company they capitalized simply crashed, like so many other start-up firms? Fly could be angry about that as well as feeling scorned.

Or was Marc Daly the rogue con man Fly made him out to be?

five

◈

By that afternoon, Cassie found she needed to close her office door in order to concentrate. In the lobby was a team of two locksmiths working on the outer door at the same time three other men from a security company were installing closed-circuit cameras in the stairwell and where they could see every angle and view of the inside of Dewell Investigations.

The security team drilled into the walls to string wire and the supervisor briefed April on how to download the appropriate software so that the camera views could be seen not only on the computer monitors within the office but remotely.

Cassie was impressed with April. April got things done. She directed the workers, asked questions, took notes, and kept the work moving along.

Isabel, on the other hand, was flustered by the intrusion but not flustered enough not to flirt with the owner of the lock shop. The owner seemed to be her type: long gray hair, a drooping David Crosby–like mustache, and an easy smile. He spoke in a loopy cadence that suggested a long history of smoking weed.

Cassie closed her door when she heard her mother say to him, "I see that you move around kind of stiffly. Have you considered yoga? I'm in a class that meets three days a week . . ."

* * *

Cassie was now officially on the Marc Daly case.

Over the past few hours, Fly had returned the signed contract and wired the retainer to Cassie's business account. She'd followed the transaction with the reports written by the missing PI as well as the few photos she'd mentioned.

In the photos, which were as poor as Fly had described them, Marc Daly was too far away to be seen clearly. He was also moving when the shots were taken because he appeared blurry. Cassie assumed that it was on purpose.

Daly was over six feet tall with sandy hair cut long and a trim mustache. He towered over Fly, who was much shorter in the photos than she'd appeared on the Zoom call.

In one photo, Daly was standing behind her and nuzzling Fly's neck with his head down. Fly had a big smile on her face.

In a second photo Daly was in the back of a group of people in what appeared to be the lobby of a restaurant or hotel. The Gasparilla Inn? The group was well-dressed and in their sixties or seventies. They looked rich. While everyone else looked at the camera, Daly turned his head toward the right and apparently shuffled his feet at the last moment. His profile was blurred but he appeared to have an aquiline nose and square-cut jawline.

In the third and last photo, Fly and Daly were ballroom dancing on a crowded dance floor. Daly's back was to the camera while Fly peered around his arm and beamed at the photographer.

The reports shed no new clues, either, Cassie found. Fly had done a good job summarizing them. The "reports" were primarily expenses rung up on his nationwide search for Marc Daly.

J. D. Spengler's text message thread to Fly was more interesting. Although he didn't detail his findings to his client, they revealed that he'd been to multiple states in the past month on the trail of Marc Daly. Each time, before he booked tickets and a rental car, he asked Fly for authorization and she'd agreed.

Spengler had been to New York City, apparently to confirm that no one there in the financial sector had ever heard of Empire Capital or Marc Daly. After that, he flew to LA for reasons not specified, then Atlanta, then Chicago, then Auburn Hills, Michigan, then on to Billings.

The only clue to why he was going to so many locations was a simple text sent after he left Los Angeles.

It read: You were right. There are other women that he defrauded.

Fly's reply: I knew it!

Cassie made a note to ask Fly if she had any names or the circumstances of the other women. She found it puzzling Fly hadn't given her more information about other victims on the Zoom call.

There were two Marc Dalys in Montana, according to the Tracers and TLO, the specialized people-finding software the agency subscribed to. Tracers was the database Cassie preferred because it was vast and cost less than a hundred dollars a month. In addition to finding people, it often provided addresses, contact information, relatives and associates, and a map option for directions on how to find the subject.

The first Marc Daly was a seventy-six-year-old rancher near Ekalaka in eastern Montana. The location brought back memories for Cassie. She'd passed through the tiny ranching community when she was searching for Kyle Westergaard and Raheem Johnson, who had disappeared from North Dakota. She wondered if she'd driven past Marc Daly's ranch.

But he was obviously not Candyce Fly's Marc Daly.

The second Marc Daly in Montana was a graduate student at Montana State. Cassie looked him up and found a spindly ginger with big aviator glasses and an awkward smile.

Strike two.

Of course, Cassie really didn't suspect that she'd find him so easily. He had obviously lied to Fly about everything else, so why would he reveal his actual name? But for Cassie, ruling out possibilities was often as important as speculating on possible scenarios. There was no doubt that a Montanan by the name of Marc Daly who was Candyce Fly's paramour didn't exist.

To further rule obvious things out, Cassie logged out of her specialized databases and did a simple Google search. "Marc Daly" in the search field revealed more than twenty million results. She rolled her eyes and started scrolling.

Most of the hits pertained to a Black entrepreneur and businessman who was married to the star of a reality television series. There were also photographers, engineers, and contractors with the name. None of them fit.

They were followed by search results that listed "Mark Daly," not "Marc." And they went on forever, it seemed.

Then Cassie changed the search criteria to "Marc Daly Montana," which resulted in nearly three million hits. But even on the landing page, most of them were "Marks."

She sat up, though, when she saw the fourth listing. Google had changed the name she sought not to "Mark" but to "Marcus." Marcus Daly.

The description read:

Marcus Daly (December 5, 1841–November 12, 1900) was an Irish-born American businessman known as one of three "Copper Kings" of Butte, Montana, United States.

And she said, "Hmm."

Cassie was familiar with the man from her Montana State history class in college.

She recalled that Marcus Daly had traveled from a mine in Utah to Montana in 1876 to oversee work at an underground silver mine in the hillside of what was now Butte. A self-taught geologist, Daly came to the conclusion that the mine not only offered a modest return in silver, but that within the hill was a massive deposit of copper ore. With partners, he purchased other mines in the vicinity and soon confirmed that what he'd found was one of the largest deposits of copper known in the world at that time.

Soon after, the electrification of America began and copper wire was in high demand. Daly became the owner of the Anaconda Mining and Reduction Company.

He dubbed Butte "The Richest Hill on Earth."

Daly was an ambitious go-getter. He built a state-of-the-art smelter for the copper ore as well as a railroad to transport the rock to the smelter. Then he built a town in the valley beneath the smelter to house his workers and named it "Anaconda." The workers came from all over the country and all over the world and they were paid in Anaconda company script.

It was an empire.

By the time he died in 1900, Daly also owned a bank, a race-track, a thoroughbred racehorse that was named "Horse of the Year," lumber interests in the Bitterroot Valley, and mansions across western Montana. A US Navy ship was named for him during the Second World War.

Cassie sat back in her chair and pondered it all.

Marc Daly. Marcus Daly. Marcus Daly founded Anaconda, which is where J. D. Spengler was headed when he disappeared.

Had the con man who defrauded Candyce Fly chosen that name for a reason, or was it pure whimsy? She wondered if the imposter who took the name—and Candyce Fly's money—had a sense of humor. It seemed more than coincidence and it was an additional tie to Montana.

Was the name Marc/Marcus Daly the reason why Spengler went to Anaconda? Or was there more?

Cassie knew there was only one way to find out, and she'd need to set aside the treasure hunt case for the time being.

six

⊹⊷◉⊶⊹

Matthew Annan drove up the crumbling switchback road
on the side of the mountain in a light rain. It was dusk. On the top
of the highest peak within his sight was the statue of the Virgin
Mary called Our Lady of the Rockies. The ninety-foot statue was
bathed in orange from a last-gasp sun and it looked like a bizarre
highway cone set against a darkening sky.

The city lights of Butte were blinking on in the distance in the
valley below him. The air was fresh and cool and it got cooler the
higher he climbed. It wasn't a downpour—yet. If that happened
he feared driving back down the mountain on the rain-slick road.

But he'd deal with that possibility when and if it happened. Tonight, he had a job to do that couldn't wait much longer.

Annan was a calm and confident mountain driver. He knew when
to gear down when ascending and how to slow down on blind corners. And he knew that if he got into trouble on a slick ascent on a
muddy road he should do the counterintuitive thing and speed up.
Sliding backward could be a disaster all around.

He'd made sure before he left that the motor and tires of the
1995 Dodge Ram 2500 long-bed pickup were in good shape for
the drive. He'd borrowed the vehicle because he didn't want to
be seen in his own SUV on the side of the mountain. The Dodge

Ram didn't stand out and if it was seen it would likely be assumed that the driver was out four-wheeling or scouting game. It was a workingman's truck.

To look the part, he wore an old flannel shirt with a hole in the elbow and an oil-stained Montana State Bobcats cap pulled down low.

Annan was tall and rangy and he was proud of the fact that at fifty he could still wear the same-sized jeans he had worn in college. He kept himself fit and he credited his workout regimen, his diet, and his genes for making his features appear younger than he was and cheerier than he felt. His light blue eyes, without a wrinkle around them at all, winked back at him in the rearview mirror.

He saw mule deer ghosting through the tall mountain juniper at the lower elevations and now he saw a cow and calf elk running away from his vehicle in the trees, their half-moon-shaped white rumps bobbing like Ping-Pong balls.

He kept on.

Annan knew all the old roads up there. He'd grown up exploring them. And there were old roads everywhere. It was notable, though, how the mountains were starting to reclaim their own from century-old rapacious exploitation. Many of the old roads were breaking apart and washing out. Mineshafts dug a hundred years before or more were collapsing in on themselves or filling with poisoned water. Once impressive wooden structures were bleaching out and falling down on themselves, and metal tools and implements long left behind were rusting into the soil.

Someday, he thought, the mountains would be wild again. He just wouldn't live to see it.

The road leveled before it reached the top of the summit and the trees encroached on both sides. Annan could see there were no tire tracks before him in the moist surface of the two-track road. That was a good sign.

He slowed as he entered the grove of trees. They'd overgrown to the point that they scraped the sides of the pickup and slapped at the outside mirrors as he passed through. After a few minutes, he sensed the turnoff before he saw it.

There was an opening in the trees to the left and he squeezed the pickup into it. Weeds scraped at the undercarriage of the vehicle.

Then, about two hundred yards from the feeder road, he found what he was looking for.

Annan killed the motor and got out. He loved the smell of the mountains when it rained. It was almost sensory overload.

He walked down the cutoff trail where he'd driven moments before. His pant legs got wet as he walked through the beaded grass. When he got close to the feeder road he ducked into the trees and underbrush and waited.

Within the next half hour, the gray Chevy Malibu was scheduled to appear. The Idaho plates had been removed and destroyed, and all the identifying VIN numbers and other serial numbers on the dash, doors, and inside the motor itself had been ground away.

Since his drive up the mountain had gone easily, he saw no reason that the Chevy couldn't accomplish the same thing. The sky was clearing and it was unlikely there would be more rain, he thought. The drive down the mountain in the pickup should be smooth.

Annan heard it coming long before he saw it: the hum of the motor and popping of small stones beneath the tires as it approached. Then the glimpse of the chrome bumper strobing through the openings of the trees. Once he saw the gray Malibu come slowly down the overgrown feeder road he stepped out and waved.

The Malibu had two men inside. The passenger, Tim White, waved back. Doug Duplisea raised two fingers from the wheel in a "Butte Salute."

Annan took a step back as the Malibu came to a stop next to him and the driver's side window whirred down.

"You made it," he said.

"I'll admit I got a little worried a couple of times back there, especially on that steep part," Duplisea said. "Tim was shitting his pants."

"Oh, I was not," Tim said. He didn't enjoy being ridiculed in front of Annan.

"The weight in the trunk helped, I think," Duplisea said. "But it's starting to stink."

"That's why we had to do this now," Annan said. He could smell it as well. "Another day or two and it would really be noticeable."

"I feel like gagging," Tim said.

"Then get out," Annan said. "Get some air. The mineshaft is down the trail. It's right where I remembered it was."

Tim and Doug followed Annan along the grassy trail past Annan's pickup. Annan asked over his shoulder, "Did anyone see you drive up?"

"Nada," Duplisea said.

"Good. I didn't see anyone, either. And there weren't any tire tracks up here on the road before me."

Annan had grown up with both Doug and Tim. They'd lived blocks apart; walked to school together; played on the same baseball, basketball, and football teams; and sometimes triple-dated at the drive-in movie theater. College had split them up since Annan went and his two friends didn't, opting instead to work in the mines and make real money. Until the mines shut down, anyway.

Even though they were the same age, Annan thought, it was remarkable how different they looked. Both of his friends appeared rougher and much older than Annan. Tim was skeletal, with missing teeth and hollowed-out cheeks. His eyes were rheumy and he walked with a limp. Although he tried to hide it from Annan by keeping his hands out of sight, he shook when he wasn't drinking. And he drank a lot.

Tim had been in and out of rehab during the last fifteen years. He'd just recently gotten his driver's license back.

Duplisea was stout and although he was starting to stoop, he was still intimidating to most. Black Irish with a volatile temper and full-sleeve tattoos, Duplisea had jet-black hair sprinkled with gray and dark, close-set eyes. His fists were the size of small hams and his knuckles were scarred from bar fights.

"Does the key work?" Duplisea asked Annan.

"We'll find out. Did you bring the WD-40?"

"Tim?" Duplisea asked Tim.

"I got it," Tim answered.

The old mineshaft opening, which was twelve feet high and fourteen feet across, was set into a solid rock wall. The opening was blocked by iron gates that looked almost medieval. They were held closed by a heavy chain secured by a substantial padlock. Both the chain and the lock were covered in rust.

There were hundreds of abandoned mineshafts in the county, and scores of underground tunnels. Every year, it seemed, a tunnel collapsed or the ground opened up to reveal a deep chasm.

Annan dug in his pocket and came out with a key. He said, "One of you guys have a flashlight?"

"On my phone," Duplisea said. He found it and turned the light on as Annan tried to fit the key into the lock. It wouldn't insert all the way.

"Give me that spray," Annan said.

Tim handed it to him. Before he took it he paused and noted Tim's trembling hand. Duplisea saw it too. Annan took the can without comment and shot the fluid into the locking mechanism and into the holes of the U-shaped shackle.

While they waited for the WD-40 to dissolve the rust, Annan said, "I remember being up here thirty years ago. I think you guys were with me, right?"

"Probably," Tim said.

"Yeah, I remember it," Duplisea said.

Annan said, "I remember thinking that if I fell into this shaft no one would ever find my body. It goes straight down. Do you remember when we stole the key from that old guy down the street who used to be a safety engineer? It was in his shed out back."

Duplisea said with a chuckle, "If I remember, we were looking for his stash of booze. We came out of that shack with half a bottle of Old Crow and his key ring."

"Who'd have thought I'd keep that key ring all these years?" Annan asked. "But I did."

Duplisea turned to Tim. "You don't remember any of this, do you?"

"I didn't say that," Tim responded. But it was obvious that he didn't.

"Okay," Annan said. "I need the light again."

He worked the key into the lock and was able to turn it this time but the shackle didn't release.

"Here," Duplisea said, stepping in. He grasped the lock and jerked it down hard. The shackle snapped open.

"Good work," Annan said. He moved to the side and doused the metal hinges of the gates with WD-40. Then: "Let's open it up."

The gates moaned loudly as they were swung back revealing an inky black maw. Annan got his own phone out and turned on the flashlight and shone it down.

It was as he remembered it. There was a solid rock shelf fifteen feet into the hole that led to an opening that went straight down. The top of an iron ladder stuck up a few inches from the rim.

Annan entered the mineshaft and went as far as the edge. He shined his light down. The reflection of his beam on a pool of brackish still water was at least thirty feet down. The ladder vanished into the black water.

He recalled seeing old photos in the local museum of trussed-up mules being lowered into the mines with ropes and cables. The mules were there to labor and they were not brought to the surface again until they eventually died. The animals were sometimes blinded so they wouldn't get any ideas and try to bolt toward the light.

Mining in those days was unspeakably cruel, Annan thought. Miners weren't treated much better than the mules.

"Okay," he said. "Let's go get the Malibu."

Duplisea drove the car to the mouth of the opening and got out. He put the transmission in neutral. Annan found a football-sized rock and threw it through the back window.

"Why'd you do that?" Tim asked.

"So the air can escape, douche," Duplisea explained.

The three of them got behind the Malibu and pushed. It rolled slowly at first and Annan got a grotesque whiff of the smell from the body in the trunk as he pushed the car.

"Push it all the way in," Annan said, "but don't follow it."

"Gotcha," Duplisea said.

It rolled more freely when the front wheels hit the stone shelf.

"One, two, three . . ." Annan said. "Now!"

They gave it a hard shove and backed off. The Malibu rolled toward the lip of the shaft and seemed to dive straight in. Annan caught a glimpse of its undercarriage as it pitched forward and dropped.

A second and a half later there was a tremendous splash that reverberated in the mine like thunder. The disturbance also released an invisible cloud of fetid stench.

The three of them stood shoulder to shoulder on the lip of the shaft. Annan and Duplisea held their hands over their mouths and noses against the smell. Tim winced and fidgeted.

Annan could hear the car sink slowly into the water. Air from the interior of the vehicle whooshed out through the hole in the back window. When the car was fully submerged the surface of the water appeared to be boiling with released gases from inside the vehicle.

Then Duplisea stepped back and shoved Tim hard in the back with both hands, sending him headfirst into the hole. Tim's arms windmilled as he flew. It was such a powerful shove that Tim's head hit the rock wall on the other side of the shaft with a sickening *pock* sound before he plunged lifelessly into the water behind the Malibu. Tim didn't get a chance to cry out.

The body was spread-eagled and it sunk out of sight. They waited for a minute in silence to make sure he wouldn't struggle to the surface. He didn't.

Annan asked, "Do you think he knew it was coming?"

"I think he had an idea," Duplisea said. "He was pretty quiet on the way up. You know how unusual that is with Tim. He knew he fucked up."

"If he could have only kept his mouth shut," Annan said.

"He never could when he was drinking," Duplisea said. "Fucking motormouth was what he was. He couldn't help himself."

"I worry about Karen," Annan said. "What's she going to do?"

"Don't worry about her," Duplisea said. "Tim had life insurance. She'll be okay. She'll probably be a little relieved when he doesn't come home, if you know what I mean."

"Still, he was our buddy for a lot of years."

"He was," Duplisea said. "We had some good times together, man. But he was always self-destructive and he was getting worse the older he got. It was like his filter was removed. We flat couldn't risk it anymore."

"Yeah, I know. But still . . ."

"You didn't push him," Duplisea said. "I did. And I can live with it."

A particular feature of Doug Duplisea was his complete lack of remorse. What was done was done as far as he was concerned. He'd always been like that. Annan recalled Duplisea's reaction when he learned that the teenage daughter he'd thrown out of the house in the winter died of exposure: a shrug.

Annan sighed. "Yeah, well. Let's get this gate locked back up and get out of here. I'll drive."

"Maybe we should stop and get a beer and a shot at the club," Duplisea said. "You know, to honor Tim's memory."

The Club Moderne was one of Tim's favorite watering holes.

"Let's not," Annan said. "Someone will notice that we're there without him. That might get some tongues wagging when he turns up missing."

Duplisea grunted, which was his way of agreeing halfheartedly. "What if someone asks us where we were tonight?"

Annan waved it off. "We'll work up an alibi on the way down the mountain. Don't worry about it."

seven

❖❖❖

Early the next morning, Cassie took I-90 West and shared it primarily with long-haul truckers and construction workers headed to their job sites. Later in the day the highway would fill with vacationers on their way to Yellowstone Park to the south or Glacier Park to the north, along with other cross-country traffic.

She stopped at a convenience store on the outskirts of Bozeman for coffee. *Just coffee,* she told herself. *No donuts.*

Cassie stood in line behind six young men dressed in Carhartt clothing, ball caps, and work boots. She guessed they were a highway crew headed out based on the fact that the cuffs of their jeans were stained black by asphalt. The crew held the items they were going to purchase in their arms: energy drinks, hot dogs, chips, candy bars. Probably both breakfast *and* lunch, she thought.

She found herself feeling very grateful for these men. They weren't college-educated professionals on their way to the office and they likely came from tough circumstances. With males in that age group there were probably a few substance-abuse issues as well as some trouble with the law. But they were up early and on their way to work outside with their hands in the sun and rain so the roads were maintained for everyone else. They'd worked outside through the pandemic while others worked from home and ordered in food. Yet no one gave them a second thought.

Cassie hoped Ben pursued a different path in life, but she wanted to encourage him to do blue-collar or construction work on the way there. It would toughen him up and make him appreciate the fact that life wasn't easy for everyone and that dirty jobs had a nobility of their own.

As she waited for the road crew to pay—one by one, they used credit cards instead of cash, which slowed things down—she wished she could give them an economics lesson before they headed out for the day about how much money they'd save over the long run if they grocery shopped and packed their own lunches instead of buying high-priced processed foods at a gas station. But she didn't.

At the last second before buying her coffee she snatched a box of mini-donuts from the endcap just behind her and tossed it on the sales counter.

She hated herself for it.

Cassie had learned as a cop that there was no better way to obtain good information than to hit the streets and talk to people. Tracers, TLO, and social media were certainly good tools to build a framework around a case or a puzzle, but without getting out there to the actual locations and asking around it was generally inefficient to actually complete a proper investigation.

There was plenty to be learned by the demeanor of interviewees and by their body language. Sometimes their words didn't really matter. Even in an age of all-pervasive social media, face-to-face interactions in small towns were invaluable. She knew because she'd grown up in one and even now she was still a little flummoxed at how quickly news, rumor, and innuendo traveled by word of mouth. And how silence itself was sometimes a confession or a tactile admission of guilt.

PIs who spent most of their time working their databases and staring at computer monitors might be successful on some cases, but Cassie had no doubt that getting out and walking around was a fine and very effective tactic even if she didn't have a list of subjects to interview. By walking around and observing, she'd found, it was remarkable how many times people of interest sought *her* out. Often, it was the guilty party attempting to steer her in other directions.

Rachel Mitchell, the attorney Cassie worked for on retainer, observed that Cassie had unique characteristics that aided her in her job. She said Cassie came off as "nonthreatening" and "empathetic." She didn't stand out in a crowd and she didn't intimidate subjects like so many LEOs did. Rachel said Cassie could get people to tell her things that they'd never tell Rachel, including some of her clients. Cassie took the observations as a compliment of sorts. Rachel was brilliant, attractive, aggressive, and stylish. She could also be intimidating. Cassie conceded to herself that there were times she wished *she* was thought of that way.

She punched up the Bluetooth on her Jeep and placed a call to the sheriff's office in Deer Lodge County, where Anaconda was located.

"Anaconda–Deer Lodge County Law Enforcement Center," said the receptionist. The woman had a husky voice that was all business.

"Hello, my name is Cassie Dewell and I'm with Dewell Investigations in Bozeman. May I please speak to the sheriff?"

"Sheriff Westphal isn't in yet," she said. "He usually gets here between seven thirty and eight. Is there a message I can give him?"

Cassie said, "Please. I'm driving up there from Bozeman today to investigate a missing private investigator from Florida whose last-known whereabouts was Anaconda two weeks ago. I've also got some general questions about people of interest in the area I hope he'll be able to answer. Do you know what his day looks like?"

"Not really," she said. "He keeps his own schedule. He comes in, checks things out around the office, and usually goes to coffee around ten. I can give him your message and I'll ask him to call you."

"Thank you," Cassie said. "I appreciate it."

"Cassie Dewell," the receptionist repeated.

Cassie spelled out her name.

"Got it."

The receptionist paused, then said, "He might not call you back right away, you know." She sounded apologetic in advance. "Sheriff Westphal isn't real fond of outside investigators."

"You mean PIs?"

"Yes."

"It's okay," Cassie said. "I'm used to it. But I make it a policy to always inform local law enforcement when I'm in their jurisdiction. I used to be a deputy sheriff myself and I always appreciated the heads-up.

"So I have to ask," Cassie said, "How many times a day do you have to say, 'Anaconda–Deer Lodge County Law Enforcement Center'?"

"Hell, lady, I say it in my dreams." The receptionist laughed.

"And you are?"

"Margaret."

"I look forward to meeting you, Margaret."

"Thank you. I'm at the front desk."

Cassie punched off. It was always a good idea to get acquainted with the frontline staff of a law enforcement office. They often knew much more about what was going on than their bosses, she'd found. Especially bosses who kept their own schedules and went to coffee every day at ten.

Although it wasn't part of her initial plan, Cassie tapped on the brakes to disengage the cruise control when she saw the exit for Manhattan coming up a mile ahead. There was no reason why she couldn't multitask, after all.

Sir Scott's Oasis was on a corner in the middle of Manhattan, population fifteen hundred.

The town actually was a kind of oasis of its own, she thought as she left the buzz of the interstate behind her. It was green and leafy and quiet and there was a grade-school kids' soccer practice going on in the town park. Unlike Bozeman just a few miles behind her on the highway and so many other Montana communities, Manhattan hadn't exploded with new growth and transplants from other places. Yet.

Her tires thumped over railroad tracks and before she knew it she nearly drove through the town. Knowing she'd probably missed the restaurant, Cassie made a U-turn and cruised back and parked on the curb in front of Sir Scott's. The throwback sign read: SIR SCOTT'S OASIS CLUB.

The building was shambling and low-slung and Cassie shut off her engine and got out. Even from the street she could drink in the aroma of decades of broiled steaks and fried seafood that had been absorbed by the walls of the building itself.

Out-of-town steak houses were a tradition in the mountain west, she knew. She could recall a dozen of them in Montana and Wyoming alone: restaurants established in the 1940s or 1950s a short distance away from a much larger city. Out-of-town steak houses usually specialized in massive cuts of beef, fried seafood, goblets of alcohol, and at one time clouds of cigarette smoke. Generations of locals made pilgrimages to those steak houses for anniversaries, birthdays, prom night, and other special occasions.

Cassie looked at the ancient sign and the steel front door and she realized she'd been there before.

It wasn't a good memory.

She'd gone there with Jim following a camping trip in Yellowstone Park. They were on their way back to their trailer in East Helena.

At the time, they'd been married seven months. Jim was having trouble opening up his life to her, she thought. He had yet to adjust to marriage. He liked to go out with his friends at night and on weekends just like he had in high school.

She'd told him that was difficult for her and he had apologized. He seemed to feel genuinely remorseful about his behavior and he'd suggested the camping trip to get away and "reset" as a couple. She didn't love camping or the crowds in Yellowstone, but she didn't want to complain when he seemed so sincere.

It had been her suggestion to splurge and go out to a restaurant on their way back home. Jim had suggested Sir Scott's in Manhattan. He'd heard about the big steaks there from his uncle.

Cassie told Jim she had something important to tell him at dinner. Jim had replied that he had something important to tell her as well.

Jim was drinking more than usual as they waited for their food to arrive. He got no clue about her pending announcement when she ordered iced tea instead of red wine, just like he hadn't noticed that she hadn't had any alcohol during the camping trip. Jim was often oblivious to things.

As she started to speak he blurted out his news: "I joined the Army."

Stunned, she said, "I'm pregnant."

Cassie couldn't recall what they ate or the drive back to East Helena.

Eight months later, Jim Dewell was killed in the Battle of Wanat in Afghanistan along with eight other Americans when two hundred Taliban guerillas attacked the village in the province of Nuristan.

Cassie shivered involuntarily as she walked to the front door of the restaurant and grasped the handle. She was surprised to find it unlocked.

The lights were muted inside and there was no one sitting at the tables. A heavyset woman with braided silver hair looked up from behind the bar and said, "I'm sorry but we aren't open for lunch yet."

"I'm not here for lunch," Cassie said.

As her eyes adjusted to the darkness she saw that the woman was wiping down the bar. A short man about the same age emerged from a back room with a plastic milk carton filled with liquor bottles to restock the back bar.

"Want a drink?" he asked her with a grin.

"Bert!" the woman scolded him.

"It's a little early in the day for me," Cassie said.

"Suit yourself," he said with a wink.

"What can we help you with?" the woman asked. Then: "Are you one of those treasure hunters?"

"Not really. I was hoping I could ask you a few questions about the poem, though. Are you the owners?"

"Would we be here at seven thirty in the morning if we weren't?" the man replied with resigned good humor.

Cassie introduced herself and showed them her laminated PI credential card. The woman read it carefully and said, "I don't think I've ever met a real private investigator before. I've watched plenty of 'em on TV, though. Mannix is still my favorite. Or maybe Jim Rockford."

Their names were Bert and Yvette Scott and they'd owned Sir Scott's Oasis for forty-five years. Bert seemed to be a very natural glad-hander and Yvette was more suspicious and businesslike.

"I'm not looking for the treasure," Cassie assured them. "I'm actually trying to find the man who hid it."

"You and hundreds of other nuts," Yvette said. "I'm afraid there isn't much we can do to help you."

"There it is," Bert said, pointing over Cassie's shoulder. She turned.

On a whiteboard was the handwritten poem in black dry-erase marker.

"We've had so many people come in here to look at it that we covered it with Plexiglas," Bert explained.

"We also covered it because you said you were going to erase it," Yvette said to Bert.

Bert shrugged. "That's the truth. I was going to erase it because that's the board where we write the specials of the day. I had no idea what a big deal it would turn out to be. When we found it I thought it was garbage and I was going to clean it up. But somebody called the restaurant and asked about it because I guess it was posted on Facebook or something. I don't do that internet stuff. Yvette does, though."

"Can you please tell me the circumstances of how you found it?" Cassie asked.

Bert and Yvette shared a look. Then Yvette said, "We came in to open up the place that morning a while back and it was there. That's about all we know about it."

"So was the poem written while the restaurant was closed?"

"Yes," Yvette said. "Otherwise we would have seen who did it. Either us or one of our people, anyway. They would have said something if they saw a guy erase the daily special and write that stupid poem instead."

"How did the guy who wrote it get in here?"

The look again. Cassie realized a longtime couple like Bert and Yvette spent so much time together at work and at home that they almost didn't need to talk to each other anymore. Not when a look between them would do. Bert sighed heavily. "I closed the night before," he said. "I guess I didn't lock the back door on the way out."

"He didn't," Yvette said. "I've talked to him for years about double-checking that the building was locked up. But it's just like the front door you found open just now. Bert closed last night and forgot about that as well."

"Hell," Bert said with a shrug. "This is Manhattan, Montana. No one locks their doors. Most of us don't even lock our cars."

"Sometimes Bert enjoys a few cocktails when he's tending bar," Yvette said with a roll of her eyes. "That leads to forgetfulness."

"Do you have any ideas about who could have written it?" Cassie asked.

Yvette shook her head. "We've been asked that so many times and we still don't have an answer."

"Do you think he was local? Like maybe that's why he chose this place?"

"No clue, but I doubt it," Bert said. "Somebody would have said something by now. We're a pretty tight little town.

"But I'll tell you what—it's been good for business. You'd be surprised how many people have come in here over the last couple of years and asked us that question. Sir Scott's has always been real popular in the area but that poem there has really brought a lot more in. That and the steaks. Have you had our steak fingers?"

Cassie thought that she might have that night with Jim, but that evening was still a blur.

"*Some* of the treasure hunters stay for food," Yvette said. "Most of them just poke around and ask a bunch of questions like you have and go on their merry way. Those types are a waste of our time. So it hasn't been all that great for business if you want to know the truth.

"We've even been accused of writing it ourselves," Yvette said with anger. "Like we'd do something like that for the publicity or something. I can *promise* you we didn't write it."

"I can hardly spell," Bert said with a chuckle. "Ask anybody. We don't need a dumb poem to get people in here."

"Or a story about Jane Fonda," Yvette said. Bert shook his head in agreement.

"Excuse me?" Cassie said. "Jane Fonda?"

"That was a good one," Bert said. "There was a rumor a few years ago. It was way before the poem appeared."

He told Cassie that a story got started that he and Yvette turned away local ranch owners Ted Turner and Jane Fonda when the two were married and lived part-time in the area. Although it never actually happened, military veterans from all over the country made a

point to visit Sir Scott's as their patriotic duty because he'd refused
a table to antiwar Fonda.

As Bert told the story, the front door behind Cassie opened and
a young man entered looking sheepish. The figure was tall and pale
and he wore a stocking cap and a week-old beard. His movements
were unsteady. He looked cautiously around the restaurant until his
gaze settled on the poem.

"There's one of 'em now," Yvette said to Cassie. "Another treasure hunter. Let's see if he asks to order food or not."

When the man saw Cassie he blanched and turned on his heel
and flew out the door. Cassie was confused.

"Do you know him?" Yvette asked Cassie.

"I don't think so," she replied.

"He acted like he knew you," Yvette said.

Then it hit her.

Cassie pushed through the door to the sidewalk and looked both
ways. She saw a glimpse of him as he turned around the corner
of the restaurant. He was in a hurry, with his arms swinging at his
sides. She recognized that awkward gait. It hadn't changed.

"Hey," she shouted. "Stop."

She ran down the sidewalk and turned around it just in time
to see the man opening the door of a five-year-old Toyota Tundra
with North Dakota plates.

"*Kyle*," she cried. "Don't run away."

Her voice apparently made Kyle Westergaard pause. He stood
there with his back to her with the truck door half-open. But he
didn't jump inside the cab.

"Kyle!"

He turned slowly as she approached him. His greeting to her
came off like a weighty obligation, which she found puzzling. She
slowed so she wouldn't be too winded when she got to him.

Kyle was a man now, nineteen years old. He was tall and lean and he wore an oil-stained white T-shirt, jeans, and sneakers. His arms and face were tanned and his hair had lightened some since she last saw him. His eyes were the same though; a little vacant, a little unfocused.

"Kyle," she said. "It's you. Why did you run when you saw me?"

"I'm sorry," he said, looking ashamed.

"You look great," she said. "I almost didn't recognize you."

Before he could respond, Cassie hugged him. After a beat, he hugged her back but with less fervor.

Cassie had last seen Kyle Westergaard five years before when Kyle and his Grandma Lottie were at the Bozeman airport waiting for their flight back to North Dakota. Cassie had pursued the kidnapped boy across both states until she finally located him at an isolated mountain cabin taken over by Ronald Pergram, the Lizard King.

Kyle had been born with a mild case of fetal alcohol syndrome and his speech was impaired, but he'd been smart enough to leave clues for Cassie along his route. He'd also been instrumental in taking down Pergman using the trucker's own custom-made explosive device.

"Hi, Cassie," Kyle said. Then he quickly looked away.

"You *do* recognize me," she said. "So why did you run?"

Kyle shrugged and looked at his boots.

"What are you doing here?" she asked.

He stared at the town park across the street and didn't answer. Cassie knew Kyle well enough to remember that look. Kyle felt guilty about something. She was pleased to know that he still couldn't lie to her.

"I need to get going," Kyle said.

"Not before we have a cup of coffee together and catch up," Cassie said. She looped her arm through his and gently steered him down the sidewalk.

He sighed and reluctantly agreed.

* * *

They found a diner on the next block and took a booth away from other patrons. Cassie ordered coffee and Kyle ordered a Mountain Dew.

"Really?" Cassie chided him. "Just soda?"

"I *am* kind of hungry."

"Then order what you want."

A grin formed on his mouth as if he was smiling at a secret joke. He ordered pancakes, eggs, hash browns, biscuits and gravy, and two orders of bacon. He'd always been a big breakfast eater and by the look of him, she thought, he hadn't eaten recently.

"So what's going on, Kyle?" she asked. "What brings you back to Montana?" She asked it in a friendly way and she deliberately steered away from using her interrogation voice.

He paused and for the first time that morning his eyes met hers. "I'm trying to find Sir Scott's Treasure."

"Ah. And are you making progress?"

"I don't know. I think so."

"You didn't know I was in that restaurant before you came in?"

"No. I shouldn't have run away. It surprised me that you were there. I feel kind of stupid about that."

"You wanted to see the poem in person?"

"Yeah."

"I almost didn't recognize you," Cassie said. "You've really matured."

"Thanks, I guess," he said.

Kyle's speech had improved measurably over the past five years, Cassie observed. Although he likely still sounded slow and disjointed to people he encountered for the first time, he could at least be clearly understood. He no longer slurred his words and he remembered to pause at the end of sentences.

"Why?" she asked.

He looked up.

"Why are you spending your time trying to find the treasure? Don't you have a job?"

"I've got a job in the oil patch in Bakken County," he said. "I deliver parts to the wells. But I get three weeks of vacation."

And he was spending it looking for a chest full of gold. "What if you found it? What would you do with the money?"

"I need it."

"But do you?"

"Yeah," Kyle said, "Grandma Lottie needs help. She's got dementia but she wants to stay in her old house. I gotta help her before something terrible happens or the county hauls her away to some kind of home. Last month she was making lefse and she forgot to take it off of the griddle. She nearly burned her kitchen down and she would have if I didn't stop by and smell the smoke. I found her sleeping in her recliner. She could have burned up."

Lottie had been Kyle's primary caregiver while he grew up. His mother, Lottie's daughter, had been a meth addict and alcoholic until she was killed.

Cassie reached across the table and placed her hand on his. "Kyle, I'm sure there are programs that could help her out. Like in-home health care. Have you checked into them?"

"She won't take no welfare," Kyle said. "She's told me she'd rather die than count on the gov'mint. So I gotta help her. I need to hire a nurse or something. I can't stay with her all day and I worry about her when I'm out at my job in the field."

"That's very admirable, Kyle."

"She took good care of me," he said. "She's all I got."

"I know that. But is treasure hunting your only option?"

"You know, it isn't easy," he said. "You have to know that a guy with my issues can't ever really make real money out there. I'm never going to be no supervisor or anything like that. I'm about as high on the totem pole as I'll ever get."

He said it in a matter-of-fact way that broke Cassie's heart.

"So you think finding the treasure will do it, eh?" she asked.

"I know it would. I know it."

The waitress returned with a cup of coffee for Cassie and a big platter of steaming food for Kyle. He dug right in. As he ate, Cassie studied his face. His expression was as guileless as it had always been. She wondered if in a strange way his disability had been a blessing, considering what he'd gone through in his life. None of the trauma he'd experienced seemed to reflect in his face or his outlook.

As he ate, he talked.

"You know I always liked puzzles. It's something I'm pretty good at. I can do puzzles even though other things I'm not so good with. At all."

She smiled.

"Well, I studied 'Sir Scott's Treasure Poem' for months. I got out my maps and I memorized that poem. I could tell you it word for word right now if you want."

"That's okay."

"I read that poem and I said: *It's got to be in Montana*. You know I've only been to Montana that one time and it was pretty awful for me, but I didn't forget how it looked and how it felt. It was so different than North Dakota. I just *know* that treasure is in Montana. I didn't even know about Sir Scott's Oasis right here. When I found that out it made me even more sure."

She sipped her coffee and urged him on. As he delved into the lines of the poem his enthusiasm was palpable.

"First, that line, 'Begin where the rivers marry,'" he said. "That can only mean the confluence of two or more rivers, right? Montana has plenty of 'em. You remember how I used to know all the rivers?" he asked.

"I remember."

It was true. Kyle and his friend Raheem spent months planning their river expedition from Grimstad to New Orleans on a boat they'd equipped themselves. It had been a wildly ambitious and dubious expedition for two fourteen-year-old boys to float on the Missouri to the Mississippi River to the Gulf of Mexico. Kyle had made lists of the gear they'd need and he'd scrounged river maps so they'd know where to navigate. Unfortunately, after the two boys set off on their adventure they'd been intercepted by Ronald Pergram.

"You've got the Missouri, that's the big one," Kyle said. "Lots of rivers flow into it: the Yellowstone, the Judith, the Marias, and others.

"Before that there's the Yellowstone. Rivers that flow into it are the Clark's Fork, the Bighorn, the Rosebud, the Tongue, and the Powder River. That's not to mention Three Forks, where the Jefferson, Madison, and Gallatin all come together."

"That's a lot of possibilities," Cassie said.

"It is, it is. But you gotta figure the treasure isn't on private land. It's got to be somewhere on public land where it could be hidden. Otherwise, it wouldn't be fair at all."

"Who says the guy who hid it is fair?" Cassie asked rhetorically.

"I just think he is," Kyle said. "He wants it to be found. He says so and I believe him."

"Okay."

"Then those lines about 'walls closing in.' So a canyon. And 'depending on the season.' That means the river doesn't have a constant flow, I think. Which says to me it isn't downstream of a dam where they regulate the flow.

"There's a lot more to it," Kyle said, mopping up the last of the pancake syrup on his plate with a strip of bacon. "I could keep going for hours. Like the burn thing. Where do rivers meet near a canyon that had a forest fire? That's what it boils down to."

"So you go out to where rivers come together and hike around?" Cassie asked.

"I've been to twelve places in the last two years," Kyle said. "I'm narrowing down the others. None of them have had everything I'm looking for. But I'm getting close. I can feel it," he said.

"Do you see other treasure hunters around when you're looking?" she asked.

"Some. But I don't talk with them."

"Do you spend a lot of time online in those treasure hunter chat groups?" Cassie asked.

He shook his head. "Too much bullshit on them for me. I think most of those guys are making it all too complicated. I want to figure it out on my own."

"How would you characterize the man who hid the treasure?" Cassie asked. "What do you think he's like?"

Kyle looked up suspiciously. His eyes narrowed. That was a tell, Cassie thought.

"I think he's fair, like I said. I gotta trust him."

"Have you learned much about him?"

Kyle looked away. Cassie could see Kyle's neck redden.

"Did you find anything worthwhile when you broke into my office?" she asked.

Kyle jerked as if he'd been slapped. He wouldn't meet her eyes. And he didn't deny it.

"How did you get in?" she asked.

He looked away. "There's a key under the mat outside."

"There is?"

Cassie thought it must have been left there by an earlier tenant. She'd never thought to look. She made a note to herself to do a better job of hiding a key to the new locks when she got back to her office.

"How did you know I was working for him?" Cassie asked.

"He made a post that said he hired a private investigator to find him, and you're the only private investigator I know. Plus, you're in Montana. I feel really bad about this. I really do. You've only ever been good to me. You and Grandma Lottie."

"Kyle?"

"I didn't steal anything," he said. "I didn't break anything. I really didn't. I'm really sorry."

"Did you take anything with you?"

He shook his head. "I wasn't in your office long enough to find anything useful," he said.

"So how did you know he hired me?" Cassie asked again.

He sighed and said, "I did what I learned from you. I kept to myself and I listened."

She arched her eyebrows indicating he should go on. It worked with Ben and it worked with Kyle.

"I came to Bozeman thinking I'd see you and Ben since I was there. I went to your old office and somebody there told me about your new one so I went downtown. I stopped at that coffee shop in your building to wait for you to come back. While I was down there the waitresses were telling each other about some envelope that somebody dropped off with them for you and that it all had to do with Sir Scott's Treasure.

"I'm really sorry I did what I did," he said. "I feel like shit about it."

Cassie was suspicious of the story. How would the baristas downstairs have any idea of who Cassie's new client was? All they'd been involved with was making sure the manila folder was delivered. Then she realized what had likely happened.

Isabel had coffee down there every day. She'd befriended most of the employees. Isabel liked to talk.

Cassie wanted to kill her at the moment.

"Why didn't you just come to me?" she asked. "Why all the sneaking around?"

"Because I knew you wouldn't tell me," he said.

She started to argue but she knew he was correct. She wouldn't divulge any confidential information about a client—even to Kyle. He knew her well enough to know that.

"I won't press charges," she said. "But you better not do it again. I have to say I'm disappointed in you, Kyle."

His eyes filled with sudden tears. "I'm disappointed in my own damn self," he said. "And I didn't really learn nothing. Other than you think the guy is from Montana, too."

Maybe because he was upset his speech pattern reverted to his younger self. *Dish-appointed in mah own dam shelf.*

"How do you know that?" she asked.

"You wrote it on the side of your report. You wrote, 'He's from Montana.'"

She hadn't remembered scribbling it but she was sure Kyle was right.

"How did you know it was me?" he asked.

"It was a guess," she confessed. "But usually when a burglar breaks in they do some damage, even inadvertently. You were careful not to mess anything up. That seems like you, Kyle.

"I don't know the identity of my client," Cassie said. "I don't think I'm breaking any rules by telling you that."

Cassie sat back and drank the last of her coffee. Kyle squirmed across the table. He couldn't wait to leave.

"How long will you be around?" she asked.

"Another week or so," he said. "Then I need to head back."

"Where will you be?"

He hesitated, not wanting to answer.

"Kyle, I could care less about the treasure," she said. "Whatever you tell me stays with me."

"I'm going to go check out Three Forks," he said. "Where the three rivers meet. Then the Little Blackfoot River."

"Where are you staying?"

Kyle gestured to his pickup. "It isn't so bad," he said. "I got a sleeping bag and everything."

"Let's keep in touch while you're here," she said. "I know Ben would love to see you before you go. He talks about you all the time."

"He's a good guy," Kyle said.

"I agree."

"I bet he's different now that he's older."

"He's much taller, for sure," she said. "But he's still my gentle boy."

They exchanged cell phone numbers.

"I've gotta go as soon as we get the bill," he said.

"It's covered," she said.

"Now you make me feel even worse."

"Good," she said with a wink.

Out on the sidewalk, they parted ways. As Kyle lumbered toward his truck he said, "I'm really sorry, Cassie."

"It's not okay but it doesn't mean we can't move on," she said. "Is Lottie still at her old number?"

"Yeah, she doesn't believe in cell phones."

"I'll call her."

"She'd like that."

"Keep in touch, Kyle. And good luck."

He did an awkward skipping move and flashed her two thumbs-up in the street before continuing to his pickup.

Cassie thought, *If anyone deserves to find that treasure . . .*

eight

◆━◎━◆

Cassie got an early lunch in Butte on her way to Anaconda
and she couldn't stop thinking about her encounter with Kyle
Westergaard. Despite what he'd done, he made her smile.

Kyle was a survivor, a kind of sweet feral operator who did what
he had to do to keep going. Kyle had a unique and fearless naivete
in how he approached life. When he wanted to visit New Orleans
in his early teens before he could legally drive, he set out to accomplish it by boat. When his Grandma Lottie needed financial help, he
decided to find the treasure that hundreds of people were scouring
the West to find. That he'd broken into Cassie's office to try to find
information on her client but made a point not to disturb anything
fit into his profile. She sent him a quick text: It was good to see you,
Kyle. Keep in touch.

He didn't reply.

The Uptown Cafe was located in the heart of Butte. Inside it was
intimate and well-appointed, with white tablecloths and beautifully
presented food. Bankers, attorneys, and doctors seemed to occupy
most of the tables. Or at least people who *looked* like bankers, attorneys, and doctors.

The building where the Uptown Cafe was located had been
there since Butte was the most important city in Montana, and if

the walls could talk she knew she'd get the skinny on the boom-
time schemes and machinations in the "Richest Hill on Earth."

From her small table in the corner, Cassie observed Butte's executive class as they entered and discussed issues at their nearby tables.
Golf scores, bond issues, and the physical moving of one of the city's
biggest Copper King mansions out of town to another location.

"I can't imagine putting that house back together," said a ro-
tund bald man in a suit. "What a ridiculous project."

She ordered heirloom tomato salad and clams maison with iced
tea and she felt quite smug about it. When she was through, she
charged the meal to her company credit card and silently thanked
Candyce Fly for lunch.

Butte was unlike any other city in Montana and she was reminded of it when she went out of the restaurant to her car. The
city block she was on looked a lot more like historic San Francisco
than rural Montana with closely packed multistory brick buildings
lining narrow streets. The steep hillside where the city was built
gave it a vertical rather than horizontal feel.

She looked up the street. A faded painted sign on the side of
a building read: BRONX LOUNGE/SUPPER CLUB/ITALIAN CUISINE. The
neighborhoods—some restored, many crumbling—were diverse
with bars on every corner and churches on every block.

The charm of uptown Butte was countered by the Berkeley Pit
that hemmed in the east side of town. The Berkeley Pit, now closed,
had been one of the largest open-pit mines in the world and was
now a Superfund site. The stunning colors of the water within the
massive hole—azure, gold, green, blue—were due to the toxic mix
of arsenic, cadmium, copper, zinc, and lead within it. The vibrant
colors, when Cassie had first seen them as a teenager, had reminded
her of thermal pools in Yellowstone Park. She recalled a controversy
a few years back about a flock of geese who landed on the water of
the pit and had all been poisoned to death.

Having grown up in Montana, Cassie knew that residents of Butte were proud, almost clannish (they referred to their community as "Butte, America"), and they sometimes came off as having chips on their shoulders associated with the fact that their city's prominence was behind them and their statewide ascendency had been denied due to the cold decisions by multinational mining companies.

There was no doubt Butte's importance had declined. In the boom years of the 1920s, it had more than forty-two thousand residents. It now had barely thirty-four thousand. Butte had been such an up-and-comer in the Roaring Twenties that Dashiell Hammett set his novel *Red Harvest* there.

Along with Anaconda, Butte was the heart of the strident western labor movement and it was known at one time as the "Gibraltar of Unionism." Although it still had more residents of Irish descent by percentage than any other city in America, Butte was the most diverse community in Montana with distinct Italian, Polish, Slavic, Scandinavian, and Chinese neighborhoods.

Now, Our Lady of the Rockies towered above the community and watched it change and cope.

Before leaving town, Cassie drove up the hill to the twenty-three-room Copper King Mansion that had once belonged to Montana senator William Clark. The historic home had been restored and tours were offered to visitors. Across the street, another mansion had been converted into a bed-and-breakfast.

Next to the Copper King Mansion was a gaping hole. She assumed that the missing structure was the one she'd heard the city fathers talking about at the restaurant.

As she took the ramp to I-90 West, Cassie's phone pinged with a text message. It was from April:

Man, there are A LOT of writers in Montana. Can you tell me where to start?

Cassie used Siri on her phone to reply:

Rule out the female writers and all the dead ones.

She drove the twenty-four miles to Anaconda, past the exit to Fairmont Hot Springs and the state highways to Wisdom and Opportunity. The immense lone smokestack rose into the sky above her as she approached the town and she drove past the mountain of jet-black coal slag that sparkled in the high sun.

Although the two towns were inexorably linked—Butte mined the copper ore and Anaconda smelted it—they couldn't be more different, she thought. There were no tall buildings in Anaconda and the homes were solid little bungalows sometimes no more than a foot apart. It was as if the early residents hadn't quite grasped how much space there was available in Montana. The town had the feel of an enclave.

Mountains rose straight up on all four sides of the town, which was crowded into the valley floor. She noted HOME OF THE COPPERHEADS and ANACONDA STRONG posters in the windows of retail shops and individual homes.

Cassie used the map feature on her phone to find the Deer Lodge County Courthouse on Main Street. It was a magnificent neoclassical three-story stone building, backed into a hillside, that looked to have been built to preside over an eventual metropolis that would never quite fulfill its promise. Carved in stone over the front door was AD 1898.

Near to the courthouse was the Anaconda–Deer Lodge County Law Enforcement Center. It was built of modern blond brick and it looked out of place next to the historic courthouse. Three police cruisers were lined up at the entrance. Cassie pulled into a space designated for visitors and got out.

Inside the lobby was a counter protected by ceiling-high Plexiglas. A woman behind the counter looked up as Cassie entered.

She was striking, Cassie thought. Mid-fifties, slender, coal-black hair, light green eyes, very pale complexion.

"Are you Margaret?" Cassie asked.

"I am."

Cassie recognized her from her voice.

"I'm Cassie Dewell. I talked to you this morning."

Cassie dug her credential out of her purse and slipped it through the opening on the bottom of the Plexiglas. Margaret retrieved it and looked it over.

"Bozeman," Margaret said. "I think I've heard of you."

"It's possible," Cassie said. "I've been involved in some high-profile cases around the state."

"You were in the middle of that cock-up in Lochsa County a couple of years ago, right?"

Cassie nodded.

"That was a wild one," Margaret said. "I remember reading about it on Facebook."

No one read the local newspapers anymore, Cassie thought. Not even law enforcement personnel.

"So," Cassie said, "have you given the sheriff my message? I'd like a few minutes with him if possible."

Something passed over the receptionist's face. She looked down at her hands, apparently embarrassed.

"Actually, I haven't seen Sheriff Westphal today. So I haven't given him your message."

"Could you call him?"

Again, the look. "He isn't picking up."

Cassie frowned. "That's kind of odd, isn't it?"

Margaret looked over her shoulder to see if anyone had come into the lobby from the back. Cassie assumed the officers' workstations were all beyond the back wall, as well as the county jail. That's how most sheriff department facilities were set up.

Assured no one was there to overhear, Margaret said, "It is just sort of odd. Sometimes he doesn't come in if there's nothing going on. It's been really quiet in town except for the usual stuff—traffic violations, public intoxication, that sort of thing. But it is unusual that he hasn't checked in at all."

"For how long?" Cassie asked.

"A few days," Margaret said. Again, she checked over her shoulder.

"You haven't seen the sheriff in three days?"

Margaret shrugged.

"Isn't this something you should be worried about?" Cassie asked.

"It isn't my place to say," Margaret said. "I haven't heard anything from our officers about it. Maybe the sheriff has been in touch with them individually, I don't know. I'm just the receptionist, as I told you."

Cassie studied Margaret's face. She believed Margaret's story about the sheriff but thought there must be something else she wasn't being told.

"Well," Cassie said, "is there someone else I could talk to? At least until the sheriff decides to show up?"

"The officer in charge is the undersheriff and chief investigator," Margaret said. "He has both titles."

"That's impressive. Is he here? Could you please put me in touch with him?"

"I can call him," Margaret said.

Cassie folded her arms across her breasts and waited. After what looked like an internal conversation with herself, Margaret mounted a pair of headphones on her hair and punched a button on her phone set. Then she rolled back her chair and swiveled around with her back to Cassie so she couldn't be heard her through the hole in the Plexiglas.

The conversation lasted less than fifteen seconds. When Margaret turned back around her face was flushed red.

"Did you talk to him?" Cassie asked.

"I did."

"Did you convey my request?"

Margaret nodded her head.

"And?"

"He said, and I quote because I don't use these kinds of words myself: 'Please tell her to fuck off and go home.'"

Cassie raised her eyebrows. "Seriously, that's what he said?"

"I'm afraid so. I'm sorry."

Cassie slipped her business card to Margaret across the counter through the opening. "Here's my card," she said. "Please ask the sheriff or the undersheriff to contact me. This is an official request. I'm not going to fuck off and go home. And if I have to come back here without hearing from either of them, I'm showing up with friends who can make their lives miserable."

"Friends?" Margaret asked.

"*Friends*," Cassie said. "They'll know who I mean."

Before going back to her car, Cassie paused at the door.

"Margaret, I know this isn't about you. You've got a job to do and being the go-between is part of that. My problem is with your bosses."

Margaret nodded wordlessly.

"Feel free to call me anytime," Cassie said. "But you might want to do it off premises and from your own phone, if you know what I mean. I can meet you anywhere."

"I try to stay out of things the best I can," Margaret said. "That's how I keep my job around here."

To cool down and regroup, Cassie didn't go straight to her car but instead strode across the lawn outside to the courthouse next door.

Amid historical plaques about city hall and the Butte–Anaconda Historic District, she thought over her threat to show up again at the justice center with friends.

Who were her friends? She had no idea. But she'd worked in the heart of sheriff departments before. Sheriffs and under-sheriffs were political animals. As such, they had people to avoid at all costs and enemies to be kept at bay. The enemies might be journalists, county commissioners, the mayor, or local activists. If the political animals in that building thought they might be con-fronted by their adversaries, it might give them the incentive to cooperate with her.

She'd let *them* determine who the enemies might be who would accompany her.

It had been a calculated risk, and one that might not pay off. If it didn't, her leverage was shot to get their cooperation.

Cassie paused and looked down the hill at the compact town of Anaconda that stretched across the valley floor.

She thought: *Here we go . . .*

She spent the early afternoon visiting local hotels and motels. There were five within the town of Anaconda and another dozen within thirty miles. In Montana, thirty miles were nothing.

None of the local accommodations were chains and all were privately owned. They ran the gamut from the large-scale Fairmont Hot Springs Resort to the east to crumbling motor lodges.

After her experience in Lochsa County staying in a motor lodge, she now saw them in a different—if undeserved—light.

At each, she introduced herself and showed the desk clerk a photo on her phone of J. D. Spengler. She'd copied the portrait from the website of Spengler's agency in Florida but had cropped it so it looked like it was in her own personal photo archive. As if she'd taken it herself.

"He should have checked in on May nineteenth," she said.

At the fourth local motel, called the Flint Creek Motor Court, she got a hit.

The man behind the counter wore a heavy flannel shirt and suspenders, despite the warm day. He had tufts of white hair above his ears and a bald, freckled head. He narrowed his small brown eyes at the mention of the name. Cassie felt a satisfied flutter in her stomach.

"Yip," he said. "He checked in for two nights and disappeared."

"Do you mean he walked out on his bill?" she asked.

"No, not that," the man said. "I got his credit card when he checked in. I charged him for both nights."

"Then what do you mean?"

The man shrugged. "He checked in and I never saw him again. He left his suitcase in the room and never came back for it or called later to ask if we found it. I'm not sure he ever really used the room at all. Our housekeeper said he didn't sleep in the bed or use any towels."

"So he checked in, dropped off his bag, and went back out?" she asked.

"Yip. I never saw him again."

"That's interesting."

"Yeah, kind of strange. But we get all kinds," the man said. "Two nights ago a couple from Oregon left two goats in a room when they went to dinner at Fairmont. We allow pets, but goats aren't pets. They defecated on the carpet and chewed up a lot of the wallpaper. Have you ever had to clean up goat shit?"

"Not that I can remember," Cassie said.

"It ain't no fun," the man said. "The smell lingers."

Cassie nodded. "Did Mr. Spengler have any visitors while he was here?"

"None that I seen."

"What did you do with Mr. Spengler's bag?"

"I still got it," the man said. "I didn't know what to do with it. There's no name tag or nothing on it."

He sighed. "People leave stuff here all the time. You know, clothes, that kind of stuff. Phone chargers are the worst. I put that stuff in storage and wait for the guest to call and ask that whatever it is can be returned. I get their credit card and charge a modest service fee and send it back to them. Sometimes it takes weeks to figure out what they forgot to pack. I kept waiting for Spengler to call me but he never did. I called the number he left on his registration form and it went straight to voicemail."

"Interesting," Cassie said again. "Do you think I could take a look at his bag?"

The man eyed her suspiciously. Then: "I don't know if I should do that or not. Are you related to him in some way?"

"He's my uncle," Cassie said. "He was on the way to our family reunion in Helena and he never showed up. The last we heard of him he was going to stay over in Anaconda and come up on the weekend."

Since she'd become a PI, Cassie found it easier and easier to lie. She tried to do it only when the stakes were low and she couldn't think of another way to get the information she wanted. It was a line she rarely crossed when she'd been in law enforcement, but she knew she'd been the exception.

"Man, I don't know," the man said, running his palm over his scalp. "It doesn't seem right. It's your uncle's property."

"Yes," she said. "But it might give me an idea where he went after this. I don't know."

"I don't know, either," he said.

"Would a hundred dollars help?" she asked. "You can consider it your service fee."

"A hundred?" he asked.

"A hundred and fifty, I meant," she said.

He looked her over carefully, obviously considering what he'd do next. Then, without a word, he turned and walked across the lobby to a door that said STAFF ONLY.

"You coming?" he asked over his shoulder as he opened the door and went inside.

She followed him into a storage room. An industrial washer and dryer sat in the back. High shelves were piled with thin folded white towels, cases of thin shrink-wrapped bathroom soaps, older television sets that had been removed, and a large container in the corner of items that had apparently been left by guests in individual rooms. A nondescript black rolling bag was next to the box.

"There it is," he said. "That's where we put our lost items. You can put his suitcase on that folding table over there but please put it back where you found it. And don't take nothing."

"I won't," she said, digging into her handbag for three fifty-dollar bills. She kept a roll of them specifically for bribe money. "Thank you."

He slid the bills into his back pocket and shouldered past her back to the counter.

The contents of the bag revealed nothing, she determined. A few shirts were folded neatly inside, as well as two pairs of trousers. Spengler had "borrowed" a pillowcase from somewhere to use for soiled underwear.

His shaving kit was jammed with items he'd also taken from other motels as well as a razor and a pack of condoms. There were three plastic bottles in the kit prescribed to Jonathan David Spengler. She recognized the drug names. One was for high cholesterol, another for heart disease, and the last was mail-order Viagra.

Condoms and Viagra, she thought. That told her something about the man when he traveled.

In the bag there were no receipts, documents, or notebooks. No weapons or other gear. Nor cell phones, laptops, or digital recorders.

For a PI in the field, she thought, he traveled *very* light. Unless he kept his weapons and working gear inside the rental car with him at all times.

She took a photo of the items displayed on the table with her phone but she wasn't sure it would be of any value.

Cassie repacked the bag and placed it in the rolling bag of recovered items. She glanced inside the container. She'd never seen so many phone chargers in one place.

As she left the room she noticed that the motel manager was peering intently out his window toward the parking lot. She wondered for a moment if J. D. Spengler had come back.

"Looks like you've got company," the man said.

She paused at the lobby door before going outside. A sheriff's department SUV was parked outside and a large officer in uniform leaned casually against it. He wore dark aviator glasses and he had a toothpick in his mouth.

He was obviously waiting for her.

Cassie turned to the manager. "Did you call him?"

"Didn't need to," the manager said. "He called me. I said you were just about done looking through your uncle's possessions in the storeroom."

She glared at him.

On her way out the door, she activated a compact digital audio recording device and left it in her handbag.

nine

⊷⊶

The only reaction the deputy displayed as Cassie walked across the parking lot toward him was the dance of the toothpick in his mouth. He remained there leaning against his vehicle with his arms crossed over his chest and his left leg bent so that his boot sole rested against the exterior of the SUV.

He'd parked so his cruiser blocked the exit of Cassie's Cherokee. She assumed it was deliberate.

Cassie noted that the edge of the business card she'd left with Margaret poked out of his meaty grip.

Her ploy had worked.

"Yes, Officer?" she said. "Can I help you?"

He was a big man with large features and thick limbs. His head was huge and shaped like an overinflated football. She guessed he was in his late fifties but the flap of loose skin under his jaw made him look older. She imagined that if she reached out and squeezed his bicep she'd find flab, not muscle.

"Are you Cassie Dewell?" he asked. He pronounced her last name as "DOOL."

"I am."

He nodded and the toothpick froze in place. "I'm Undersheriff Duplisea. I understand you'd like to have a chat."

"I'd appreciate that."

"First of all, what were you doing in there?" he asked, chinning toward the Flint Creek Motor Court. "I understand you've been driving all over town harassing our business owners."

"That wasn't my intention. I didn't harass anyone."

"I heard different. But anyway, what are you doing here?"

"I'll show you," she said.

"Show me what?"

"I'm going to reach into my purse to get my phone."

She was deliberate in her movements. Even with the notice, she could tell that Duplisea tensed up a little when she did so.

Cassie could think of dozens of scenarios where civilians had been shot because a police officer came to the snap judgment—justifiably or not justifiably—that a subject they encountered was reaching for a gun.

She glanced at Duplisea to see if he was wearing a body cam. He was not.

She drew out the phone by pinching it with two fingers.

"I was hired by my client to find this man," she said, pulling up the shot of Spengler and showing it to the deputy. "His name is J. D. Spengler and he's a licensed private investigator out of Florida."

Duplisea thrust his face forward to view the screen but he didn't reach for the phone. Then he leaned back to his original position. Cassie didn't think the deputy looked at the photo very carefully.

"I don't know the man," Duplisea said.

"He's her uncle," the manager of the motel chimed in from behind Cassie. She hadn't heard him come out.

"Is that the case?" Duplisea asked.

"Not really," she confessed.

"That's what she told me," the manager said. He was irritated.

Cassie could feel her face flush hot.

"So you lied to him?" Duplisea asked.

"I told him a fib. But it doesn't matter. I still want to find Spengler and I thought the contents of the bag he left here might help my client."

"Are you gonna take her in, Doug?" the manager asked. Cassie noted the first-name basis.

Then she turned on him. "Please stay out of this. Or give me back the hundred and fifty dollars I paid you to look inside the suitcase."

The manager turned on his heel and walked back to the motel office. Duplisea chuckled at the scene playing in front of him, and Cassie felt humiliated.

"So you lied to the man," Duplisea said to Cassie. "Now tell me more about this guy you're trying to find."

Cassie recovered and said, "He vanished on or about May nine-teenth. His rental car was a gray 2021 Chevrolet Malibu four-door with Idaho plates."

"Doesn't ring a bell," Duplisea said.

"Anaconda was his last-known location."

Duplisea grinned. "Known by who?" he asked.

"Pardon me?"

"You said his last-known location was my town. What I'm asking you is by whom? Who knows he went missing here, of all places?"

Cassie hesitated. "That's my client's recollection," she said. "Spengler sent her a photo of the 'Welcome to Anaconda' sign on the edge of town."

Duplisea's grin curled into something cruel. "So no one here saw him?"

Cassie shook her head. "That's not true, Deputy. Spengler booked two nights in the motel. He dropped his luggage here but he never retrieved it. The manager inside recognized him and he has his registration on file."

"Well, that's *something*," Duplisea said skeptically. "What I'm wondering is why I'm just now hearing about this. Did your client call our office to report this?"

"She didn't," Cassie said, "but my understanding is that his office did and a missing person case was opened."

"Are you sure about this?"

"No. It's secondhand information."

Duplisea shook his head. "This is pretty weak stuff. You must have a dumb client. Who is this client, anyway?"

"I can't say. I'm sorry."

Duplisea simply looked at her. She wished she could see his eyes but they were hidden behind the dark lenses.

He nodded in the direction of the motel. "I think you might have defrauded that man with your lies. I need to look up the specific offense but I think we're talking about a misdemeanor. Defrauding an innkeeper? Does that sound right to you?"

"You've got to be kidding me," she said. But she knew that if a police officer was determined to find a charge against someone, odds were on their side.

"My job isn't to protect out-of-town PIs," Duplisea said. "My job is to protect and serve the good people of Anaconda. Especially when folks blow in here and try to deceive them."

"I need to call my lawyer," Cassie said. She knew her face was red now. "Have you heard of Rachel Mitchell?"

For the first time, Duplisea visibly flinched.

"So you have," Cassie said.

"We all have," he said. "She's the one who goes after the cops for doing their duty whenever she can. Yeah, we've all heard of her. She's a snake.

"*Miss Dool*," he said, "I think I have a good idea how we can resolve this dilemma of yours and then you can be on your merry way. It doesn't have to involve charges or goddamned lawyers."

"How's that?"

"Follow me back to my office. We'll sit down and file a missing person form on this Spengler guy. I'll circulate it through the office and post it on all the appropriate sites. You can tell your client you did all you could to find him and then you can go back to Bozeman knowing you did your job. How's that sound?"

Not good, she thought. But she could use the interaction to her advantage if she played it right.

"By the way," she said, "I'm recording this conversation."

He flinched again. He had a very quick fuse. For a half second Cassie got the impression he was going to assault her. He glowered, and leaned forward as if poised to lunge. She stepped back.

Duplisea took a deep breath, straightened back up, and the faux smile came back.

"I think we may have gotten off on the wrong foot here," he said. "So if you'll just come with me we can get everything sorted out."

"I'd rather follow you in my car. That way, you won't need to bring me back here."

And my car will be in public view parked in front of the Justice Center if I go missing, she thought.

He narrowed his eyes, calculating. Then: "Suit yourself."

She nodded.

Cassie sat in an uncomfortable hard-backed chair across the desk from Duplisea. He'd invited her to his office through the lobby after telling her she'd need to leave her belongings in a small locker mounted to the back wall.

"I don't have my weapon on me," she'd said.

"Protocol," he'd replied. But what he really meant was that he didn't want the conversation they were about to have recorded. She had no choice but to comply.

Cassie filled the locker with her handbag, keys, and phone. The recording app was still active and she didn't turn it off.

The sheriff's department space was open concept, with four desks shoved together in the middle for officers. Only one deputy, a fresh-faced slight man with a starter mustache, sat at a desk. When

Cassie and Duplisea came in she noted a wordless exchange between the two men. The deputy grabbed his cap and stood up and left the room. Cassie wasn't sure what the undersheriff had signaled to the deputy aside from, "Clear the room."

She followed Duplisea into one of two individual offices on the right side of the room. The other office had a plastic SHERIFF PHILLIP WESTPHAL plaque in the corner of a window that looked out at the rest of the office. It was dark inside the sheriff's office.

"Okay," Duplisea said, adjusting the tilt of his computer monitor and tapping a few keys to wake it up. "Give me a second here." He put on a pair of reading glasses. The monitor faced away from her on the desk. With his sunglasses removed she could see his dull brown eyes. They were not the eyes of a kind man. They were hard and mean.

He said, "There, I found it. '2021 Montana Code Annotated Title 70, Chapter six: Defrauding an Innkeeper.'"

Cassie rolled her eyes. "I thought we were through with that."

He didn't acknowledge her and he kept reading and quoting from the screen. "'70–6–501, Innkeeper's liability as to property of guests—dollar limitation.' Nope, that doesn't apply. '70–6–512, Innkeeper's responsibilities—limits.' I guess that doesn't apply, either."

"Of course it doesn't," Cassie said. "You're just wasting my time here."

"Maybe so," Duplisea said. "But I thought it was best to check. I wouldn't want you to think I wasn't thorough. You might have to report that to your lawyer friend."

"Can we get on with this?" Cassie asked.

He leaned back in his plush office chair and turned to her. "By all means," he said.

Then he said nothing. He simply stared at her for nearly a full minute. She stared back. Cassie knew the dead-eye stare to be an effective interrogation tactic at times. Cops did it to suspects hoping the uncomfortable moment would compel them to fill the void by talking.

"Go ahead," he said finally.

"As I told you back at the motel, I've been hired by my client to find a missing PI from Florida. I called your office this morning to let you know I'd be here in your community because I consider that a professional courtesy. I was also hoping I could speak to you or the sheriff about the missing man. Despite you making this as difficult as possible, here we are."

Duplisea nodded. Then: "This just doesn't make a lot of sense to me. Why would a client hire a private investigator to find another private investigator? Is there some kind of dispute between them?"

"Not that I know of," Cassie said.

"So what was this other guy investigating in the first place?"

Cassie chose her words carefully. "My client alleges that a man defrauded her of millions of dollars and that he may have fled here. Or that he may be a local. The missing PI tracked him across the country and apparently came to the same conclusion. I was hired to find either man—or both if possible."

Duplisea looked amused. Cassie wanted to lean across the desk and slap him.

Finally, he asked, "What's the identity of the so-called fraud-ster?"

"I have a name but I'm pretty sure it's false," she said.

"And that is?"

"Marc Daly. Marc with a C."

Duplisea laughed out loud and shook his head. "Marc as in Marcus Daly? The founder of Anaconda? He's been dead for a hundred and twenty years. I think you and your client are being played."

"I said it was a false name," Cassie said. "Maybe you should take notes."

"Oh, not necessary," Duplisea said while pointing to his big head. "I'm keeping it all up here."

Cassie didn't give him the pleasure of a reaction.

He said, "So, because this fraudster gave his name as Marc Daly, both you and the missing PI figured out he must be from Anaconda. Is that it?"

"The other PI had that theory. That's why he came here. But, as you know, he's gone missing. I'm here following up."

"Maybe he's holed up in Missoula with a working girl?" Duplisea said. "Or maybe he's in Las Vegas having the time of his life on his client's dime? He could be anywhere."

The undersheriff's speculation was ridiculous and meant to humiliate her further, she knew. But she tucked it away and didn't respond.

"Yes," Cassie said. "He could be anywhere. But I thought I'd start here. And I thought you might be able to help me at least rule it out. But you don't seem interested in helping me at all."

"I don't know why you'd say that," Duplisea said, showing her his huge palms.

She said, "I've started a file on the missing PI. I'll be happy to forward it to you. Think if it as my gesture of goodwill, the sharing of information."

"Okay," Duplisea said. His feigned interest didn't fool her.

"Do you know anyone in Anaconda who might be the type to trick a woman out of her fortune? My guess is he's done this before."

Something passed over Duplisea's face at the question. A shadow. A tell of some kind.

"Can't say that I do," he said. "Oh, we got all kinds, just like any town. But you'd think I'd notice if one of our locals suddenly turned up rich. In a small town like this that kind of thing would get around."

Cassie gestured to the empty office next door. "Where's your sheriff?"

"He's not in at the moment, as you can clearly see."

"Margaret said he'd been gone for two or three days," Cassie said. "Aren't you concerned?"

"Why would I be?" Duplisea said. He sounded defensive. "I can handle things around here. I was the undersheriff when Westphal got elected and I'll be the undersheriff when he moves on. I've got three years left before I retire. I can ride it out no matter what happens."

"I have to say I find that very odd," she said.

"You shouldn't," Duplisea said. "It's not your concern. Look," he said, lowering his voice, "the man has a bit of a drinking problem. This isn't his first bender. When he's off the sauce he's a damned good sheriff and I'd even call him a friend. He'll show up any day now all remorseful. It's kind of a pattern."

Cassie nodded as if she understood.

"We take care of our own around here," Duplisea said. "It isn't like other places where they throw people to the wolves if they screw up. We're tight here. We've been here a long time. We're Anaconda Strong," he said.

"I've seen the posters."

"And you probably thought it was funny, didn't you?"

"I thought this was a town with pride," she said.

He rolled on as if she'd said nothing. His voice rose as he went on. "If it were up to all the newcomers in this state, they'd like this town to dry up and blow away. They're *embarrassed* by us. We don't fit the profile of Montana these days. We're not Teva-wearing metrosexuals mining bitcoin on their laptops at some Bozeman wine bar, or fly-fishing with a two-thousand-dollar fly rod. We're made up of four generations of hard rock miners here. People from all over the world: Irish, Scottish, Polish, Russian, Lithuanian, Italian—you name it. We did diversity before diversity was cool, you know?"

Duplisea prodded the desktop with his index finger as he made his points.

"But it doesn't matter where they came from because they have one thing in common. They stick together. *We* stick together."

He raised his arm and pointed toward the window and to the town the Justice Center overlooked.

"Those people out there are from stock that put their lives on the line every day for shit wages and shit safety conditions. If you don't know anything about the 1917 mining disaster, I suggest you read up on it to see what it was like."

"I've heard about it," Cassie said. "I'm from Montana."

"Bozeman isn't Montana," Duplisea said. "Maybe it used to be at one time, but it sure isn't now."

By now his face was crimson. He scared her.

"I think I'll be going now," she said. "I know you already have my card. I'll follow up with the file and send it to your email address, as promised. I hope you'll give me a call if you find anything out about the whereabouts of Mr. Spengler."

"What if I find Marcus Daly?" Duplisea said sarcastically. "Should I call you about him?"

Cassie stood up. Before turning to get her items from the locker in the lobby, she said, "Tell me something, Deputy Duplisea."

"What's that?"

"Earlier, you speculated that Spengler could be holed up with a prostitute in Missoula or living it up in Las Vegas."

"So what?" Duplisea said, his eyes narrowing.

"I'm just curious why you went in that particular direction if you were totally unfamiliar with him. Who's to say he wasn't an extremely devout Christian family man who was devoted to his loving wife in Tampa? It's almost like you knew he had condoms and a pill bottle of Viagra in his shaving kit."

Duplisea's eyes got larger and Cassie could see that quick fuse lighting again.

"What in the fuck are you implying?" he said.

"Oh nothing," she said.

She opened the door quickly and let it wheeze closed behind her while she retrieved her belongings. Duplisea was right behind her and he snatched her phone out of the locker before she could get it. He quickly deleted the recording and handed it back to her before retreating to his office.

"Must be fun working with that guy," she said to Margaret on her way out.

"It's like every day is a party," Margaret said wearily.

ten

◆━━◉━◉━━◆

It was midafternoon on June 1 when County Sheriff Phillip Westphal circled the block in his SUV around Club Moderne on Park Avenue. He found what he was looking for.

Undersheriff Doug Duplisea's civilian GMC pickup was parked on Ash Street on the side of the club and Matthew Annan's BMW was in the alley behind it. He looked around for Tim White's Silverado but he didn't see it.

Westphal had been in town long enough to know that locals kept a good eye on him and his movements. He knew that if he parked behind Duplisea's truck and went inside for very long there would soon be rumors about it.

Why did the sheriff meet up with his undersheriff in the middle of the afternoon on Doug's day off?

Or worse: was the sheriff starting another of the benders he was known for at Club Moderne?

After all, he'd done it before.

So he swung around the building and parked behind Annan's aging BMW. His vehicle couldn't be seen from the street that way. He knew Annan favored that parking location for the same reason.

Westphal killed the motor, got out, and hitched up his uniform pants. It was unseasonably hot. He wiped his forehead with his sleeve and clamped his brimmed hat on tight as he walked around the corner to the front. This was official business, after all.

Phil Westphal had a thick red gunfighter's mustache peppered with silver that looked like strands of tinsel. His thick middle strained the buttons of his uniform shirt. He had deep-set dark eyes and jowls that quivered above his shirt collar when he walked. His deep voice came from three decades of chain-smoking Camels. Instead of reaching for his pack of smokes, he popped a 6mm tab of nicotine gum and chewed it fast as he walked. The sensation was not as satisfying as filling his lungs with smoke, but it would do.

The Club Moderne was an iconic bar in Anaconda. Built in 1937 in a style known as Streamline Moderne, it was a quaint corner neighborhood tavern with a wrap-around façade of Carrara glass. It had been fully restored to its art deco roots the previous decade after a fire.

He entered and tipped his hat to the barmaid. She said, "Hey there, Phil. It's been a while."

"It has," he said.

"The usual?"

"No thank you. But I'll have a ginger ale."

She looked at him sidewise as if amused.

"Seriously," he said. "Ginger ale."

Three retired locals sat shoulder to shoulder at a long table watching *Family Feud* on a television mounted on the wall. Two of them looked away when he eyed them. He knew them, too. All too well.

"Art, Ted, Howard," he said. "Good to see you. Who's winning?"

The three old-timers were retired miners who watched *Family Feud* every afternoon and shouted out their answers to the questions. Ted kept track of who was winning. They sipped light beer on tap while they did it.

"Howard," Ted said. "But I'm right on his heels. Do you want to join us?"

"Not this time, thanks."

"We kind of miss you around here," Ted said.

Westphal nodded and approached the bar. It had moody back-bar lighting that looked great when it was dark outside. The place didn't have the same vibe in the afternoon, he thought.

A local newsbreak came on the television and the finely coiffed newsreader announced the recent sale of the Montana ranch that had served as the location for the movie *A River Runs Through It* for one hundred and thirty-six million dollars.

Behind him, the table erupted.

"A hundred and thirty-six million?" Art hollered. "That's ridiculous!"

"Who in the hell bought it?" Ted asked.

"You have to watch at ten to find out, I guess," Howard said.

"It's fucking ridiculous," Art said again. "I keep telling you guys—we're gonna get priced out of Montana."

"I wonder what my house is worth?" Ted said.

"Nobody wants your house. Besides, where are we gonna have to move? North Dakota?"

"I ain't moving to North Dakota," Ted said.

Westphal ignored them. "Is Doug in the back?" he asked the barmaid.

She nodded as she handed him his ginger ale.

"Thank you," he said.

"On the house," she replied.

Westphal grinned. "That's a new one."

"So's ginger ale for Phil Westphal."

He carried his soft drink through the small bar to a larger room in the back. The room had been added on sometime in the sixties and it didn't have the charm of the art deco bar. Instead, it had pool tables, shuffleboard, and high-backed booths lined up along the side wall. A poster advertising a gopher hunt sponsored by the Anaconda

VFW had been tacked above the booths. The winner was eligible to win a .30–06 rifle.

"There you are," he said to Duplisea when he approached the last booth in the room. "I thought I'd find you here on your day off."

Duplisea greeted him warmly and told him to grab a chair. Westphal did.

In the booth with Duplisea was Matthew Annan, as expected. Annan couldn't have been nicer, offering to buy the sheriff another round.

"What are you drinking?" he asked.

"Ginger ale," Westphal said.

"Bullshit," Duplisea said.

"Really. I'm on duty."

"When has that ever sto—" Duplisea started to say but caught himself before he finished. Westphal was his boss, after all.

Westphal let it go. "Where's Tim?" he asked. "Don't you guys travel in a pack?"

Duplisea, Annan, and Tim White were rarely not seen together. They'd grown up in the town and Annan, at least, was a kind of royalty.

Annan's great-grandfather, Frank Annan, had been one of the early labor leaders who fought against the copper barons for better wages and fewer hours. He'd been famous all over the country at the time, and he was one of the reasons Anaconda was known as the heart of the American labor movement. He'd been beaten and lynched for a crime he didn't commit by surrogates of the mine owners in 1919. There was a bronze plaque in his honor on a wall of the courthouse.

Matthew Annan was a charmer. He had an easy manner and he was well-liked in town and he did a lot for the community. Westphal had once heard Matthew portrayed as "all the men want to be like him and all the women want to be with him."

In response to the question, Duplisea and Annan both shook their heads.

"We haven't seen much of Tim lately," Duplisea finally said. He didn't offer any more.

"How's Jillian doing?" Annan asked.

"She's doing better," Westphal said. "The radiation treatments were rough on her but her hair is coming back. She's doing all right for now."

He didn't want to tell either Doug or Annan that his wife Jillian's bout with cancer had scared him straight. She'd stuck with him over the years for reasons he couldn't quite fathom but he was grateful for it. Years of drinking, vanishing, running for office, ignoring her and their two children. Even when she first got sick he didn't realize how bad it was at the time because he was in a fog of alcohol.

Once the realization of her condition hit him, he'd vowed to keep sober and clean so he would be more attentive if and when the cancer came back in full. He'd accompanied her to her chemo and radiation treatments and he'd cooked for her when she was too weak to get out of bed. The doctors had given her a 45 percent chance of a full recovery.

"So what can I help you with?" Duplisea asked.

Westphal glanced at Annan, indicating that what he was about to say was meant for Duplisea alone.

Duplisea shook his head. "Anything you have to say you can say in front of Matthew. I'm not going to ask my good friend to leave."

Annan watched the exchange between Westphal and Duplisea wordlessly as if he were watching a tennis match.

Westphal cleared his throat. He said to Duplisea, "Do you have any idea where your buddy Tim is? The owner of the welding shop he works at called me and said he hasn't been to work since May 22.

I checked with his live-in and she says she hasn't seen him around since then, either."

"Yeah?" Duplisea said. "So why are you asking me?"

"Because you two have been tight all your lives, I thought. Everybody says that. I thought you might know—"

"Well, I don't," Duplisea said, cutting him off. "We kind of had a falling-out and I haven't been keeping track of him lately. I wouldn't be surprised if he's in rehab somewhere."

"Hmm."

"What are you hmm-ing about?" Duplisea asked, red-faced.

"I guess I was hoping for a better answer. And there's something else."

"What?"

"You know Lyla Hayes, I'm sure."

Hayes was a local woman in her mid fifties who pushed a shopping cart filled with her possessions from one end of Anaconda to the other, then repeated the process. Her brain injuries, it was said, had been the result of a car accident when she was in her teens. She was a familiar sight to anyone passing through town.

Most of the locals took pity on Lyla and made sure she was fed and clothed. Although there were facilities for the homeless in both Anaconda and Butte, Lyla refused to stay in them longer than a day or two.

Duplisea rolled his eyes. "Of course I know Lyla. I've brought her in to jail to sleep it off or stay warm a half-dozen times over the years. She's pretty harmless."

"I know she is," Westphal said. "She came in this morning with a story to tell and a question to ask."

Both Duplisea and Annan nodded, urging him to continue.

"Well, Lyla said about two weeks ago she was pushing her cart on the sidewalk up on Seventh Street when she saw something suspicious."

Westphal noted that when he said "Seventh Street" that Annan's expression froze.

"Lyla said she saw a gray four-door sedan with out-of-state plates pull up in front of the construction site. You know which one I'm talking about," Westphal said. "She said a portly gentleman got out of the car and approached her. He asked Lyla if she knew who owned the lot across the street. Lyla said sure—everybody knew who owned that lot."

Both Annan and Duplisea remained silent.

"A half hour later, Lyla said, she saw your patrol vehicle show up at the location," he said to Duplisea. "She said you and the portly guy had a pretty heated argument and she pushed her cart the hell out of there. She asked me if I knew what happened to the fat guy. Was he arrested for something? Was he escorted out of town? I had to tell her I had no idea what she was referring to.

"So I checked the duty log for May nineteenth, which is when she said she saw the incident. There was nothing on the log about any kind of interaction or confrontation with a man driving a gray car with out-of-state plates."

Westphal leaned forward toward the two men in the booth but his eyes fixed on Duplisea.

"You may know this, but we have an open missing person notice in our office. The person who called it in said their man went missing on or about May nineteenth. He was described as an overweight private investigator from Florida named J. D. Spengler. He was last known driving a gray Chevy Malibu with Idaho plates.

"I'm just wondering," Westphal said to Duplisea, "if you can help enlighten me a little on this odd coincidence."

Duplisea's face remained blank but Westphal noticed that the blood had drained from it.

"First," Duplisea said, "why are you relying on the testimony of a mental defective like Lyla? Who knows what she saw when?"

"I'll grant you that," Westphal said. "She isn't exactly reliable. But for some reason, I believed her. Maybe it's because she doesn't appear to have any reason to lie."

"She doesn't know the difference between the truth and a lie, Phil," Duplisea said.

"Maybe. Are you saying you didn't encounter this missing man on May nineteenth?"

Duplisea hesitated, then looked away. He said, "I'm not saying that at all."

Westphal sat back, a little surprised. Annan looked puzzled as well.

"I was on the street and I saw him parked there looking at the construction site," Duplisea said. "I noticed he looked out of place and I saw he had Idaho plates. So I stopped and asked him if I could be of any service. There was no 'heated argument' or confrontation of any kind, Phil. Lyla made that part up."

Westphal said, "You didn't note this in your duty log for that day."

"Of course not," Duplisea scoffed. "Do you really think I document every time I help a lost visitor with directions? I mean, come on."

Westphal conceded the point. Then: "But this guy obviously matched the description of this Spengler. And his car does too."

Duplisea shook his head with emphasis. "No, Phil, you're reading this all wrong. I had no idea there was a missing person report on file when I met the guy. I wasn't looking for him, you know? I didn't call his plates in or anything. And I didn't put it together that this guy might be Spengler until you just told me."

Duplisea's eyes went cold and he said, "Phil, I resent the hell out of you coming in here on my day off and making these kinds of accusations. You, my friend, are *way* out of line."

"I'm not making accusations," Westphal said, holding up both of his palms in surrender. "I'm just trying to clear something up."

Duplisea glared at Westphal and he seemed to cool down. "I can't believe you'd take something Lyla Hayes said and run with it. I've been an officer in the sheriff's department for nearly twenty years. I hope to hell you'd believe me over her."

"Of course I do," Westphal said. "Thank you for telling me otherwise."

"Are you sure I can't get you a drink?" Annan offered. He was obviously trying to bring down the temperature of the conversation.

"I'm sure," Westphal said. Then to Duplisea: "What was Spengler trying to find?"

The question took Duplisea aback. "What?"

"You said he was asking for directions—that he was lost. What was he trying to find?"

Duplisea's face flushed red and it was obvious to Westphal his undersheriff was trying to hold back his anger.

"Do you want me to show you?" Duplisea asked with heat. "Do you want me to show you what he was trying to find?"

"You mean now?" Westphal asked.

"I mean now," Duplisea hissed.

"Can't you just tell me?"

"No. Not after all this shit has gone down. Not after you practically accuse me of doing something wrong."

Duplisea launched himself out of the booth and Westphal had to scoot his chair to the side to avoid being bowled over.

"Come on, Phil," Duplisea said. "My truck's out front. Follow me, goddammit."

Duplisea stormed out of the room into the bar area.

Westphal turned to Annan. "What just happened?" he asked.

"I don't know," Annan said. "Doug can be a hothead, as you know. But I suggest you follow him."

Westphal pushed back and got up. He said, "I guess I will."

Annan's look, the sheriff thought as he clamped on his hat and pursued Duplisea, was an odd mix of pity and sorrow.

★ ★ ★

Westphal followed Duplisea's pickup down Park Avenue. His undersheriff was driving too fast, likely because he was so angry. Westphal hoped their speedy departure wasn't observed by any of his more critical constituents.

But he was also annoyed at Doug. Duplisea was obviously keeping secrets from him, which was unacceptable. If he knew of the location of a missing person, he should have revealed it days before and he better have a damned good reason why he hadn't.

Duplisea didn't signal when he took a sharp left toward the Old Works Golf Course. The course was designed by Jack Nicklaus on an Environmental Protection Agency Superfund site, and had once been the location of a copper smelter. Westphal rarely played golf, but when he did it was with county commissioners on the Old Works.

Why was Duplisea taking him there?

His answer came a few minutes later, when his undersheriff proceeded past the entrance to the golf course and he turned onto an old asphalt-paved road that wound up into the foothills. The surface of the road was breaking up and was marked with potholes. Westphal was grateful for the potholes because they made Duplisea have to slow down.

They wound up and over a hillock into a wooded pocket nestled into a gulley. Westphal recognized the old house there as one used at times as a safe house by county law enforcement. It had been pointed out to him by Duplisea himself after he was hired.

The old structure was a shambling Victorian two-story home with graying wood shingles and faded yellow paint. Duplisea drove straight up to the front of it and his brake lights flashed.

Westphal parked his SUV next to Duplisea's pickup and climbed out.

"He's here?" Westphal asked. "Why?"

"I'll show you," Duplisea said.

As they walked toward the front door, Westphal got a sudden bad feeling. The house looked unoccupied, and there was a layer of dust on the front steps that appeared undisturbed. Duplisea faded back as they approached the porch.

Westphal heard a creak of leather from behind him and when he felt cold metal on the back of his neck he reacted by turning his head and darting sharply to his left. The muzzle of Duplisea's Glock exploded at the same time.

The sheriff almost couldn't comprehend what had happened until he clapped his right hand over the side of his temple. His ear had been shot off and blood pulsed through his fingers. The detached ear lay like a potato chip in the spring grass in front of him.

He wheeled around to find Duplisea in a shooter's stance with his weapon out.

"Doug?" Westphal asked.

"I'm sorry," Duplisea said a half second before he shot the sheriff three times in the heart.

Duplisea stood over the dead sheriff and drew his cell phone out of his breast pocket. He speed-dialed the second number on his contacts list, the name and number directly below Phil Westphal's.

"Yeah," he said, "everything went pear-shaped. All I could think of at the time was to get him out of there. Do you still have that key to the gate for the mineshaft?" he asked. Then: "Yeah. We'll need to drive up there again tonight, I'm afraid."

eleven

❖

Cassie spent the remainder of the afternoon haunting the streets and alleyways of Anaconda, soaking it up. She had often found that insights and revelations came to her while simply driving around, and she tried to sort out her two interactions with Undersheriff Doug Duplisea with what she knew about Spengler's disappearance. Things simply didn't add up, but she came to no conclusions.

She drove by the fenced-off remains of the industrial area in town: massive soot-covered brick buildings that now housed ancient machinery or nothing at all. There were a few vehicles inside the enclosure and she wondered what the people did for a living inside the district now that mining and smelting copper was no longer viable.

At Mount Olivet Cemetery she marveled at the number of memorials and effusive arrays of flowers on the gravestones. She'd never seen such an audacious display at any other cemetery in her life, and she chalked it up to how seriously locals maintained their devotion and loyalty to their departed relatives. It was both moving and unusual.

Downtown, Cassie had noted a thin, haggard woman dutifully pushing a shopping cart filled with her possessions toward the western outskirts of town. Later, as Cassie approached her, she saw the same woman pushing the cart back the other way when one of its wheels slipped over the curb. She lost control of it and it rolled into the street.

Cassie braked so she wouldn't have a collision with the cart. The woman scrambled after it and grasped the push bar to stop it from crossing the street. While she did she shot Cassie an angry look.

"You nearly hit me," the woman said. She wore oversized lace-up boots and several layers of clothing. Her hair was bound back in a ponytail and her eyes were wild. Her deeply tanned skin was wrinkled like the bark on a cottonwood tree. She was younger than Cassie would have guessed—likely in her fifties—but a victim of hard living and obvious mental illness.

While Cassie put her hands up in frustration, the woman wheeled the cart around the front of the Jeep and bumped it up against the driver's side door. Not hard enough to leave a dent, but hard enough to annoy Cassie.

"Please move aside so I can go," Cassie said after powering down her window.

"I'm Lyla," the woman said. "Who the hell are you?"

"Cassie."

"You nearly hit me."

"I stopped so I wouldn't hit you, Lyla."

"Yeah, well," Lyla said. She was still disturbingly angry. She leaned over her cart and thrust her face toward Cassie's open window. Cassie shrank back. Lyla's odor was pungent.

"They're still out there," Lyla said. "They're still doing the things they always did, only now it's worse."

"What are you talking about?"

Lyla thrust a bent finger toward Cassie's nose. "You remember them from high school. You remember what they're like."

Cassie shook her head and looked for a way to disengage. She didn't want to peel away and risk injuring Lyla, but she wanted no part of this.

"You remember," Lyla said again.

"Do you think we know each other?"

"Don't play stupid," Lyla said. "Tim, Doug, and Matty. You still got to watch out for them. Do you remember when they passed me around like a piece of meat? That was before my accident. Didn't they pass you around in high school?"

"I'm not from here," Cassie said. "Please back off. I've got to go."

Lyla thrust the finger at Cassie again. "Watch out for them! If anybody goes missing around this town it's because of one of them or all three of them. Watch out!"

"Okay," Cassie said. "Thank you."

Lyla nodded triumphantly, as if she'd finally made her point. When she backed the cart away from Cassie's open window, Cassie pulled away.

She watched Lyla roll the cart back to the sidewalk in her rear-view window. Lyla was still shouting and gesticulating as she did so.

Cassie slowed down her Jeep when she passed the construction site on Seventh Street because it was so striking. There, among older homes in various stages of disrepair, was the obvious relocation and refurbishing of a magnificent early twentieth-century Victorian brick mansion. The home stood out like a beacon, primarily because there were so few other new homes.

It was nestled with its back into the hillside and it looked out on the town that was spread out below it. It had turrets and gables with new windows fitted into old brick window openings. Through the huge glass windows on either side of the heavy double doors she could see a wide staircase inside leading up to the second floor and a crystal chandelier the size of her car hanging from the ceiling.

There were pallets of lumber on the side of the residence and virtually no landscaping on the churned-up grounds.

There was a lone figure out front—a man loading large rocks into a wheelbarrow. She couldn't help but notice that he was tall and fit and very well-built. He wore jeans, work boots, and a dirty white T-shirt that clung to his sweaty chest and abs. His muscles bulged from the hard work he was doing.

He didn't *look* like he was part of a construction crew—no hard hat, no tool belt—so what was he?

Suddenly, he glanced up as she drove slowly by and their eyes met. He had tousled dark hair and sharp blue eyes and a three-day beard. He was, she concluded, *ridiculously* good-looking.

Because he had caught her staring at him, she pulled over to the curb and turned off her car.

He paused and eyed her as she got out.

"Hello," she said, trying to maintain her composure.

"Hello."

"I'm Cassie Dewell. I'm a private investigator from Bozeman."

"Matthew Annan," he said. "I'd shake your hand but mine is really dirty, as you can see. So what brings you here?"

He had a natural, easy manner and, damn it, a wonderful smile. She dug into her handbag for her phone and punched up the photo of J. D. Spengler.

"Do you know this man?" she asked. "Have you seen him around here?"

Annan squinted. "I'm sorry—I'm having trouble seeing it in the sun."

She stepped from the sidewalk to the rough ground and offered him the phone. Her heels sunk into the loose dirt.

He took the phone from her and fished a pair of readers from his front pocket. She was grateful he had the same flaw she did. He looked closely at the photo. She got a whiff of him. Not unpleasant.

He handed the phone back. "No, I'm sorry but I can't help you. Why are you looking for him?"

The readers went back into the pocket.

"He might have gone missing in this area two weeks ago," she said. "I've been hired to try to find him."

"I hope you do," Annan said. "I'll keep my eye out for him." Then: "If I see him, how do I reach you?"

She felt a thrill pass over her and settle just below her abdomen. It was entirely unexpected.

"I mean, do you have a card or something?" He smiled again. He asked rhetorically, "Do people still carry business cards?"

"I do and I'll get you one," she said. Her mouth was dry, all of a sudden. She chinned toward the house. "That's quite a place. Is it yours?"

He turned and looked at it with her. "Yes. I bought the lot fifteen years ago. There was a little bungalow on it that had been vacant since the 1940s but as you can see the view is to kill for. We finally knocked that bungalow down and replaced it with . . . this.

"Moving that house here has turned out to be quite an adventure. I didn't know what I was getting myself into." He chuckled.

"Are you remodeling it yourself?"

"No, not entirely. I'm not a craftsman, and that place needs real old-school craftsmen. I just do what I can—which isn't much." He chuckled in a self-deprecating way. "Like picking up rocks. That, I can do."

"It's really beautiful," she said. Cassie felt a little dumb for saying it. She sounded like an old-home fangirl, which she really wasn't.

"I want to restore the house to what it once was," Annan said. "I've got some old photos and we found the original plans. At one time it was really something."

She recalled the businessmen at lunch talking about some foolish man moving a home from there.

"Is it from Butte?" she asked.

"Good call." He nodded. "That house used to be one of the famous Copper King mansions. I grew up here, but all of the big-shot owners of the mines and the smelters that were in Anaconda lived someplace else."

He gestured toward Anaconda in the valley below them.

"*These* are the people who did all the work. Some of them died doing it. Asking these good folks to work for you but not having your own home here just seems wrong to me, you know. So I like to think I'm doing my little part to right that wrong.

"God," he said, laughing. "That sounded so self-righteous that I can't believe it came out of my mouth. Can you just forget I ever said it?"

She looked at him. "Sure."

"Thank you, Cassie."

He called her by her name. Another thrill. Cassie felt like she was in high school and the handsome star quarterback had suddenly noticed her in the hallway. She was ashamed of herself.

"It's been really tough," he said. "Tougher than I thought it would be. Everything costs two or three times what I budgeted. We had to number every brick before we took it down to reassemble it over here. The woodwork inside was dried out and brittle and really tough to take apart and put back together. That chandelier you can see took nearly a month to carefully take apart. We couldn't dare risk breaking any of the crystals because they just don't make them like that anymore.

"And the toughest thing of all is to get reliable help. Craftsmen are hard to find on their own, but it's hell to simply hire day workers for things like I'm doing—picking up rocks. All these unemployed kids around here—and no one wants to work. All they do is stare at their phones all day and collect unemployment checks from Uncle Sugar.

"Look," he said, "I offer them twenty bucks an hour. That's much more than minimum wage. But when they show up and see this wheelbarrow, well, all of the sudden it's too much. They don't come back the next day. I can convince transients to do some manual labor but they leave, too. I guess that's why they call them *transients*," he said with a wink.

"I know finding people to work is a problem," Cassie agreed. "Every restaurant owner I know says the same thing."

"It's a national tragedy," Annan said. "And one of our own making. Our country doesn't value hard work anymore."

She nodded. She didn't know how to respond to that.

"I'm sorry to go off on that rant," he said. "It's just that I grew up taking every dirty job I could get so I could get a car, go to community college, all that. Sometimes I worked two or three jobs at a time. I didn't love it, but I didn't turn my nose up at hard work. Crap, there I go again."

He shook his head and said, "Pretty soon I'm going to say, 'kids these days.' I never thought I'd say *that*."

"No worries," she said. Then: "I hope you can find some help. Your house will be spectacular."

He looked at her. Deeply. It was thrilling and unnerving at the same time.

"If you weren't on a case I'd love to show you around inside. They don't build homes like this anymore. I have a feeling you'd appreciate the details."

"Thank you for the offer," she said. She knew she was flushing. "Maybe next time."

"So you'll be back around here?" He arched his eyebrows as he asked.

"I'm sure I will."

"I'd say that is about the only good news I've heard all day." He grinned.

She turned and walked back to her Jeep. She hoped she wasn't using that stiff-legged gait she sometimes lapsed into when she was nervous or distressed.

As she reached for her door handle, Annan called out.

"Cassie?"

She paused.

"Your business card?"

"Oh, right."

She fumbled for one and he was right there when she turned.

"Dewell Investigations," he read. "Well, it was a pleasure to meet you," he said, slipping the card into the back pocket of his jeans. His *tight* jeans. "I hope you find the guy you're looking for."

"It was a pleasure to meet you as well, Mr. Annan."

"Call me Matthew," he said.

Cassie circled the block and found a place to park so that a huge untrimmed hedge blocked her view of Matthew Annan's home. She attached a long zoom lens to her digital camera and got out.

Through an opening between hedgerows she snapped a series of photos of Annan working in his front yard. He never looked up to spot her.

Then she backed down the street out of view.

Cassie was careful to keep below the speed limit as she drove out of Anaconda on her way home. Cassie didn't want to give Duplisea or any of his deputies an excuse to pull her over.

She wasn't that surprised, though, when she glanced at her rear-view mirror to see that a sheriff's department SUV was tailing her as she drove out of town. Had they been watching her all day, she wondered? Or had they picked her up on Main Street?

The cruiser followed her as far as the entrance to I-90 East. Once they were sure she was headed back to Bozeman, it slowed to a stop and turned around.

Although April called her on her cell phone, Cassie let it go to voice mail. The reason was she was having a hard and somewhat painful conversation with herself.

Matthew Annan was charming, attractive, and charismatic. He lit up the room even though he was wearing a dirty T-shirt and he was outside. She shifted uncomfortably in her car seat when she thought of him.

She knew she'd think of him later, when she was alone in bed. His pull was that powerful.

But she also knew that a man like that wouldn't normally make a play for her like inviting her into his house. He was unusually interested in learning her name and getting her details, she thought. Annan acted like he was anxious to see her again—but was he?

He *knew* what kind of effect he had on her and probably 99 percent of all the women out there.

He was too good to be true, which was painful to concede to herself. He was the kind of man, she thought, who could approach an unattached older woman on a golf course and say, "*If you'd like me to, I'll wrestle that alligator to get your ball back.*"

Cassie pulled over and parked on the side of the highway. She scrolled through the photos and tagged five good ones that clearly showed his face and upper torso. After transferring them to her phone via Bluetooth, she emailed them to Candyce Fly with the question, "Is this him?"

Between Butte and Bozeman, Cassie returned April's call.

April said, "I've put together a pretty good list of male writers, I think. Once I dropped the ones who were dead, too old, or had moved from the state I came up with fourteen names."

"Excellent job," Cassie said. "Let's go over them first thing tomorrow. Pay special attention to the ones who describe themselves as poets. Even the ones who are really bad poets—maybe self-published types."

"I love this," April enthused. "I love finding pukes."

"He isn't necessarily a puke," Cassie said. "How many are in the Bozeman area?"

April paused as she scrolled through her list. Then: "Five. Most of these guys live in Missoula or the Flathead Valley. A couple in Billings."

"I'm not surprised," Cassie said. "And I might have something else for you. You and Ben, I mean."

"Me and Ben?"

"How would you like to do some manual labor? Putting in sod, planting trees and bushes? That kind of thing?"

April got quiet.

"You'd be doing that work, but you'd also be keeping a close eye on the homeowner."

"You mean spying?"

"I mean spying," Cassie said.

April said, "Cool."

twelve

"I want it found legitimately, not because they know who I am and have therefore traced my history and writings."

Those words repeated themselves in Cassie's mind the next morning as she reread the list of possible suspects April had come up with. All five were located in the Bozeman area with two in town, one near Belgrade, and the last two in Livingston.

Since she'd not heard back from Candyce Fly in regard to the photos she'd sent her, Cassie had decided to devote the rest of the day to her other pending case. It was a little surprising, though, that Fly had not reacted either way.

They'd renamed the case file from "Sir Scott's Treasure" to "Bad Poet" because their search wasn't for the treasure but for the man who wrote the poem.

It was a process of elimination, she knew. There were more than a hundred men who self-described themselves as authors or writers in the database of Humanities Montana, the state agency that kept track of such things. Of that list, April had been told to key on local authors, which she had.

Cassie had no doubt there were more out there who for various reasons hadn't made the list. Would a wealthy eccentric who self-published his own autobiography be on the state list, she wondered? Then she answered her own question: doubtful. She thought about how many ranch houses she'd visited over the years that displayed family histories or self-penned autobiographies on their coffee tables.

It was very likely none of those authors existed on a semi-official state list.

And what if the man who'd hired her had deliberately planted the words "my writings" into their conversation to steer her the wrong way? That was certainly possible, she thought. But the way he'd said it in the most offhanded way made her think otherwise.

On her pad, she wrote down attributes she hoped to identify in the writers she would try to interview that day.

OLDER THAN SIXTY
ECCENTRIC
EGOTISTICAL/PRETENTIOUS
WEALTHY
FAMILIAR WITH THE AREA
BAD POET (although he thinks otherwise)

With April, they'd struck one of the five authors on the list before Cassie even began. Regis Stanhope of Belgrade, a literary novelist with three long books set in the Middle Ages, had recently been sentenced to prison in Deer Lodge for manslaughter, driving while impaired, and reckless endangerment. She recalled the case.

After drinking too much at a reception at a local ranch, Stanhope had driven home by himself and he had struck a hitchhiker on the side of the road. Although Stanhope had denied any recollection of the accident, state troopers found the victim still wedged into the passenger side of Stanhope's vehicle while it was parked in his garage.

Although Stanhope met several of the criteria, Cassie determined there was no way he could have hidden the treasure, penned the poem inside Sir Scott's, phoned her, *and* engineered the cash retainer drop from prison.

She drew a line through his name.

That left two writers in Bozeman and two in Livingston.

It was important, she thought, not to notify them in advance of her arrival. She wanted to see their faces when she introduced herself, and listen carefully to what they had to say—and how they said it. The Bad Poet who had called her had a certain formal cadence to his voice even though it had been electronically distorted. She thought she'd be able to identify that cadence in person as well as his choice of words.

She'd start in Bozeman with T. A. Ravalli and Courtney Wyoga.

Ben had been barely able to contain his excitement when he showed up at the office that morning for his assignment with April.

"Play it cool," she told them both. "Arrive separately and say you saw the ad for labor in the *Anaconda Leader*. It's okay later to admit that you know each other because the key to these kinds of undercover jobs is to keep your cover story as authentic as possible so you don't trip up. If you start making up stories it's harder and harder to remember them, especially under pressure. So what are your cover stories that we discussed?"

April said, "I'm April Pickett, a ranch girl from Wyoming and I just moved to Montana because I needed some space from my parents and because I want to wind up with a job as a wrangler on a horse ranch or a dude ranch. I couldn't find one right away so when I saw the ad in the paper I thought I'd check it out. I'm a hard worker but I'm also not looking for a career as a common laborer. Mainly, I like the idea of twenty bucks an hour."

Cassie had nodded and turned to Ben.

"What's your name?"

"Ben Stafford."

"Good."

A quick Google search of the name would take the user to Ben Stafford, a junior at Bozeman High. The resemblance between her

Ben and Ben Stafford was uncanny, and both teachers and school counselors had often confused them.

"Why are you there?" Cassie asked.

He flushed when he said, "I'm taking some time off from high school because I need to make enough money to buy a pickup. I met April downtown and when she told me about the job I followed her. I mean, who wouldn't?"

April rolled her eyes and Cassie laughed uncomfortably. Ben's cover story was just a little too on the mark, she thought.

"Remember," Cassie said, "don't ask too many questions or appear too curious about the owner. He's a very smart man and he'll figure you out if you do. Just hang back, work hard, and keep your eyes and ears open."

Both of them nodded that they understood.

"Most important," Cassie said to them sternly, "under no circumstances will you do or say *anything* that puts you in harm's way. You have to promise me that if anything seems hinky or questionable you'll both pack up and get the hell out of there. Immediately, without looking back. Promise?"

They promised. But while they did it she wished she didn't sense both defiance and ambition in their attitudes. April and Ben wanted to break this thing. She wanted them to as well, but not in any way that would threaten their safety.

T. A. Ravalli was shooting arrows at a large hay roll on the side of his house when Cassie arrived. He lived on the edge of town in a fine three-story home with a Hummer and a Toyota Land Cruiser out front. She noted that the target on the hay was of a Middle Eastern terrorist with a scowl on his face and an AK-47 in his arms.

Ravalli was balding and in his mid-fifties, but his demeanor was tight and coiled like a snake. He moved quickly and his eyes darted all around as if looking for an ambush.

"Sorry," he said to her. "If you want an interview you need to go through my publicist."

"I'm sorry to just show up like this," she said.

"Yeah, no kidding."

His eyes narrowed while he studied her Jeep, apparently to see if there was anyone else inside.

"It's just me," she said, extending her hand. "Cassie Dewell."

He clutched the grip of the compound bow in his left hand. It was a complicated weapon that Cassie only partially understood with its wheels and sights and stabilizers. There was a broadhead arrow shaft poised on its arrow rest that she wished he would disarm. He reached out with his right hand and shook.

"It's never too early to get ready for elk season," he said as a way of explanation. There was something crazy and penetrating about his light green eyes. But there was no tell that he knew her.

"I'm not a journalist. I'm a private investigator," she said. "I'm working for a client—"

"I write about PIs," he said, cutting her off. "My guy is named Lynx Mattis and he's a PI out of Philly. Real badass. Ex-Special Forces. Wears an eye patch and carries a .45 Sig in a shoulder holster and a .32 in an ankle holster. Drives a tricked-out Humvee and he has a cigarette boat in a slip he liberated from some baddies. Oh, and he's also a pilot."

"I have few of those qualities," Cassie said.

Ravalli looked her over like a predator. He refrained from agreeing with her out loud.

He said, "I've got a shitload of books in what is called the 'Tap' series. *Double Tap, Triple Tap, Savage Tap, Primal Tap* . . . ?"

"I'm afraid I'm not familiar with them."

"There's plenty of time to catch up!" he said with a wolfish grin. "Most of my readers are men but there are plenty of ladies who like them, too."

She already knew he wasn't the Bad Poet. He was a bit too

young and his rat-a-tat style of speaking had no resemblance to the man who had called her.

"So," he said, "I'm guessing you want to pick my brain."

At first, she was confused. Then she realized Ravalli assumed she'd shown up to get some pointers on how to be a *real* PI. The kind who flew airplanes and owned boats.

"I'm simply eliminating suspects in a case," she said. "You're eliminated."

"So quickly?" he said, genuinely hurt. "Just like that?"

"Yes. I spoke to the man I'm looking for. You're not him."

"Too bad," he said. "I could really let you in on some tips and techniques. I'm in touch with operators all over the country and I do a lot of research. I might be able to really help you do your job."

"I'll keep that in mind."

"Fine. You obviously know where I live."

He turned quickly and fired the arrow toward the target. It sailed over the top of the hay bale.

"You never saw that," he said quickly.

"Indeed I didn't," she said.

Courtney Wyoga lived in a modest two-story home on Covey Court in the older North Star neighborhood. It was shaded by mature cottonwoods and overgrown hedges crowded the step-up walkway to the front door.

Cassie noted the NO SOLICITING sign taped inside the screen door as well as the small security camera mounted above the door itself when she rang the doorbell.

A high male voice responded with, "Just leave it on the front porch."

Cassie stepped back and showed her open empty hands to the camera. She tried to demonstrate that she was not delivering food or a package.

"What do you want?" the same voice said, this time closer to the door.

"I'm in the midst of an investigation. I'm talking to well-known Montana authors."

"Is that what I am?" he asked.

"I'd say so, at least according to Humanities Montana."

Playing on the vanity of subjects usually worked well. She guessed that writers might be especially susceptible to flattery given the solitary nature of their work.

"I'm hoping I can take a few moments of your time today."

"Are you sure you aren't selling something?"

"I'm sure. I'm a private investigator working on a case."

She dug her license out of her handbag and showed it to the camera lens, then shifted it toward the peephole in the door.

"Do you have a mask?" the man asked.

"A mask?"

"A proper face covering," the man said, obviously irritated.

She rifled through her bag. Finding none, she said, "I think I might still have one in my car."

Cassie located a crumpled blue paper face mask in the console of her Jeep and she pulled it over her mouth and fastened it behind her ears. It smelled of onions, likely from the last hot dog she had eaten the year before when masks were mandatory in some public buildings.

She was immediately reminded how much she hated wearing useless paper masks during the pandemic. But she returned to the front door with it on.

"Just a few minutes, okay?" the man said. He undid the chain lock and stepped back, leaving her to push it open.

She found Courtney Wyoga inside seated in a recliner on the other side of the room at least twenty feet away. He wore a mask *and* a plastic face shield over it. He gestured toward a chair near the door where she stood.

It was dark inside the living room and it took her a full minute to be able to see it all. The television was on and tuned to CNN but muted. A monitor from a laptop displayed several views from closed-circuit cameras on the periphery of his house. The curtains had been pulled closed and the only light came from narrow bands of it above and below the shades. She could see his kitchen table through a doorway to the kitchen. It was covered with spray bottles of disinfectant and boxes of cleaning wipes and disposable gloves. She recalled washing her own food for about a week in March of 2020 before giving up on that.

Cassie kept the front door slightly open and sat down. She thought it would make Wyoga more comfortable that she hadn't sealed herself into his space.

"I usually don't let people in," Wyoga said.

"Are you concerned about COVID?" Cassie asked.

"Anybody who isn't is a damned fool. There will be another strain coming. Anyone who doesn't take precautions is taking their life in their hands."

Cassie nodded. There was no need telling Wyoga that she had had the virus, recovered, and now rarely thought about it anymore. She repeated that she was in the process of interviewing local authors in regard to a case she was involved with. As she said it she nodded toward a narrow bookcase that held at least a dozen copies of books he had written. She could see his name on the spine of them. They looked old.

"Are you working on a book now?" she asked.

He erupted: "I don't know what these publishers expect! They're mad. They seem to think you can write on demand like some kind of automaton. They don't understand the creative process—that you can't just turn it on like a light switch and produce a hundred thousand words."

She said, "I take it you haven't been able to write due to the pandemic."

"Of course not! How can I when I spend all my time social distancing and trying to figure out when I have to go to the store? And constantly hounding places to get things delivered? It's a twenty-four-hour job in itself. There's no time for writing in there. You can't just turn off the worst pandemic in the history of the world and work in a creative field. They just don't understand."

"It's got to be tough," she said.

"My wife's in Romania, where she went to visit her family nearly two years ago," he cried. "She hasn't been able to come back."

Wyoga tried to cover his face with his hands but the shield prevented it. Instead, he slipped his hands up underneath it and rubbed his eyes. "It's a crime what they expect of me. Can't they see I'm paralyzed?"

"I can certainly see that," Cassie said. "For most people the pandemic is over."

"They're fools," he said. "We should all be locked down for our safety."

"What I think about is all of the people out there who work—and worked—to keep you alive and well. Like the delivery food drivers, the grocery store workers, the truck drivers, and so on. They didn't have the luxury of staying inside their homes."

"Collateral damage," Wyoga said. "Nothing I can do about them."

In addition to being heartless, she could also see that unless Courtney Wyoga was one of the greatest impromptu actors in the world that he wasn't capable of planning and carrying out Sir Scott's Treasure scheme in his current condition. Much less venturing from his home all the way to Manhattan to launch it.

"I'm sorry to bother you," she said. "And I'm sorry about your wife. I wasn't aware of the travel restrictions into our country."

"No one is," he moaned. "And no one cares. No one cares about anything or anybody anymore."

"I don't know if that's true," she said. "Maybe if you went out a little? There are a lot of happy people downtown right now."

"Happy virus carriers, you mean. *The unvaccinated*." He said "the unvaccinated" with such hateful contempt that Cassie had no response.

"I don't think there is any reason to take up any more of your time today," she said.

"Really? That's it?" He seemed slightly hurt there wasn't more.

"That's it."

She stood up and sidled through the door to the porch and closed it behind her.

Her mask was wadded up in her handbag before she got to her Jeep.

Before grabbing lunch-on-the go and driving to Livingston, Cassie checked her messages.

There was nothing from Candyce Fly, so Cassie re-sent the email from the evening before.

But . . .

We're in, April had texted. Ben, too. He's got us picking up rocks.

Then: P.S. I really like the guy.

"Of course you do," Cassie said aloud.

With T. A. Ravalli and Courtney Wyoga out, Cassie's target list consisted of William Reichs and Buck Wilson of Livingston. She remarked to herself how lucky she'd been thus far locating her first two subjects at home when she visited and she hoped her luck would continue. PI work rarely went so smoothly. She spent a lot of her time in her car waiting for subjects to come home. Writers were different, she thought.

They had no other place to go.

thirteen

❖

Kyle Westergaard rolled up his sleeping bag in the bed of his pickup and cinched it up and placed it in an oversized plastic garbage bag so it wouldn't get wet if it rained later in the day.

He'd spent the night in an unpaved parking lot off of the highway and not far from the unincorporated location known as Bonner. There had been a few other vehicles in the lot when he arrived the night before, but one by one they'd left during the night. He was now the only person there.

He could hear the Little Blackfoot River through the thick trees, and it excited him. Three Rivers had been a bust.

The pine trees surrounding the lot were tall and dark and the sun had not risen high enough yet to cut through them. It was cold, and he wore his oil field Carhartt parka as he balanced his camp stove on the open tailgate of his pickup and started it with a wooden match. He very much liked the hissing sound of the flame when he got it going.

Kyle reached into the bed of his truck and grasped the butt of his 20-gauge shotgun and pulled it out. It was a pump-action Remington he'd bought at a pawn shop in Dickinson and he'd used it to hunt grouse and rabbits. It was in a Cordura case and he slept better knowing that he could defend himself if anyone showed up to cause trouble during the night. He slipped it behind the seat of his pickup for safekeeping.

The Little Blackfoot River excited him because it met one of the important criteria of the treasure poem.

On the evening before, he'd crossed the confluence where the Little Blackfoot poured into the Clark's Fork.

Begin where the rivers marry

Kyle opened a can of pork and beans and placed it on top of the flame. The loaf of white bread he'd purchased at a convenience store the day before was handy and he pulled out two slices and placed them next to each other on a blue enamel plate he'd owned for many years. His spork was in his backpack and he fished it out.

Many years before, Kyle had assembled a survival kit for his adventure on the Missouri River with his friend Raheem. Most of the items he'd gathered were from Dumpsters or garage sales in Bakken County, North Dakota. Even though the adventure had gone horrible awry when they encountered Ronald Pergram, he still treasured his survival kit and he took it with him everywhere. Kyle wondered why everyone didn't use sporks—a utensil that combined a spoon and a fork into one. It made a lot of sense to him.

When the can was bubbling on the stove, Kyle poured the beans over the slices of bread. He liked the way his plate steamed and the food was delicious when he dug in and shoveled it into his mouth.

When he was through, he wiped off his plate and spork with wet wipes and returned them to his kit. The beans would give him gas but being flatulent while hiking was no big deal. It wasn't like he was going to a wedding.

Kyle checked his phone. He had only a few numbers in his directory: work, the pizza delivery place in Bakken, Lottie's doctor's office, and Lottie herself.

He punched up Lottie's number. It was a landline because

Lottie had never even turned on the cell phone he gave her for Christmas. There was no answer and she didn't have voice mail set up.

That concerned him because it was too early in the day, he thought, for her to be out of the house at her daily hair appointment.

A couple of other cars arrived in the parking lot while Kyle got ready. Men got out of the cars and started pulling on waders and assembling fly rods. Kyle watched them out of the corner of his eye and envied them.

A burly man with red hair walked across the parking lot with a Thermos and offered Kyle a cup of coffee.

"No, thank you," Kyle said. "I don't drink coffee."

"What do you drink?" the man asked.

"I'm a Mountain Dew man, myself," Kyle responded.

"Sorry, I don't have one of those."

"That's okay. It was nice of you to offer."

"Are you going fishing?" the man asked, letting his eyes stray over the gear in the back of Kyle's pickup. No doubt he was looking for waders, boots, and rods.

"Not today," Kyle said. He didn't want to tell the fisherman what he was doing. *I'm hunting for a hidden treasure chest* sounded too goofy.

"Well," the man said finally, "have a good day."

"You, too."

Lottie answered the phone when Kyle called back. She sounded exasperated, but he was grateful she was there.

"I just wanted to make sure you were okay," he said.

"Of course I am, Kyle. It's just that my right ear is a little cold."

"I don't know what that means."

She hesitated. Then: "I guess I left the phone in the refrigerator overnight. I just now found it." She sounded irritated. Lottie always sounded annoyed after she'd done something stupid, as if it were someone else's fault and she was put out about it.

"So the phone is cold?" Kyle asked.

"Isn't that what I just told you?"

Kyle nodded. "This is why we need to get you some help."

"This again! Maybe you should just come back."

"I will soon."

Then she launched into a story about squirrels coming into her backyard and eating all the bird food she put out. Kyle had heard it a million times. He waited her out.

Finally, she asked, "Where are you again?"

"Montana," he said. "I've told you that over and over again. Maybe you should stop feeding the birds."

"What if I decided not to feed you when you were little and you showed up at my house?" she asked. "How would you feel about *that*?"

"Love you. Don't leave the phone in the refrigerator."

Kyle set out for the day with his backpack and a walking stick he picked up along the way. It got warm quickly as the sun rose and he shed his jacket.

The way the sun dappled on the grass through the walls of tall pines made him happy. He drank it in and wished he lived there, although it would be impossible to convince his Grandma Lottie to move with him. She'd only once been west of the Montana state line, and she was perversely proud of the fact. Lottie thought

Montanans were arrogant and that they looked down their noses at North Dakotans. Maybe with her dementia he'd be able to convince her to come, but that thought made him feel terrible.

And take the hidden trail,

There were established trails along both banks of the river. He guessed they were used primarily by fly fishermen. Kyle thought the trails were too prominent to be the right ones.

He climbed up along the slope of the river into the timber. The river was to his right and below him.

Stay in the shadows and you will prevail.

As he climbed he stepped over a faint grassy trail that cut across the slope parallel to the river. It was a game trail—the mountains were filled with them—but it sunk into the loam, indicating it had been there and had been used for a number of years. Kyle felt a flutter in his belly and it wasn't just the beans working.

As he hiked he looked down. There were a few fly fishermen in waders in the river. He stopped and admired them—their clothing, their gear, the way the line looped gracefully when they cast. The ruddy man from the parking lot was one of them. The man looked up and glared at him. Apparently, he didn't like to be observed.

No fish were caught that he saw. Kyle quickly moved on.

There were a few small creeks to cross that flowed into the Little Blackfoot, but none of them were big enough to be considered a river, he was certain. The Little Blackfoot wasn't even all that wide, but it was pretty. Although there were several hillsides that had burned over the years from forest fires, he decided that the burns were in the wrong order to apply to the poem.

★ ★ ★

At five and a half miles in, the walls of the canyon rose sharply on both sides and the trail he was hiking on disappeared.

From there you'll have to summon strength
The walls are closing in;

Kyle climbed down the slope to the river itself. The Little Blackfoot was squeezed between two dark rock walls. There was no way to walk along it anymore.

But it comported to the poem! His hands trembled as he pulled his boots and socks off and replaced them with a pair of river sandals. He tied his bootlaces to loops in his pack and gingerly stepped between a pair of large rocks to enter the river itself.

Kyle held his pack up over his head as he slipped into the river. The stones on the bed of the river were slick and he stumbled a few times but he didn't go down. It was remarkably cold and at one point the current was just below his armpits and it was powerful enough to sweep him away and wash him down the river.

Depending on the season,
You may have to wade or swim.

He wasn't a good swimmer, but he was committed too far into the canyon to bail out. For a moment, he stood and braced against the current and breathed deeply again and again, trying to remain calm. Then, using a technique where he leaned back slightly against the flow and stepped ahead using his heel first one step at a time, he made it through the narrowest part of the canyon. It was so narrow at one point that he could almost reach out and touch both walls.

He kept going and somehow didn't lose his footing.

After a few more minutes of inching ahead, Kyle could see that it was opening up ahead of him. The river was lower on his back and sun splashed the water ahead.

> *If you've been smart and found the burn,*
> *Look west to spy the treasure,*

He *so* wanted to emerge from the canyon to find a burn that he could visualize the place where he'd discover the treasure.

It would be in a pool of shadow at the base of a pine tree to his left. Although the metal on the chest would be discolored from the weather and dried pine needles would have fallen on it, it would be there. He could see himself lifting it up by its handles and moving it into the sunlight. It was heavy. He had no idea how heavy gold was until that moment and he started to worry about carrying it all the way back to his pickup miles away.

But when Kyle emerged from the narrow canyon he was disappointed. There was no burn. Instead, there were grassy meadows on each side of the Little Blackfoot. On the north bank, there was an old miner's cabin without a roof tucked up into the trees.

On the left bank, where he'd expected to find the treasure, it was flat and grassy with no features except for half-buried rocks.

Still, he spent an hour looking over every inch of the west bank. He even went about ten feet into the trees to see if he'd missed anything. He hadn't.

Kyle sighed and crossed the river to the cabin. Maybe the poet got that wrong?

All he'd found inside the cabin when he entered it were a few old beer cans and a discarded condom that looked like a thick white worm. Pretty gross.

* * *

Disappointed, Kyle worked his way back on the other side of the river to where he'd parked his truck. Rather than fight the current in the river, he climbed very high until he was on top of the narrows and he stumbled his way down the other side back to the bank.

He told himself he was not discouraged. Kyle was *never* discouraged, because it meant he could now draw a line through the Little Blackfoot River on the list of Montana rivers he'd made in his notebook. There were only four other rivers on it he'd not explored: the Marias, the Judith, the Rosebud, and the Powder River. Which meant he was getting closer.

fourteen

❖⟹⟸❖

She was halfway up Bozeman Pass when Cassie noticed the speck of a silver GMC pickup in her rearview mirror. Her antennae went up because it hung back at a respectful distance—not gaining on her nor falling behind.

She had the cruise control on the Jeep set at eighty-two miles per hour (the speed limit was eighty) and she toggled the control on her wheel to take it down to seventy-seven. The GMC slowed down as well.

When she goosed it up to eighty-five as she reached the summit, the GMC hung right with her.

"Who are you?" she asked aloud.

If she was being followed as she now suspected, the driver was experienced at this kind of thing. She was dealing with a professional.

As she emerged from the timbered canyon just seven miles from Livingston, Cassie knew the summit of the hill behind her obscured her location for a short while from vehicles to her rear. She tapped on her brakes and eased the Jeep off of the interstate as quickly and as safely as she could and came to a stop just outside two delineator posts. A roll of dust washed over her vehicle and she turned in her seat to catch a glimpse of the driver of the pickup as it passed her.

She waited ten seconds, then twenty. Then a full minute.

Small passenger cars, minivans, and a stream of tractor-trailer rigs roared down the highway, blasting by her and shaking her Jeep on its springs. The semitrucks always sent a chill through her, ever since her encounters with the Lizard King. She wondered if she'd ever be able to see a big truck on the highway and not experience a shot of terror.

Had the silver pickup been among them in the other lane and she'd somehow missed it? Cassie could see the vehicles a long distance in a straight line bound for the Livingston exits. The pickup was not among them.

Which meant the driver of the silver GMC had known or discerned that she'd stopped, and pulled over himself.

Which meant he *was* following her after all.

She thought for a moment about crossing the eastbound lanes, driving down into the borrow pit, and coming up on the westbound highway. She could then drive back over the summit and observe the parked silver pickup from that vantage point.

But there were too many cars coming from both directions. Making that maneuver would be reckless and dangerous. It was less than half a mile from the summit and if a vehicle was speeding it could T-bone her Jeep if she pulled out across the highway. Same with the westbound lanes. There was a stream of cars coming.

Instead, she moved out into the emergency lane and built up speed. Then she slipped back into the stream of traffic. She assumed the driver of the pickup had done the same thing on the other side of the mountain.

Her suspicion was confirmed as she took the first exit into Livingston. The pickup was back.

But rather than take the same exit and end up directly behind her, it sailed by the ramp. She couldn't see the driver because of the angle of her car.

Cassie assumed the pickup would take another exit into town and find her or wait patiently for her to get back onto I-90 when her business was concluded. Either way, she vowed to keep an eye out for it.

How the driver of the pickup knew she'd stopped flummoxed her. And then, thinking about it, she came up with a possible answer.

Author Buck Wilson lived in a shambling modern log home on ten or so acres on the bank of the Yellowstone River. It was the kind of home Cassie pined for—and knew she would never live in. It had a vast lawn and old-growth evergreen trees and she could see the sparkle of the afternoon sun on the rippling surface of the river.

There was an assortment of brightly colored Big Wheels and other children's toys in the grass on the side of the house. She liked that but the toys suggested Wilson might be too young to meet at least one of her qualifications.

Cassie took a circular drive and parked near the main entrance. When she got out of her Jeep she dropped into a squat and leaned over to peer under the carriage of her car. She reached down and felt along the inside of the wheel wells until she found it: a stubby metal attachment about the size of a pack of cigarettes. It was fixed to the metal with magnets.

Instead of pulling it off, she lowered her phone under the wheel well and took a photo of it. It was a tracking device. She recognized its make and model from her years in law enforcement.

Who had placed it there and when? She'd have to retrace her movements to narrow it down.

But rather than pull it free and dismantle it, she left it there. There might be a way to use the device against the person tracking her movements—no doubt the driver of the silver pickup.

She'd just have to figure out how to make that work.

"Ma'am, can I help you?"

It was a female voice and it came from the doorway of the home on the other side of Cassie's Jeep.

Cassie rose. Her knees hurt as she did so.

Standing on the front porch was an attractive, athletic-looking woman holding a small baby and wearing a full long-sleeved shirt and yoga pants.

"I'm sorry," Cassie said. "I must look stupid pulling into your drive and ducking down behind my car."

"Kind of," the woman said.

"I had a shimmy when I was driving," Cassie said. "I wanted to look underneath my car to see if I could figure out what was happening."

"Did you find it?"

"No, to be honest. But let me start fresh. I'm Cassie Dewell. I'm a private investigator out of Bozeman. I was hoping I could speak with Buck Wilson if he's available."

"Ah," the woman said with a bit of hurt in her voice. "I'm Jessie. And here I thought you were here to see me."

Cassie was confused.

"We're looking for a part-time nanny and I was hoping you were here to apply for the job."

"Do I look like a nanny?" Cassie asked.

"You look like what I hope a nanny looks like," Jessie said. "So far, the only applicants we've had are teenagers covered in tattoos and body jewelry or they look like they've just been released from the Montana state women's prison."

"Well, I'm sorry," Cassie said. "I'm here to talk to Buck Wilson."

"No one ever wants to talk to the *wife* of the big-time author," Jessie said.

Cassie felt guilty until Jessie smiled to indicate she was kidding.

"Buck's my husband but he's out right now."

Cassie's theory that every writer would be at home fell apart in a second.

"Can you tell me when he'll be back?"

"What's this about?"

"I'm doing an investigation on behalf of a client," Cassie said. "As part of the investigation I'm interviewing Montana writers and authors."

"That's not very clear."

"I can't really divulge much more, I'm afraid," Cassie said. "I'm sorry about disturbing your morning. I'll come back later. When would be a good time?"

Jessie said, "Buck takes the kids to school and comes home to work for a few hours. Then he takes a long walk to clear his head before he starts his afternoon session. He's on his walk now so . . . maybe an hour?"

"Thank you."

Cassie felt the guilt again. Jessie seemed open and guileless and Cassie felt a little like an oily PI on the make. And she had disturbed Jessie's morning.

"If it's okay with you I'll come back later this afternoon," Cassie said. Then: "I don't suspect your husband of anything at all. It's more a matter of ruling people out."

"Ruling people out of what?"

"Involvement in a . . . situation."

"Buck's probably too busy to be involved in a situation, I'd guess."

"I'm sure he is," Cassie said. Then she thanked Jessie again.

As she climbed into the Jeep she paused. To alleviate her guilt, she said, "Is there anything you need that I can bring you? Diapers, formula, take-out food? Anything?"

"A part-time nanny who looks like you would be nice."

Cassie smiled. "I'll keep my eyes out."

"Thank you," Jessie said. "I'll tell Buck to expect you later."

As Cassie drove around the circular drive she scanned the road for the silver pickup but she didn't see it. Then she thought: Why would he even have to stay on her when he could track her every movement? He was probably parked on a side street with an iPad on his lap, watching her Jeep move around Livingston.

William Reichs *was* home, and as Cassie pulled into a parking area near his extremely impressive river-rock home off of US 89 on the way south toward Emigrant, she got a tweak of intuition she hadn't been expecting.

The home was well established and it reeked of old money, yet it was a bit pretentious and showy at the same time. A huge bronze statue of a bull elk doing battle with a small pack of wolves dominated the front lawn. There were magnificent views of the Yellowstone River and the Beartooth and Absaroka mountains to the east.

She approached the massive hardwood double doors and noted a substantial bronze knocker over the words:

WILLIAM H. REICHS
AUTHOR/NOVELIST/POET/ESSAYIST

Who would describe himself like that? she thought.

Inside the alcove was another brass plaque with the last stanza of a Robert Frost poem that even she, not a student of poetry, recognized:

> *I shall be telling this with a sigh*
> *Somewhere ages and ages hence:*
> *Two roads diverged in a wood, and I—*
> *I took the one less traveled by,*
> *And that has made all the difference.*

"Hmm," she said.

Cassie used the knocker and heard it echo inside. A fleet of small dogs started yapping, followed by a stentorian voice telling them, *"Stop!"*

The door was swung inward by a tall portly man wearing a dark red smoker's robe and holding a pipe. He had long silver hair that swept straight back over his pate and flowed an inch over his collar. Reading glasses perched on the tip of his bulbous nose and his light blue eyes sparkled with wry devilry. His fleshy face was lined with small veins that made it resemble an ancient porcelain teacup.

"Greetings," he said. "What is the reason for you calling on me today, young lady?"

Cassie stammered out the intro she'd used three times that day although she suspected it might be unnecessary. She played heavily on the "prominent and important" writer aspects. Reichs weighed her words, puffed on his pipe, and stepped aside and invited her in.

"There is a reason you're not giving me more specifics about your client and your case," he said. Then he winked at her and said: "You're here to size me up."

She went over her criteria again:

OLDER THAN SIXTY
ECCENTRIC
EGOTISTICAL/PRETENTIOUS
WEALTHY
FAMILIAR WITH THE AREA
BAD POET (although he thinks otherwise)

So far, several of the boxes had been ticked.

"Let's have a seat and discuss this," Reichs said, gesturing to a pair of overstuffed chairs in what Cassie could only describe as a parlor. "Is there anything I can get you? Coffee? Tea? A stiff drink, perhaps?"

"No thank you," she said.

"When you're through sizing me up I have a question for you," he said as he settled into his chair. "It's about a particular poem that has created quite a bit of public interest these days. So much so that a private investigator might choose to become involved with the hunt for buried treasure."

Cassie felt her neck get hot. She studied his face for confirmation but he carefully maintained his air of aloof, but friendly, superiority.

"It's very telling that you brought up 'Sir Scott's Treasure Poem,'" she said.

"It's a terrible title they've given it," he said. "Why not something like, 'The Road to Riches,' or 'Journey to Gold,' or something tantalizing like that?"

"Is that what you would have called it?" she asked.

"I don't know. But it certainly would have been better than 'Sir Scott's Treasure Poem,'" he said with a wink. Then: "I've been thinking a lot about that poem and the interest it has generated. I've been thinking about using the whole premise in a new novel. But I can assure you I'd do it differently."

Cassie sat on the edge of her chair. She didn't want to sink back into it. She continued to study his face and gestures, looking for a tell. But he was good. And there was no doubt he enjoyed toying with her.

"How would you do it differently if you were writing about it?" she asked.

"I would add"—he paused and leaned into her—"*danger*. I would actually hide four different caches. Three of them would be booby-trapped, set to explode and kill or maim the treasure hunter. It would all be spelled out in the poem itself, of course, so the searchers would be warned in advance. Otherwise that would be a very cruel trick. But the fourth cache would be genuine. And whomever found it would be rich and set for life.

"In my novel," he continued, "we would follow four treasure hunters as they searched for the gold. One would be a piggish heir to a fortune who doesn't really need the money. The second would be an ex-con who will do anything imaginable to thwart others and secure the gold himself. The third I'm still working on although I'm sure my publisher would insist on a person of color or another minority of some kind. The fourth would be a young boy or girl who needs to find wealth to pay for a life-saving medical procedure for their mother. We would root for the fourth character, of course."

"Of course," Cassie said.

Reichs said, "But the third character would be very sympathetic and perhaps they'd join forces with our hero at some point. You can't kill off characters like that or you get in trouble.

"Although I *could* defy all expectations and have the piggish heir find it, only to be killed before he could exploit it. There is poetic justice in that as well."

Cassie shook her head. "I don't think I'd like that ending."

"You're probably right," he said. "I'm still hashing it all out in my mind. Here's something very important you should know, Cassie Dewell. Just because a writer isn't, you know, in the act of writing that doesn't mean the writer isn't working. So much of writing is done up here," he said as he pointed to his head.

Cassie looked from Reichs to his bookshelf. She asked, "In your novel, which of your writings would lead an investigator to the poet himself?"

Reichs hauled himself up and strode across the carpet and pulled a thin volume from the shelf. He returned with it and handed it to Cassie. It was a book of poetry entitled *My Sacred Journeys*.

She opened it. The book was a collection of very short poems about locations Reichs had visited in his lifetime, it appeared. There were sections on Europe, Scandinavia, and Australia and New Zealand. But the largest section by far was devoted to the American West, and the Rocky Mountains in particular.

She flipped to the title page to see that *My Sacred Journeys* was published not by a major publisher, but by a printing company in Billings twenty years before.

He said, "Yes, I see where you're looking. It's a sad fact that the big boys in New York simply don't like publishing poetry because they're convinced it doesn't sell."

"How many copies of this book did you have printed?"

His face reddened. She couldn't tell if it was anger, embarrassment, or the tell she was looking for.

"A few hundred copies, I believe," he said. "Most were given to friends and libraries."

She looked up at him. "If a treasure hunter found this it could be quite literally a guidebook to where the treasure might be found because all these places are familiar to you."

Reichs looked at Cassie with a blank expression. Then he tapped out his pipe in a bowl for that specific purpose.

He said, "It appears that you're confusing the premise of the novel I might write with something else entirely, Miss Dewell."

"Am I?"

"Most certainly you are. But it's a mistake often made by laypeople. They assume that everything they read in a novel *must* come from somewhere in the author's life. They have trouble believing that fiction can be wholly conjured from the air, that not every character is actually based on a real person the author knows. They refuse to believe in the magic of fiction. Additionally, too many academics spend too much time analyzing the work to figure out where an author got this or got that because that academic is incapable of writing their own novel. These literature professors don't have the spark of creativity necessary to produce fiction."

Cassie nodded, then offered her hand to him. "That'll be

twenty-five thousand dollars, I believe. I can take it as a check or I can give you my bank details for a direct deposit. There isn't any need to pay in cash again."

Reichs stared at her hand in disbelief. He said, "This sounds like a shakedown."

"You set the terms," she said, feeling a little giddy.

"I set no such terms," he argued.

Cassie stood up and smoothed her jeans. "I'll send a bill," she said. "But I'd strongly suggest you call off the treasure hunt before anyone else gets hurt. If not, I'll blow your cover and I'm sure you wouldn't like that."

"Blow my cover?" he said, offended. "I'm well-known. I don't have a cover to be blown."

"I'll see myself out," she said.

Cassie was grinning to herself as she approached her car and checked the side roads for the silver pickup. It wasn't there. As she reached for the door handle to get in, a female voice called out to her from the Reichses' house.

She turned to find an elegant woman in her sixties striding quickly down the pathway. She'd come from a door in the back of the house. The woman wore a smart pantsuit and she had bobbed silver hair and a concerned look on her face.

"I'm Eugenia Reichs," she said, extending her hand. "Bill is my husband."

Cassie shook Eugenia's hand and found it chilly.

"I couldn't help but hear the conversation you had with Bill. I was in the next room."

"Yes?"

Eugenia looked over her shoulder to see if Reichs had followed her out. Assured he hadn't, she said, "Bill has nothing to do with the hidden treasure, I can assure you of that."

Cassie looked at her skeptically.

"He'd like for you to think that he's responsible for it, I'm sure. But he had nothing to do with it."

"I don't understand," Cassie said.

Eugenia leaned in close to Cassie and lowered her voice. "Bill had two very successful novels back in the late eighties. That's when I met him and we got married. But since then it's been very, very tough for him. He wrote another novel but none of the big New York publishers wanted it. Since then, well, writing has been a struggle for him. He doesn't like to talk about it and he maintains a very convincing literary presence, which I'm sure you'll attest to. But he's basically suffered from writer's block for the last eighteen years."

"So that's really a thing?" Cassie asked.

"It is with Bill."

Cassie gestured toward the home and said, "But all of this?"

"I'm a Cotherman," Eugenia said.

The name made Cassie step back. "Of the Cotherman ranches?"

"Yes."

The Cothermans were the largest landholders in eastern Montana. They also had massive properties in North Dakota, Wyoming, Idaho, and Texas. The family was Montana royalty. Eugenia was obviously one of the three daughters who were heirs to the fortune.

"This is all very interesting, but it doesn't mean he couldn't have hidden the treasure or written the poem," Cassie said.

"Actually, it does," Eugenia said. "There's no way he could have amassed millions of dollars in gold to hide. He makes a few thousand dollars a year in royalties from those early books, but that's it. Last year, it was less than two thousand."

"But this place?"

"It's owned by the family trust. You see, Bill has never been good with money. He used to waste a lot of it on poor investments and other schemes. It was his own money, so that was his business. But he ran out of it a long time ago. Our family trust met and we put him on an allowance many years ago. A stipend, if you will. It's not a big stipend. This is a very sensitive topic in our household, as I'm sure you understand."

Cassie was flummoxed. "Then why did he lead me down the path he did? He's the one who brought up the treasure poem, not me."

"He's obsessed with the Sir Scott treasure," Eugenia said. "He'd love to find it and be independently wealthy again. He's been going out on weekends for two years trying to find it. It's a shock when he *doesn't* bring up that poem within the first five minutes of any conversation."

"Are you being completely truthful with me?" Cassie asked.

"I am. And there's one more thing."

"Which is?"

"He probably wouldn't mind being publicly named as the man who hid the treasure and wrote the poem. It would make him famous again, and the notoriety would indicate to the world that he has money. Bill would like both of those things very much. But I wouldn't."

Cassie believed her. "Thank you for telling me all of this."

"I would have preferred not to, believe me. I'm a very private person."

"I get that."

"I did hear you mention twenty-five thousand dollars. I don't have that kind of cash laying around but I could probably get it within a week or two. I'm sure I could do ten easily enough if that would do. I feel bad that you came here in good faith and Bill led you on."

Cassie said, "Are you buying my silence? If so, please don't insult me."

Eugenia flushed bright red. "I'm sorry, I didn't mean it like that."

"I hope not."

Cassie said, "Bill's secret—and yours—is safe with me."

"Thank you. Somehow I knew I could trust you."

"Even though you tried to buy me off."

"Again, I'm sorry."

Cassie nodded and shook Eugenia's hand again.

"Do you swear it wasn't your husband who wrote the poem?" Cassie asked.

"I swear it as a Cotherman," she said.

"I believe you."

Cassie couldn't wait until the Reichses' home faded away in her rearview mirror.

"No," Buck Wilson said with a wide smile when Cassie sat down with him in his house, "I didn't hide the treasure and I didn't write the poem. That's just not my kind of thing."

"How did you know that's what I was here for?" Cassie asked.

"Bill called me just a few minutes ago. He seemed to insinuate that you suspect him—and he didn't deny it. I nodded and said, 'uh-huh,' a lot, which is what I always do when Bill calls. He thinks we're kindred spirits."

Buck Wilson was dark and lean and avuncular. He was also much too young to fit the "bad poet" profile.

"Kindred spirits?" Cassie asked.

"Since we're both writers in Livingston, I guess," Wilson said. "I don't want to break it to him that we aren't. He likes to come across as literary and hoity-toity. I just go to work every day, just like you do."

Cassie admired Wilson's bookshelf. It had far more books by him on it than any of the others she'd visited that day. And he seemed to be remarkably levelheaded.

"Let me ask you," Wilson said, "Do you ever wake up suffering from 'private investigator block'?"

"If I did I'd go broke," she answered.

"That's what I think about writer's block. You either go to work or you don't."

"Thank you for your time," Cassie said. "You have a nice family."

"I can't argue with you there," he said. "Good luck on your case. It sounds very interesting."

"Interesting, yes," she said. "But frustrating. I'm now back to zero."

"You'll figure it out," Wilson said.

"Thank you for your confidence."

"By the way, I would have written a much better treasure poem," he said with a sly grin.

Cassie exited Livingston at midafternoon and started the climb to Bozeman Pass on I-90 West. A mile behind her, the silver pickup emerged from the second exit and hung back in the right lane.

"Hello, again," she said aloud.

When her phone chimed she took a quick look at the screen. There was a voice message from an unknown number with an area code of 239. She recalled seeing that area code recently and realized it had been attached to the Zoom call she'd had with Candyce Fly. Boca Grande.

Cassie called up the message and listened to it over her car speakers via Bluetooth.

Hi. My name is Daney Tanner. You don't know me but I'm Candy Fly's niece. I'm at her house and I see you've been sending emails to my aunt Candy. Well—something terrible has happened. Please call me back at this number when you can.

Click.

fifteen

◆━◉━◆

Cassie connected with Daney Tanner via FaceTime on her iPad in her office. She'd closed her door so Isabel couldn't overhear the conversation. Although at one time Cassie had disliked video calls or meetings, she'd grown to appreciate the value of being able to see the facial features and expressions of subjects even if by long distance.

Daney Tanner was tanned and willowy like her aunt and she was obviously quite upset. She was speaking to Cassie from Candyce Fly's home. She had the same background on the call that Fly had used just days before.

"I was the one who found her," Tanner said. "I texted her this morning to see if she wanted to go out for breakfast. She didn't reply, so that was suspicious right there. Aunt Candy is never without her phone. Never. So I drove over and knocked on the door. No answer.

"I knew where she kept a spare key out front beneath a fake plastic rock, so I let myself in."

Tanner paused and looked away from the camera for a moment. When she came back her eyes were filled with tears. "I found her lying on top of her bed with her golf clothes on. The empty pill bottle of Oxy was on her nightstand. It was obvious to me that she took her own life sometime yesterday. Probably in the afternoon. The EMTs said the same thing, I guess based on her body temperature and how stiff her body was."

"I'm so sorry to hear that," Cassie said. "I really am."

"Yeah, she didn't have a lot of close friends. Aunt Candy was kind of hard to get along with, I get it. I was one of the few relations she kept in touch with. We shared things, you know? This is really a gut punch because I always thought she was one of the toughest women I knew. But it just goes to show you that you can never really know what's going on in another person's head, even someone as strong as Aunt Candy."

"Have the authorities been there?"

Tanner nodded. "It was a zoo here all morning. EMTs, cops, evidence techs. They were all here but there was really nothing they could do. The coroner has already ruled it a suicide, but that was obvious to me when I walked in. I guess it's a preliminary ruling, but I have no doubt."

"Did she leave a note?"

Cassie knew that the majority of suicide victims didn't leave notes.

"No," Tanner said. "I looked. I checked her home office and both her phone and her computer. I knew all her passwords were 1-2-3-4-5 because I'd suggested a long time ago that she change them. That's when I saw you'd been sending her emails."

"Had they been opened?" Cassie asked, speculating that it might have been the photos of Matthew Annan that had sent Fly over the edge.

"No," Tanner said.

Cassie was both grateful and disappointed. It *would* have been helpful to confirm his identity, but she didn't want the burden of causing a suicidal reaction.

"Are you aware of our professional relationship?" Cassie asked.

"Yes, she told me she hired another private investigator after the last one flew the coop. She said that she'd sent you a retainer."

Cassie nodded. "I might have had a breakthrough on her case. The timing is awful."

"It really is," Tanner said. "I think she literally sent you her last dollars."

"What do you mean?"

"Aunt Candy confided in me a few weeks ago, which was something she didn't do very often. She said after that man stole all of her money that she was in really bad financial shape. The golf club suspended her membership for lack of payment, and I think she was fighting with the utility company to keep her electricity on. Aunt Candy was a very proud woman, and her status was very important to her. When her friends started finding out she was destitute it must have killed her."

Realizing her choice of words, Tanner quickly said, "I didn't mean it like that. But it's true, you know? I think she got super depressed and she saw no way out. If I could find that stupid boyfriend of hers who took all of her money I think I'd kill him myself."

"I didn't realize what kind of situation she was in," Cassie said.

Cassie flashed back to Fly's emotional outburst during their initial call and now saw it as a possible revelation of her mental state at the time. Fly had let it break through, and Cassie hadn't recognized it for what it might have portended.

"No, she probably kept up a good front for you," Tanner said. "She didn't want you to think that she was fragile and that you might not get paid. But I know she listed her house a few days ago. That's how bad it was."

Cassie's feelings toward "Marc Daly" suddenly hardened. He'd not only bilked Candyce Fly out of her fortune but he'd pushed her toward death by her own hand.

"Did you ever meet Marc Daly?" Cassie asked.

"Once," Tanner said. "At a dinner party at the Gasparilla Inn. I sat a long way from him on the other side of the table, and Aunt Candy didn't really introduce us, which I thought was odd at the time. I figured later that he probably didn't want to be introduced to her niece."

"How did he act that night?"

"He was kind of evasive, I thought. He hovered around Aunt Candy like a kind of predator the whole night. I didn't really trust him. But Aunt Candy was head over heels about him. I thought it was just embarrassing. Let's just say I wasn't shocked when I found out what he'd done to her."

"Please take a look at the photos I sent your aunt," Cassie said. "Please tell me if you recognize this man."

Tanner made a face. "It feels really weird to be opening her private emails."

"It might help give your aunt some justice. And since I sent the emails I give you permission to open them."

Daney Tanner did. She said, "It could be him but I can't say for sure. When I met him he was wearing a jacket and slacks and it was dark inside the dining room. This guy is outside and all buff, you know? It could be him but it's also possible it's a man who resembles Marc."

"Thanks for your honesty."

Tanner looked over her shoulder from the screen. She said, "I'm sorry but I should probably get going now. I've got to figure out how to organize a funeral. I've never done that, you know?"

"I understand," Cassie said. Thinking: *I've never worked for a dead client.*

"I have a favor to ask," Cassie said.

"What's that?"

"Could you please download or print the photos I sent and show them around to Candyce's friends at the funeral? People who might have seen her together with Marc Daly? Someone may recognize him. If they do, please have them get in touch with me."

"Sure," Tanner said, though with some hesitancy. "I can do that. But what are you saying? Are you saying you're going to continue to try and find him even though we probably can't pay you for your time?"

Cassie's voice got louder. "That's exactly what I'm saying. If nothing else, I want to take down this sleazeball on behalf of your aunt. Maybe I can recover some of her money, maybe I can't. But this guy deserves what's coming to him."

"If only Aunt Candy could hear that," Tanner said. "Maybe she would have made a different choice."

Cassie winced. What Tanner had said about not really knowing someone—or what pain they were in—echoed in her ears.

After terminating the call, Cassie sat back in her chair and stared at the patterns in the ceiling tiles in her office. She retraced her steps and her theories. Was Annan "Marcus Daly"?

She had no idea.

Everything she'd done thus far in the case had been predicated on what J. D. Spengler had done before she was hired. That's what took her to Butte and Anaconda, where she met Matthew Annan. Very little of her investigation had been based on primary sources thus far. She'd been following the route of a man who was now missing.

What if she'd been operating with blinders on? That perhaps Spengler had been on the wrong track and she'd been following it without doing her own wholly independent investigation?

As she retraced her steps she recalled how long her Jeep had been parked outside of the Justice Center in Anaconda. It had been parked there long enough and unattended, she thought, for a tracking device to be placed beneath it.

Which convinced her that Spengler *had* been on to something. She doubted that her simple presence in town would have generated such suspicion without Spengler laying the groundwork and stirring things up. Deputy Duplisea would not have been following her every move—and likely following her on the interstate—without Spengler asking questions that alarmed certain people.

So Spengler it was. She needed to dig deeper into his investigation that took place before she'd been hired by the late Candyce Fly.

It was 3:30 P.M. mountain time, which meant it was two hours later in Florida. It might be too late for someone to still be in the offices of J. D. Spengler's agency in Tampa. Cassie dialed the number anyway and was surprised when it was answered after three rings.

"J. D. Spengler Security and Investigations. This is Ellie."

Cassie sat up. She'd pulled up the agency website before dialing and could see a woman named Ellie Dana listed under staff as a "research assistant."

"Is this Ellie Dana?" Cassie asked. Dana looked to be in her late twenties or early thirties and she was a stout brunette with a plain, open face.

"Yes. Who is this?"

"My name is Cassie Dewell of Dewell Investigations in Bozeman, Montana. Like your boss, I've been hired by a client to investigate a fraudulent scheme perpetrated by a man who goes by the name Marc Daly."

Dana snorted and said, "No one here has heard from our boss in weeks. That's the reason I answered your call instead of the receptionist. I thought this might be him because it came from Montana. And why didn't the receptionist pick up? Because she quit five days ago when she didn't get paid. Our business manager is threatening the same thing. The only reason I'm here is because I wanted to clean out all my private stuff from my office before our landlord locked us out of the building for skipping on rent.

"So, if you don't mind, I want to finish up here and pick up my kids and look for another job," Dana said.

"I really need your help," Cassie said. "I just need a few minutes of your time. This might be our only opportunity to find out what happened to your boss."

"He's holed up in some cathouse, is my guess," Dana said bitterly.

"That's unlikely," Cassie pleaded. "We really don't have many of those here anymore. I think something criminal might have happened to him and I'd really like to find out what it was. It's possible he's still alive. If I can find him maybe he can come back to Tampa and right the ship."

"It's probably too late for that," Dana said. But Cassie detected a slight thawing in her tone. Then: "What exactly are you asking me for?"

"My understanding is that Mr. Spengler had been all over the country before he found his way here. I don't know where he was or what he was doing. If I can find out it may help me find him."

"J.D. likes to travel, all right," Dana said. "First class all the way. Except for cars. He likes really boring cars."

"Let's start there. Do you have his travel records?"

"I'm sure we do. But I have an ethical problem with sending you records on an ongoing case. If you're a PI you should know that."

"I understand," Cassie said. "But this is an unusual situation. Your boss is missing and our mutual client is recently deceased. She committed suicide in Boca Grande. I'm sure those circumstances render the ethical concerns moot."

"What? Suicide? That's crazy," Dana said. Then: "What's the client's name? I'll see what we have."

"Candyce Fly," Cassie said. She spelled it out and she could hear Ellie Dana tapping on a keyboard.

"Yes, she was our client," Dana said. "There are quite a few files on her in our database. I'm familiar with some of them because I researched some people for J.D. and forwarded the files to him."

"What people?"

"People all over the country," Dana said. "All women, as it turns out. J.D. would text me a name from the road and I'd access our databases and build a background history on them. Then I'd forward the files to J.D. I don't know what he did with them or why he even asked. That isn't part of my job."

"How many women are we talking about?" Cassie asked.

"I don't know. Four, maybe five."

"Can you share their names with me?"

"Of course not," Dana said with a chuckle.

"Is there a file with your boss's travel records?"

"Yeah, that's all here."

Cassie tensed up. "I know this is a big ask and that you're trying to get out of there right now, but could you please send the files to me? I swear I'll keep them confidential and whatever I find I'll share only with you."

"Why? I don't give a shit. I'm quitting."

"Still, don't you want to know what happened with your boss? Wouldn't his wife?"

"They've been divorced for years. His ex moved to Miami and got remarried, I think. He does have a granddaughter, though."

"Doesn't she deserve to know what happened to her grandfather?" Cassie asked.

"I suppose so."

"And wouldn't the other people in the agency want to find out? And possibly even law enforcement if it turns out to be bad?"

There was a long pause. Cassie was afraid Dana might simply terminate the call. Ellie owed her nothing. And based on what she'd told Cassie, the agency could fold up at any minute and take the files and records with it.

"Do you swear this is all on the up-and-up?" Dana asked.

"I swear. You can look me up. I'll give you the URL."

"I've already looked you up while we've been talking," Dana said. "I'm looking at your photo right now. It looks like you've got a small agency, but you seem legit."

"I am and I'd be deeply grateful."

Ellie Dana sighed. "Okay, give me your email address and step back. There'll be a lot of stuff coming."

Cassie glanced over at her monitor and saw attachment after attachment fill her email box. Each arrived with the distinctive chime of an incoming message.

"I'm forwarding it all," Dana said. "Maybe you can make sense of it. I can't take the time to vet what it all is."

"Thank you."

"Sure," Dana said. Then: "Your website makes Montana look pretty cool. You wouldn't happen to be looking for a researcher, would you?"

"Maybe," Cassie said. "Please send along all your contact details."

"I'd be worried about the snow," Dana said. "It snows like three feet in Montana, doesn't it? I don't do cold very well."

"It snows," Cassie said.

"Let me think it over."

sixteen

❖—≡◦⊂—❖

Kyle Westergaard sat alone in a corner booth in a diner on
the outskirts of Deer Lodge, hoping he didn't stink too badly from
his excursion on the Little Blackfoot River. He thought he noticed
that when he ordered the waitress took a sniff and drew back and
quickly turned around. When she returned with his drink a few
minutes later she craned her head away from him.

As she retreated toward the front counter, he raised his right
arm and ducked his head and sniffed his armpit. Yes, he stunk. It was
embarrassing. He could either keep his arms pressed tightly against
his body for as long as he sat there, or he could try to clean up.

Kyle opted for the latter. He found a restroom door labeled
"Cowboys" and went in. He stripped off his dirty shirt and splashed
cold water under his arms and across his chest. He washed his face
in the sink and noted the gray rivulets swirling around the drain.
Then he put on his shirt and returned to the booth.

Better, he thought.

The diner was like the one he'd gone to with Cassie in Manhattan. There were deer and elk heads on the walls, faded cowboy
prints, plastic menus, and all kinds of "funny" signs (NEVER TRUST
A SKINNY COOK, LIFE IS UNCERTAIN—EAT DESSERT FIRST) behind the
counter that looked like they'd been there since he was a child.

The waitress was quite efficient and it was obvious she didn't
want to visit. That was okay with Kyle. He was horrible at small

talk and when forced to engage in it he often confused the person
he was speaking with. It was a skill he was convinced he'd never
master.

Deer Lodge was a company town, and the company was the Montana State Prison. The prison was huge, and Kyle had driven along
the side of it on the way to the river. He'd never seen a state prison
before.

There wasn't much else of Deer Lodge, though. It had just over
three thousand people, according to the sign. He guessed that most
of them worked in the prison.

So it was no surprise to Kyle—or the waitress—when the two
men came into the diner in their correctional officer uniforms and
settled into a booth in the other corner of the restaurant. Both were
large men with attitude. Kyle thought their attitude came from the
uniforms they wore. They walked by Kyle as if they didn't notice
he was there.

Kyle had always specialized in being invisible. He didn't know
why it was, but people didn't notice him. He was the opposite of
standing out in a crowd. It had always been that way. Cassie had
always been the exception. Cassie *always* saw him.

Recently, he'd been with a group of four other truck drivers
out in the Bakken oil fields when their supervisor addressed the
group. He said to the five drivers that, "I need you four to step up
your game. We've got a long list of parts that need to be delivered
and we're getting behind."

There Kyle was, one of five. Standing there shoulder to shoulder with the other drivers. But the supervisor just didn't see him.
This had happened many times before.

So it was, it seemed, with the two correctional officers.

Being invisible to others used to be humiliating to Kyle, but he was used to it now and it no longer bothered him. Just like not speaking a word the first seven years of his life hadn't bothered him even though it concerned his mother and Grandma Lottie.

Kyle sipped his Mountain Dew—it was a little flat—and he waited for the grilled cheese sandwich he'd ordered. He kept his head down as he always did.

And, like always, he listened.

He wasn't sure he liked either of the COs. They seemed overloud, overaggressive, and used to telling men beneath them what to do. One had a shock of blond hair on the top of his round head. He also had a bristly red mustache.

The other was dark with slicked-back hair and a three-day stubble. His sleeves were rolled up to reveal tattooed forearms the size of hams.

The COs debated the merits of the new Ford F-150 versus the new Toyota Tundra pickup. The dark one favored the Ford and the lighter one favored the Toyota.

The blond man said, "Tracy, you're fuckin' nuts. Don't you know they make those things out of aluminum these days? They'll crumple up like a beer can if you hit an elk."

"Bullshit," Tracy said. "F-150s are the most popular truck in America. With that EcoBoost engine they'll smoke any other pickup on the road."

"Until you hit an elk. Then goodbye, Tracy."

"At least they're made in the good old USA, goddammit."

"So are Tundras, idiot. They're built in Indiana and Texas."

"But they're still Japanese, come on."

"No more Japanese than you are, Tracy-san."

Tracy laughed with a deep rumble. It was obvious to Kyle the two men worked closely together and chided each other a lot. Trash talk like this with other men was another skill he hadn't mastered.

"I'm going with the F-150," Tracy said. "Getting a new one, thanks to Sir Scott's! And don't try to talk me out of it."

That got Kyle's attention.

Had they found the treasure? Had they beaten him to it? His heart dropped.

The waitress delivered his sandwich and the two COs followed her with their eyes and apparently noticed for the first time that he was there. Kyle heard the blond one say, "Better keep it down."

"Don't worry," Tracy said, but in a tone much lower than before.

"Still . . ."

"You're the only one I've ever talked to about it. You know that."

"Hundreds of yahoos are still out there looking for it. Did you ever think . . ."

"Hell, no." Tracy chuckled. "It's fuckin' nuts."

Kyle chewed on his sandwich but he couldn't taste it. He'd been so close, he thought.

Then the blond one said, "What do you think? Will anybody ever find it?"

"The treasure?"

"Fuck yes, the treasure."

"Who knows?" Tracy said with a shrug. "I couldn't care less. All I care about is that it helped me buy a new truck."

So they hadn't found it, Kyle thought. So what were they talking about?

"This was so much easier than smuggling something in," Tracy said. "Paid better, too."

"Shh," the blond one warned. He nodded his head toward Kyle.

Tracy said, "I don't think that loser understands a single word we're saying. Did you look at him?"

"Yeah, but you never know."

They continued to talk after the waitress delivered them their double cheeseburgers. Most of the conversation was incomprehensible to Kyle. It was shoptalk; gossip about inmates and supervisors, Block A, Block B, overtime, on and on.

There wasn't any additional mention of Sir Scott's Treasure. So what had they meant by it?

Kyle paid his bill with cash and left the waitress a five-dollar tip, which was probably too much. At least *one* Montanan would appreciate this North Dakotan, he thought.

He drove out of the parking lot past two pickups that were nearly as old as his own. Each had stickers in the windshield allowing them access to the prison complex, so he guessed they had to belong to Tracy and his colleague.

Kyle circled the block and parked on a side street in the shade of a big cottonwood tree with a good view of the diner. He dug his binoculars out of his day pack and focused them on the door of the building.

After twenty minutes, it opened and the two COs came out. Kyle didn't care about the blond one. He concentrated on Tracy.

The two men stopped and chatted before separating and going to their respective vehicles. Kyle was able to see both of their name badges. Tracy's badge said "Swanson."

Tracy Swanson.

Kyle followed Swanson at a respectable distance. When Swanson stopped at a Montana state liquor store, Kyle parked and waited. Swanson came out of the store with a twelve pack of Busch Light and a bottle of liquor in a paper bag. He didn't look around and didn't seem to sense that he was being followed.

Kyle stayed with him until Swanson pulled into the driveway of a small bungalow. The neighborhood was decent but old, made up of single-family houses that had seen better days.

He pulled over before he could be noticed. Swanson's home looked like the kind of home where a brand-new Ford F-150 would look out of place.

Kyle sat back and thought about it. He knew he couldn't tail

Swanson around Deer Lodge. The town was too small and his North Dakota license plates would be noticed. And what would he accomplish by following a CO as he went to work and made his rounds?

He wrote the name "Tracy Swanson" on a fresh page in his notebook.

Kyle was a good observer, but he wasn't a detective. He didn't know where to start to unravel Tracy Swanson's connection to Sir Scott's Treasure.

But he knew someone who might know how to do it.

seventeen

⋙———◉———⋘

While the files from the Florida PI's office arrived in her email in-box, Cassie left her office to confront Isabel. She knew it wouldn't go well. It never did.

"Mom, what happens in this office needs to stay in this office," Cassie said. "You know we've talked about this before. It's important to keep our work confidential."

Isabel looked up from her desk and cocked her head. "I have no idea what you're talking about."

"Downstairs in the coffee shop," Cassie said, jabbing her finger toward the floor. "Did you mention to the staff down there that I was looking into the Sir Scott's Treasure? That I'd been hired by the person who wrote the poem to try and find him? That a courier had delivered a retainer from him?"

Isabel blinked at each accusation as if Cassie had struck her every time.

"Maybe in passing . . ." she said, looking away.

"You can't do that again," Cassie said. "It's the reason our office was broken into."

"What are you talking about?"

"I'm not going to go into it because I'm not sure I can trust you not to blab again. But I know it to be a fact."

Isabel teared up, which is what Cassie had expected. And despite herself, even though she knew it was a ploy, she felt sorry for her mother.

She wondered what he was doing in all of those cities. Chasing
Marc Daly? She doubted it. Living high on a client's dime? Possible,
but she hoped not for the sake of the general reputation of private
investigators like herself.

No, she thought. He was onto something.

What wasn't in the tranche of emails from Florida was a day-
by-day report of what he was doing and why. That was bothersome
to Cassie and it meant Spengler didn't want to write down his
activities. Apparently, he kept his theories and overall investigation
close to the vest. That was annoying, she thought. And she couldn't
ask Candyce Fly what he had reported to her.

There were three separate files included that didn't seem to re-
late to the expense report and travel that Cassie could discern. Each
was labeled by a name: MONICA WEATHERBY, RUTHANNE SOMMERS,
and BROOKE ALEXANDER.

She opened them one by one. All three had been compiled by
"E.D." They were obviously the work of Ellie Dana, who had been
given their names by Spengler from the road. Dana had written a
bio on each, no doubt using the same kind of investigative database
software Cassie used.

Monica Weatherby, fifty-eight, was a New York socialite and
widow who lived on the Upper West Side. She was heir to a shipping fortune and her husband had died of brain cancer. Photos of
her from *The New York Times* archives showed her to be trim and
attractive with a gleaming white boxlike smile. There she was at the
Met Gala, and at a fundraiser for Alzheimer's. Cassie discerned from
the photos that Weatherby was a shy and cautious woman from the
way she held herself. She seemed demure, and unlike the ebullient
socialites who surrounded her in the shots.

RuthAnne Sommers, sixty-two, had married into an old and
established Chicago family that had once owned meatpacking facilities. She was twice divorced but known as a generous philanthropist and party girl based on the number of sightings of her at

fundraising and cultural events both in Chicago and at their second home in Sun Valley, Idaho. She'd been involved in a high-profile divorce from her last husband, Armond Sommers, which was followed closely by all the city's newspapers. RuthAnne's attorneys alleged that Armond had conducted numerous affairs and that he'd also hidden away a fortune in offshore accounts.

Apparently, RuthAnne's attorneys convinced the judge because she'd been awarded tens of millions. Most of the photos of her in the file were taken in and around the trial. She was tall and willowy with a full mouth and dark eyes that she was often dabbing with a hankie. In several of the photos she appeared to be keenly aware of the photographer.

Brooke Alexander, fifty-five, was a Realtor to the stars in Santa Monica. She was also divorced. Alexander was a hard-charging businesswoman who had run for and won a seat on the city council. Her attractive, pixie-like face was on billboards and bus stop benches throughout the city. There were press rumors of her being romantically involved with several Hollywood B-list actors after her divorce, and photos of her decked out in English riding gear on a sleek horse.

Cassie sat back. There wasn't a single mention of Marc Daly in any of the profiles. So why did they exist in Spengler's investigation?

Cassie took a chance that Ellie Dana would take her call again. This time, she called Dana's cell phone number that had been listed on the company website.

"Yes?" Dana said cautiously.

"It's Cassie again. Thanks for taking my call."

"I thought we were done. I sent you everything in the Fly file."

"And I really appreciate that," Cassie said. "Are you still at the office? I was hoping I could ask you one more favor."

Silence. Then: "You've got five minutes tops. Then I need to leave here to pick up my kids."

"Five minutes should do it," Cassie said. "Can you please tell me

if Monica Weatherby, RuthAnne Sommers, or Brooke Alexander
were clients of your agency?"

"Hmm. Those names are familiar."

"You did profiles on them," Cassie said. "But I was wondering
if they're in your database separate from the Fly files you sent me."

"This is a question for J.D. or our office manager," Dana said.
"Neither one is around."

"Can you check, please?"

Dana sighed. Cassie could hear a keyboard being tapped.

After a minute, Dana said, "Yes, all three became clients in the
last three months, which means we opened files on them."

Cassie felt a trill of excitement. "Does it say *why* they became
clients?"

"No. Our database doesn't work like that. It just gives their
name, contact details, and when we started working for them. Oh,
and whether or not they paid the retainer. Apparently, all of them
did."

"Interesting," Cassie said. "All are wealthy and single. Just like
Candyce Fly."

"I suppose," Dana said. "Who knows what kind of scheme J.D.
was working here."

"Maybe it wasn't a scheme. Maybe J.D. was onto something and
he picked up more clients along the way."

"I'll pretend I understood that," Dana said with a chuckle.

Cassie said, "I know I can look them all up from here, but to
save time could you forward their contact details? I'd like to reach
out to them. Maybe they can fill in some of the gaps when it comes
to your boss and his investigation."

"Sure, why not?" Dana said.

"Thank you," Cassie said as her in-box chimed.

"I'm still thinking of sending my resume," Dana said. "Are you
against remote work?"

"I haven't given it much thought."

"I mean, I can do research just as easily from Tampa as from down the hall in your office, you know?"

"I'll keep that in mind," Cassie said.

She reread their profiles and decided to contact RuthAnne Sommers first. Sommers appeared, to Cassie, to be the one most likely to be available and to be inclined to talk. She'd certainly not been shy about answering questions from Chicago reporters during her trial. The photos of her from her divorce proceedings showed that she enjoyed attention. She also seemed to have plenty of leisure time.

Monica Weatherby, the New Yorker, on the other hand, might seem suspicious of a cold call from an area code as obscure as 406. Brooke Alexander seemed to be too busy and hard-charging to take a call from an unknown number.

Cassie was wrong about RuthAnne Sommers. She didn't pick up. When the voice message followed, Cassie said, "RuthAnne, my name is Cassie Dewell and I'm a licensed private investigator in Bozeman, Montana. I'm currently working on a case that involves your relationship with J. D. Spengler, who might or might not be missing. It also involves a subject from Montana who allegedly defrauded an innocent woman out of a lot of money. Please call me back at . . ."

The message recording time cut short.

Cassie cursed and wished she'd been more brief. Then she realized that if Sommers got her message and listened to it she also had her callback number.

That's when line one of her handset lit up.

eighteen

✶══◉══✦

"Dewell Investigations, this is Cassie."

"This is RuthAnne Sommers. You called me."

"Thank you, Ms. Sommers. Did you get a chance to listen to the message?"

"I never listen to messages," Sommers said with a laugh. "Does anyone?"

I do, Cassie thought but didn't say.

Sommers had a husky voice that Cassie knew men found attractive. It had a little purr in it and fit with the emotive photos of her she'd seen in the file.

Cassie repeated her message but with less urgency.

Sommers said, "Mr. Spengler cashed the check for his retainer and I never heard from him again. I find that very unprofessional." She sounded genuinely annoyed.

"I understand," Cassie said. "I'm not with his firm. I'm doing an independent investigation and Mr. Spengler is tangentially involved."

"Tangentially? I don't know that word."

"It means I've been hired to investigate something else but Spengler's name keeps popping up."

"Oh, okay. Well, if you find him please tell him I'd like my money back. I don't want to get fleeced again."

That set off an alarm bell in Cassie's head, but she pushed it aside.

"How did you even know to reach out to me?" Sommers asked. "I only met the guy once."

Cassie told her about the three files she'd been sent from Spengler's office. "Yours was the most intriguing," Cassie said. It was blatant flattery, and she almost felt guilty about it.

Sommers laughed. "Yes, the last few years of my life have been . . . interesting. But if you could see me now you'd be surprised. I'm sitting on the deck of my Sun Valley house drinking wine with a lovely view of Dollar Mountain. I think you could say it all worked out in the end."

"That sounds nice."

"It is." She giggled.

"I'll try not to take too much of your time here, but I'd like to ask you a few questions."

"Will it get my money back?"

"That I can't promise," Cassie said.

"Well, go ahead," Sommers said. Cassie could hear her sip her wine.

"First, can I ask you why you contacted Mr. Spengler in the first place?"

Sommers whooped. "Hell, he contacted *me*. I'd never heard of the man before. He showed up at our, I mean *my*, town house in Chicago. He said on the intercom he wanted to speak with me about an important matter. I thought it probably had to do with the divorce, you know? Maybe he had more dirt on my ex-husband?"

"And did he?"

"No," she said. "And at first I put him off. I asked him to leave his details with the doorman. Believe me, since the divorce I've learned to be a lot more careful when it comes to strangers just showing up. It isn't exactly a secret that I've had a windfall, you know?"

"It must be difficult figuring out who you can trust," Cassie said.

"Oh, it is. But in this case, he left an envelope with my doorman.

I opened it and found a couple of blurry photos that I thought I recognized. I ran his name past the PIs we hired during my divorce and they vouched for Spengler. They said he was legit. So I called him and he came over."

"Yes," Cassie prompted.

"He told me he was looking for a guy named Daly, I think. Maybe Marc Daly. He wondered if I knew him."

"Did you?"

"No, not at all. Then he showed me a few more photos. They weren't very good ones, to be honest. But when I saw them I said, 'I don't know this Marc Daly character, but that guy looks a lot like Bill Clark!'"

"Who is Bill Clark?"

Sommers paused while she refilled her glass. Cassie could hear it clearly. She was an expert on the sound of wine being poured into a wineglass.

"Bill Clark is a con man who fleeced me out of five million bucks and then vanished into the wind. He's the reason I've become so cautious when it comes to meeting strangers."

"Okay," Cassie said, "let's start from the beginning. When did you meet Bill Clark?"

"Oh, this is all so embarrassing," Sommers said. "When I tell you you're going to think I'm just a gullible idiot."

"I won't," Cassie said. She hoped she wasn't lying.

"I didn't know Bill Clark until the divorce proceedings. I'd never even heard of him. But I couldn't help noticing this man who was sitting in the third row of the courtroom. Same row, same seat, every day.

"He was obviously taking notes during the testimony, I could see him. He had a kind of presence, I must say. He was well-dressed and really good-looking in an intellectual sort of way. I thought he must be a reporter because there were a lot of reporters at the divorce trial."

"Can you describe him?" Cassie asked.

"Oh yes, I can," Sommers said with a hard laugh. "Tall, broad shoulders, very fit. He had kind eyes and a sweet smile."

"Hair? Eyes?"

"Sandy hair, kind of longish," Sommers said. "Big brown eyes. He wore glasses that made him look smart and he had a trim goatee. Like I said, he almost looked like a college professor. The kind of professor you'd fall in love with, if you know what I mean."

"Sort of," Cassie said.

"Anyway, we kept making eye contact during the days of the trial. He seemed sympathetic to me, on my side. One day after we proved that Armond had secret accounts in the Cayman Islands that he hadn't disclosed, Bill smiled at me and pumped his fist like, '*Yes.*'"

Another sip.

"During a recess I went back into the benches and thanked him for his support. Frankly, it was kind of stupid but it was the only thing I could think of. After all, he couldn't come through the gate to the plaintiff's table to meet *me.*

"He said he was an author working on a book about me and the trial. He said he wanted to tell the truth about Armond and all of his dirty secrets. Bill asked me if after the trial would I agree to be interviewed? I mean, he was totally charming. I said sure, I'd love to talk to him and get my truth out there. You see, Armond had all kinds of PR flacks spreading rumors about me to the press. They were lies—mostly—but the Sommers clan knew how to manipulate the press and the public over to their side. They'd been doing it for years."

Although Cassie blanched at the phrase "my truth," she didn't interrupt. Sommers was on a roll.

"So after the trial where I was awarded a major settlement, we got together," she said. "I don't know how long it's been since I'd been with a man who really listened to me. I mean, *really* listened. Armond had always been such a cold fish that it was absolutely wonderful to actually be with a man who wanted to hear my story, hear my truth."

Again, Cassie thought with a roll of her eyes.

"I take it your relationship got more serious," Cassie said.

"Yes, it did. And rather quickly, I have to say. I mean, I'm *ashamed* to say."

"Did you ever suspect he wasn't who he said he was?" Cassie asked.

"I wish I could say that," Sommers said with a sigh. "But man, he was good. He gave me signed copies of two other books he'd written. One was about a high-society woman accused of the murder of her husband in Connecticut. The other was about a crazy family in California and how the siblings fought each other for the family fortune. Not that I read them, but I saw that on the jacket flaps, you know?"

"Sure," Cassie said.

"I still have the books," she said. "Each one has his name on the cover and his author photo on the back. So yes, I believed him."

She paused, and said, "Who would have ever thought that a man would go to such lengths as to make up his own jackets and put them on books actually written by real writers? Or replace the title page inside each one with his own name? Who would think to do that?"

"Someone who did a lot of preparation," Cassie said. "Someone who targeted you well in advance."

"You're exactly right," Sommers said. "That's why I feel like such a stupid airhead when I tell you about it."

"How did he get you to give him five million dollars?" Cassie asked.

Sommers moaned. "This is where I really come off as a dolt."

"You can tell me," Cassie said.

"Well, Bill claimed that the book he was working on was generating quite a bit of interest in the publishing world, which I know absolutely nothing about. He said he was already receiving offers from movie producers to film my story. I bit on that because I'm so vain," she said with a bitter chuckle.

"I don't get it," Cassie said. "If producers wanted to buy your story . . ."

"I *know*," Sommers said. "I know how it sounds. But Bill made a really good case that once we sold my story I wouldn't have any control over it. Bill said he's seen too many people be taken advantage of by Hollywood types. They could make me out to be a gold digger, or a manipulative bitch. Maybe Armond and his toadies would attract the movie people over to his side. But if *we* financed the production and hired the writers, the director, and the actor to play my part—I'd have control."

Cassie said, "When you say 'we' you mean 'you.' I wouldn't guess Bill agreed to put any money into it."

"No." Sommers sighed. "He said his cut would come when he put the deal together. He's an executive producer, whatever that is. He knew all the movie jargon and I didn't. And I fell for it."

"So you wrote him a check for five million to get the movie developed that was based on his book?" Cassie said.

"It was actually a wire transfer," Sommers said. "Which went to an account in Belize that closed a few days later."

"And he was gone by the time you realized it," Cassie said.

"Exactly. He said he was flying out to LA to get things underway. That's the last I ever heard of him.

"And when I thought about it later, it all made more sense," she said. "Bill rarely met with me at a public place during the interviews or when we were more serious. He said it was to protect my privacy, but I think it's so he'd never get caught on a closed-circuit camera or in a press photo. The newspapers were still following me around at the time. When we were out together, he always paid cash, even at expensive restaurants. I should have realized at the time how odd that was but of course he was leaving no paper trail. He said he was staying at the Four Seasons but I never went there or saw his room. When I tried to find him after he vanished they said he'd never checked in."

"Did you alert the police?" Cassie asked.

"I thought about it, but no."

"Why not?"

Sommers said, "I was a victim of my own vanity. I knew how it would be portrayed. Armond and his hacks would make sure everyone knew that I paid five million dollars to make a movie about myself. Tell me, how would that look?"

"Not too good," Cassie conceded. "So did J. D. Spengler offer to try and find Bill Clark?"

"Yes, and I took him up on it," Sommers said. "Spengler thought that Bill Clark might be an alias for another guy he was looking for. Maybe it was this Marc Daly person you mentioned."

"But you couldn't identify him from the photos Spengler showed you?"

"Not for sure. Like I said, Bill had sandy hair, glasses, and a goatee. The fuzzy photos Spengler showed me could have possibly been a different guy. I just couldn't be sure."

Cassie said, "I'm going to send you a series of photos taken very recently. Will you please look at them and tell me your conclusion?"

"Sure," Sommers said. "Send them to this phone."

Cassie sent the four clearest shots of Matthew Annan in his front yard.

"Oh. My. God," Sommers said. "Where did you get these?"

"I took them a couple of days ago."

"It's Bill all right, that son of a bitch. He's changed his hair color and shaved his face. But it's Bill."

"How sure are you?"

"This might be the wine talking, but I'd say it's Bill. I'd recognize those rock-hard abs anywhere. So where did you find him?"

"Here in Montana," Cassie said. "He's building a home about an hour from where I'm calling you from."

"I bet it's a *nice* place." Sommers snorted.

"It is."

Sommers paused. "Are you asking me to hire you to go get him?" She sounded wary.

"No. But I'm going to ask you something much harder."

"What is that?"

"I'm asking you if you'd testify against him in court if he's arrested for fraud."

"I'll have to think about that."

"Think hard," Cassie said.

Still buzzing from the conversation with Sommers, Cassie tried a wholly different approach with Monica Weatherby and Brooke Alexander. She led with her hole card: the photos she'd taken of Matthew Annan/Marc Daly/Bill Clark. She texted each woman and asked if they recognized the man in the photo and if so would they please call her right away?

The photos got results, and similar stories.

Monica Weatherby said she knew him as Auggie Heinze, a hedge fund billionaire who claimed he was "on the cusp" of financing a start-up that would combine the attributes of Twitter, WhatsApp, and TikTok into a single platform. She fell for him and his pitch and she "invested" four million into his social media company against the opinion of her financial advisors. Auggie Heinze vanished from New York shortly after and the company turned out to be a sham. J. D. Spengler had contacted her and said he was hot on Auggie's trail and she paid Spengler's retainer.

Weatherby was annoyed that she hadn't heard anything from Spengler in the last month, despite several calls to him that went to voice mail. But she was *very* angry at Heinze.

"If you find that asshole," Weatherby said to Cassie, "I want my money back. I'd like my pride back, too, but I'm not sure he—or you—can give that."

Brooke Alexander had a now-familiar story with a couple of fresh angles. The man she'd met introduced himself as Marcus Daly and he claimed to be in the business of buying town houses and apartment buildings in medium-sized US cities like Nashville and Boise where urban professionals had flocked to during the pandemic. That appealed to the Realtor, and so did Marcus Daly, whom she described as "humble, handsome, and very, very smart." She "invested" $2.5 million and never heard from the man again. Spengler came to her office in Santa Monica and she retained his services to find the man who had both seduced her and bilked her.

"I want to personally kill him," Alexander told Cassie. "I want to put my hands around his throat and choke him to death. I'm a pretty savvy businesswoman, but he totally conned me. I'll fly out there to kill him if you can get someone to hold him down."

"I'll pretend I didn't hear that last part," Cassie said. "Let's just see if we can get him into custody."

Both women said they'd testify against him if he were arrested and went to court.

Cassie sat back. She was satisfied with her work and unnerved that Annan had been so active. He was a unique kind of predator. How many more women out there had he taken advantage of in this way? Had his charms ever failed him?

Despite their wealth, she felt immensely sorry for the four women he'd targeted and duped. They'd all been alone and vulnerable and he knew it and he'd used it to worm his way into their lives. Having briefly met Annan she could see how it could have happened. Even to her.

Fortunately, she didn't have millions in her bank account and likely never would. He'd probably sensed that immediately.

What she wondered was how Spengler had identified the three as victims of scams similar to what had happened to Candyce Fly. What had tipped him off that Annan was a serial fraudster? There was nothing in his notes that linked them.

She flipped to a fresh page in her legal pad and wrote:

Marc Daly
Bill Clark
Auggie Heinze
Marcus Daly
Matthew Annan

Something about the names was familiar to her but she couldn't put her finger on it.

Cassie was about to Google the names when April and Ben blew in. Their mood was sky-high even though they both looked dirty and physically exhausted. Cassie motioned for them to come into her office and tell her about their day.

"Mr. Annan kept us working all day but he was really nice," April said. "Ben cleared rocks from the front grounds and I cleaned out the construction junk from four or five rooms in the house. I've never been in such a big house before, I'll tell you."

"Did you have any conversations with him?" Cassie asked.

Both nodded. Ben said, "He couldn't have been friendlier, really. He worked right alongside me for a couple of hours this morning. We talked NBA, elk hunting, and fly-fishing. He said he'd be happy to take me fly-fishing on the Little Blackfoot River someday. He said he hated school when he was growing up, too."

"You hate school?" Cassie asked, taken aback.

"I keep telling you that," Ben said with an eye roll.

April said, "He took our orders and went and got lunch for us. That was really cool. And he didn't take the cost of lunch out of our pay, either."

"He gave us each a fifty-dollar bonus at the end of the day," Ben said. "Cash."

"Don't be expecting that here," Cassie said. Then to April: "Did you chat with him as well?"

April nodded. "He asked me about growing up in Wyoming, things like that. He seemed really interested in what I had to say and he kept complimenting me on my work ethic. He said that if he had Ben and me working for him the whole time his house would be completely done."

"So he charmed you both," Cassie said.

"I wouldn't say *charmed* . . ." Ben said. "He was just cool, like April said."

"I'd say charmed," April said, flushing a little and looking away. "He's probably the easiest man to talk to I've ever met even though he's way too old for me. If I could find a guy my age who was like that . . ." She didn't finish.

"So what is it Matthew is supposed to have done?" Ben asked Cassie. "I feel kind of guilty spying on such a nice guy."

"Don't be," Cassie said.

"So what is it?" April asked. "There's no way you can convince me Matthew is some kind of criminal."

Cassie cleared her throat and said, "Let me tell you both something that might surprise you. I've been chasing bad guys for a long time both as a cop and now as a PI. Very rarely do people think of themselves as bad. Nearly everybody I've chased or brought down think they have really good reasons for their actions. They can justify their bad acts. Even someone as horrible as the Lizard King never took responsibility for the many women he kidnapped, tortured, and killed. He thought he was *made* to act that way by the way his mother treated him. He thought none of the things he did were his fault.

"So just because someone is nice to you or cool to be around doesn't mean he's a good, responsible citizen. Bad men don't look or act bad in everything they do or say."

"So you're not going to tell us?" April asked.

"Not yet."

"I'd still bet on Mr. Annan as one of the good guys," Ben said.

"You'd lose that bet," Cassie said. Then: "Do either of you suspect that he might be onto you?"

Ben and April exchanged glances, then both shook their heads. "He didn't seem suspicious of me at all," April said. "He said he was looking forward to seeing both of us tomorrow. I'm kind of looking forward to it, too."

He told me the same thing, Cassie thought.

"What is this intel you said you had?" she asked.

"Well, it doesn't have anything to do with Mr. Annan," April said. Cassie was annoyed at the fervor both April and Ben had shown and continued to show when they defended the man.

"It was someone else," Ben said.

Cassie arched her eyebrows.

"We were getting ready to get going when this big dude showed up," April said. "He came right into the house without knocking. When he saw me he told me to get out. It was really rude."

"What did this man look like?"

"Like April said, he was a big guy," Ben said. "But old."

"Maybe in his fifties," April said. "He had black hair and mean eyes. He walked and acted like he wanted to punch somebody. You know—arms out from his sides, fists clenched, like that."

Cassie thought: Doug Duplisea.

"Was he wearing a sheriff's department uniform?" Cassie asked.

"No," Ben said. "He was wearing a hoodie, jeans, and boots."

"So what happened?" Cassie asked.

"Well, he just stood there in the great room until I cleared out," April said. "Mr. Annan apologized to me and told me to wait a minute outside. He seemed real embarrassed. So I went outside and helped Ben finish up."

"But we could hear them," Ben said. "They were really arguing about something, really yelling."

"Not Mr. Annan," April said. "I never heard him raise his voice. But when I looked in through the front windows he looked pretty angry. And he seemed to be trying to stare down the other guy."

"The other guy did most of the yelling," Ben said. "That's true. He waved his arms around and paced. Mr. Annan just stood there, staring at him."

"*Glaring* would be a better word," April added. "Like he was really pissed off at the guy."

"How long did it go on?" Cassie asked.

April shrugged. "Who knows? Mr. Annan came out of the house and paid us and told us to drive home carefully. He seemed completely normal when he said it. Then he went back into the house and we left."

"Interesting," Cassie said. "Could you hear what this man was saying to Mr. Annan?"

"I wished I could," April said. "All I could get were the shouts. No real words. I was standing by my truck at the time. Ben was much closer."

"Ben?"

"No," Ben said. "I couldn't really make out what the argument was about. I thought I heard the word like 'Crestfall' or 'Wess-fall,' maybe."

Cassie sat up. "Was it 'Westphal'?"

"Maybe," Ben said. "I'm not sure. Oh, and I might have heard him say your name."

"My name?"

"Yeah. I thought I heard him say 'Cassie Dewell.' It might have been something else, but it sure sounded like it to me."

Cassie asked, "What was this man driving?"

April indicated she hadn't paid any attention to his vehicle.

But Ben said, "He drove a silver GMC pickup. Maybe a couple of years old, but really nice."

April looked harshly at Ben. She was embarrassed for not knowing.

"Hey," Ben said to her with a grin. "That's the kind of thing I notice."

Cassie nodded slowly. Things were starting to come together. She said, "You two won't be going back to Matthew Annan's place tomorrow. You've done good work, but that job is over."

"But we *like* him," April said. There was hurt in her eyes. "We don't want to let him down and just not show up."

"He's a man who is easy to like," Cassie said. "You'd be surprised how many people out there would agree with you."

"Can I at least text him and let him know?" April asked.

"No. We don't want him to know your number or anything more about you. Either of you," she said, moving her eyes to Ben.

"He paid pretty good, too," Ben said with a resigned shrug. "Much better than Dewell Investigations."

nineteen

ONE DAY BEFORE

Undersheriff Doug Duplisea was at his desk in his empty office. Out of the corner of his eye he picked up on a slight figure ghosting through the office aimed at him. He slipped off his reading glasses and looked up.

It was Jillian Westphal, and she looked terrible. She was wan, bent over, and skeletal in appearance. Her eyes seemed to have sunk deep into her skull and even though she wore a crocheted stocking cap there were wisps of pure white hair that tickled her jaw and neck. She looked twenty years older than the last time he'd seen her at the department Christmas party five months before. Jillian wore a housecoat and slippers and her pants bagged around her thighs and ankles.

As she approached him she shuffled her feet as if she couldn't pick them up. Her eyes darted over to the dark sheriff's office as she moved.

"Jillian, it's good to see you. What can I help you with?" he asked.

She placed two birdlike hands on the top of his visitor chair as to steady herself. Then she said, "Doug, I'm worried about Phil. He's never been gone this long."

"What, did you think he was here hiding out?" Duplisea asked, hoping he'd coax a smile out of her. It didn't work.

"I think he's been gone longer than this," he said. "I remember he was gone over a week a couple of years back."

"I'm going to sit down," she said. And she did with a heavy sigh. She placed her hands in her lap as if to keep them from trembling.

Duplisea said, "Jillian, I wouldn't worry. This has happened before—as both of us know. He'll show up anytime now with his tail between his legs and spend a week apologizing to everyone."

She looked up. Her eyes were watery and Duplisea saw both despair and desperation. "Phil is a good man," she said. "Lately, he's been . . . wonderful. He's really shown me his caring side. I'd be quite upset if he didn't come home soon. In fact, I'm upset right now."

"I understand," Duplisea said. "When did you see him last?"

"June first, three days ago. He said he was going out to find you, in fact. I don't know why but he mentioned Club Moderne. And he was supposed to stop at the pharmacy on his way back home."

"Club Moderne?" Duplisea said. He could feel his neck get warm.

"That worried me right there," she said. "He's been avoiding that place the last few months. I had this bad little thought in my mind that if he went there this could happen. And I'm afraid it did."

"Well," Duplisea said, "I'll tell you something. I *was* at the club for a while after work that day. But I never saw Phil come in. You know, Jillian, there are a lot of bars between your house and the club."

"I know that," she said. "I'm not stupid."

"I'd never even suggest that you were," he said. "I'm just saying that Phil might have had great intentions but he stopped at one or two watering holes on the way to the club. You know how it goes with him: one drink leads to another, which leads to another, which leads to another. Then he's off to the races and we don't see him for a few days."

"Can you check?" she asked.

"Check what?"

"Can you go to all the bars and find out if he was there? And if he was, can you try and figure out where he is now?"

Duplisea took a deep breath and blew it out. "I'm really pretty hammered with paperwork right now, Jillian. Maybe I could send a deputy."

She shook her head and her eyes narrowed. "I don't trust your deputies. I've heard too many bad things about them."

"I'd hate to think Phil was talking about our guys that way," Duplisea said.

"He said you hired them all. Not him."

This was the way it often was with people who were as sick and as old as Jillian, Duplisea thought. They no longer had filters when they spoke. Or if they did, they didn't care.

"I did hire most of them," he said. "I didn't realize that was a sore point with Phil."

"Well, it is. But no, never mind. I really want you to track him down and find him and bring him home. I need him, Doug. When you find him tell him I'm not angry. I just need him home."

Duplisea sat back in his chair. He didn't want to shout at her, and he needed her to trust him.

"I can maybe get to that in a while," he said. "Once I get all this paperwork done."

"My husband is more important than your paperwork," she said. "I really don't want to call the state police or the DCI. Maybe I can go to the paper or radio station. But we need to find him."

"Jillian," Duplisea said patiently, "that would be a really bad idea. For one thing, Montana doesn't have state police. For another, believe me, we don't want to get other agencies or the media involved. You know how it is. Most folks around here know Phil has gone on a bender from time to time. They look the other way because as you say, they know he's a good guy. Why would we want to shine a bright light on his behavior? Neither one of us wants to see stories in the paper about it or hear it on the radio. Do you really think he could keep his job after that?"

"I don't care about his job," Jillian said. "I care about me if you want to know the truth. I'm selfish these days because I don't know how much longer I'll be around. I need him back."

She said, "This is the first time I've driven my car in a couple of months. I'm not supposed to drive. And I'm not sure I have the energy to go to the pharmacy after this."

"I'll tell you what," Duplisea said. "I'll take you home in my cruiser. Then I'll stop by the pharmacy and bring you your prescription. Then I'll hit the bars and try to find out what happened to Phil. Does that work for you?"

"That's all I ask," she said. "Thank you, Doug."

He said, "Just leave everything to me, Jillian."

She closed her eyes and was very still. For a few seconds, Duplisea thought she might have gone to sleep.

When she opened her eyes they were wet with tears.

Duplisea stood up and helped her to her feet. She was light as air. He guided her toward the door.

"How are you feeling, Jillian?"

"Not real good."

"What does your doctor say?"

"What does he say?"

"About your condition."

She paused and looked up at him just before they reached the door. "I told him I'm not doing any more treatments. No more chemo, no more radiation. Those things are as bad as the cancer, Doug. Phil and I talked about it."

"So—what does that mean?" he asked softly. "Are we talking a few years? A few months?"

"If I make it to Christmas I'll be grateful."

Seven months away, he thought. Seven months of Jillian whining about where Phil went.

"Like I said," Duplisea said, "just leave everything up to me."

twenty

The next morning, Cassie did something she hadn't done in years and had thought she'd never do again: seek out a truck stop.

She chose the Flying J in Belgrade, west of Bozeman on I-90. The truck stop was already a hive of activity, with semitrucks and trailers rumbling and idling and belching exhaust on one side of the facility and ordinary cars and trucks using the other.

For Cassie, truck stops brought back terrifying memories of her hunt for the Lizard King, and even though that chapter of her life was over and Ronald Pergram had been taken down, they were still not places she wished to revisit. But she had a plan.

She filled up her Jeep and marveled at the high price of gasoline. As she did, she made a note to herself to revisit the standard travel expenses in her client agreements to hike them appropriately to cover her costs. She cursed the disparity that existed between urban commuters who had access to public transportation and western locals who had to drive hundreds of miles a day to earn a living. It had always been like that.

Despite the odor of diesel fumes in the air, it was a still, cloudless, and beautiful June morning in Montana. The distant mountains shimmered and she could see faraway ski runs still white with snow. It was the kind of day where she felt guilty for not having plans to go hiking or fishing or horseback riding—even though she never did any of those activities anymore.

The view mitigated her dispute with eastern commuters. They may not have to fill their gas tanks as often, but they also didn't get to see these vistas every day.

It had not bothered Cassie to leave her home that morning and head back to Anaconda. Ben was angry with her for not allowing him to return to work at Matthew Annan's house, and Isabel was giving her the silent treatment because Cassie had chewed her out at the office. She'd left them both to figure out their feelings on their own. Perhaps, she thought, they'd bond over their common enemy: her. But she doubted that. Ben and Isabel lived on different planets.

Cassie had made a point of loading her full investigative gear bag into the Jeep for the day. It was on the floor of the passenger seat. Her .40 Glock 27 was clipped to her belt and concealed by the longish jacket she wore over her top.

When the fuel tank was full, Cassie climbed into her Jeep and slowly cruised to the trucker side of the facility. Most of the drivers of the rigs had spent the night there on the lot ensconced in their sleeper cabs watching movies or surfing the internet. A few of the big units had already pulled out from the four lines of trucks to hit the road, and others were getting ready. She saw a couple of drivers testing the inflation of their tires by hitting them with rubber hammers, and a few others having a discussion about something in between the massive tractors.

As she passed by the restaurant she could see through the fogged windows that many of the drivers were still having breakfast inside.

Cassie chose a bright red Peterbilt with Washington plates. The tractor was attached to a gleaming refrigerated trailer behind it. Condensation puffed out from the twin pipes of the Peterbilt as well as from the refrigeration unit on the trailer itself. She knew from pursuing the Lizard King that the trailer was known as a "reefer."

The cab was empty as she drove by. That meant the driver was in the truck stop itself finishing up breakfast or showering, or he/she was still in the sleeper area behind the cab.

Cassie circled the rows of trucks until she was once again in front of the Peterbilt. The driver had not emerged from the sleeper so she assumed the cab was unoccupied. The sleeping curtains had been drawn back.

She parked her Jeep in front of the huge chrome grille and climbed out. There was no movement from the cab.

Cassie climbed out and walked beside the Peterbilt and knocked on the passenger door. Drivers, she knew, were always surprised when that happened. They knew—and she knew—that someone knocking on their truck door at a truck stop was likely a prostitute or "lot lizard." Just because it was early in the morning didn't negate the possibility of an intimate encounter.

There was no response from inside the cab.

Working quickly, she returned to her Jeep and bent down near the rear wheel well. Cassie reached under it and grasped the tracking device. The magnet was strong and at first she couldn't wrench it free. Then using both hands and grunting, she loosened it and she nearly fell over backward when it let go.

With the device blinking in her hand, she checked to see if anyone was observing her. Seeing no one, Cassie walked down the length of the tractor and reached under the lip of the reefer trailer. The tracking device almost leapt from her hand to attach to the metal with a *thunk*. It was well out of sight.

She brushed off her hands, looked around to make sure no one had seen her, then climbed back into the Jeep and drove away from the Peterbilt.

There was no sign of Duplisea or his silver GMC, but she knew he'd be out there.

She'd chosen a long-haul rig to transfer the tracker instead of a random passenger car on purpose. If Duplisea followed the tracking device as she suspected he would he'd be led hundreds of miles away. He'd eventually realize his target was not her Jeep but a red Peterbilt reefer, and he'd likely give up the chase. It was better to choose a big commercial semitruck than a civilian car with an innocent driver, she thought.

It was a mean trick on the semi driver, who may or may not ever even know a tracking device had been planted on his unit. But it would get Duplisea out of the picture for a while.

Long enough, she hoped, that she could turn her full attention onto Matthew Annan.

Cassie backed her Jeep into a parking space on the side of the Flying J building where she could observe the red Peterbilt. After five minutes of no activity, she ducked inside for a large coffee and a box of chocolate-covered mini-donuts. Guilt had become an almost essential part of every stakeout, and she indulged it.

After fifteen minutes, a man emerged from the restaurant and ambled toward the Peterbilt while working a toothpick in his mouth. The driver was a big guy wearing baggy Carhartt jeans, a too-tight T-shirt despite the early morning cold, and a backward Seattle Seahawks ball cap.

She watched as he climbed up into the cab and spent a minute talking on his phone. Then the big truck shook and eased out of the slot toward the highway.

It approached the exit and stayed in the right turning lane until it hit a cloverleaf that forked onto I-90 East.

She liked that. The red Peterbilt was headed away from Belgrade, away from Bozeman, and away from *her*.

She put her Jeep into gear. As she did she looked up just in time to see Doug Duplisea's silver GMC pickup flash by in the eastbound lanes. She noted his profile behind the wheel.

He never glanced over.

Cassie grinned and eased out into the westbound lane. That's when her phone lit up. The call was from Kyle Westergaard.

She punched him up via Bluetooth.

"Kyle, how are you?"

"Pretty good." He sounded groggy.

"Where are you?"

"Well, I slept in my truck at a campground last night. I'm not far from Deer Lodge."

"Can't you afford a motel?"

"I don't like to waste my money."

"Gotcha. So what do I owe the pleasure this morning?"

"Huh?"

"Why did you call me, Kyle?"

"Oh. Yeah. Well, I want to ask you for some help. Please."

"Are you still looking for that stupid treasure, Kyle?"

He paused. "Yeah."

She sighed. "Why do you think I could help you?"

"I heard some things in a diner yesterday. I think if I told you what I heard you might be able to figure it out. I got a name and a plate number but I don't know what to do with either one of them. You know how to do this and I don't. You're, you know, *smart*."

Her heart melted a little. She had a soft spot for Kyle and she always would. As long as he didn't break into her office again.

"Look," she said, "I'm on my way to Anaconda from Bozeman and I'm kind of pressed for time. Since you're in Deer Lodge, why don't we meet halfway? Say, Butte for breakfast?"

"Yeah, that sounds good."

"Start driving now. I'll call you when I find a place where we can meet," she said.

"Thank you, Cassie."

"Don't thank me yet, Kyle. I'm going to try once again to talk you out of treasure hunting."

"But what if I find it?" he asked. The optimism in his voice made her want to root for him and cry for him at the same time.

Instead, she said, "You won't find it, Kyle. But I *will* buy you breakfast."

Cassie felt exuberant as she drove. Part of it was the beautiful spring morning and the sun on the mountains, but a big part of it was the feeling in her gut that things were finally coming together. She wished she could share the feeling with Candyce Fly.

What she'd learned from the three women the day before had been the tipping point. Now she knew his game and how he operated.

She was closing in on him, and he didn't yet know it.

Cassie thumbed the speaker feature on the steering wheel and said, "Call Matthew Annan."

He picked up after four rings. He was hesitant. "Yes?" he said. He sounded out of breath.

"This is Cassie Dewell with Dewell Investigations, Matthew. We met the other day."

"Oh, I'm sorry. I didn't recognize your number."

"That's okay," she said. "You didn't enter my number in your phone. But why should you?"

"I've been awfully busy," he said. "And I'm sorry I'm out of breath. My helpers didn't show up today and I'm, well . . . it isn't important."

His tone changed quickly. "Cassie, how are you? Are you coming back our way?"

"I am. We need to meet."

"Sure," he said with apparent enthusiasm. "How about my house? You know where it is."

"I'll get there about lunchtime," she said. "Instead of your house, how about meeting at a restaurant or diner? That way you don't need to worry about feeding me."

"Okay."

"I need to ask you some questions."

There was a moment's hesitation. Then: "I'd love that. I'd like to learn more about you and about your investigation. And I'd be lying if I didn't say I've been . . . thinking about you."

She thought: *Liar.*

But she said, "I've been thinking about you as well." It wasn't a lie, really. She'd spent hours thinking about him and talking about him with RuthAnne Sommers, Monica Weatherby, and Brooke Alexander.

He chuckled. "Well, this is interesting. But I guess we're both at an age where we can just say the things we mean. We've both been around the block. It's kind of scary but it's also kind of liberating, I suppose."

"I suppose."

"I'm glad this isn't a video call," he said. "Otherwise, you'd see how uncomfortable I am right now."

She laughed a genuine laugh. "So where should we meet? You know Anaconda a lot better than I do, given that you grew up there and all."

"Hmm, let me think. Would you be okay to meet in a bar rather than a restaurant? There are too many local gossips in the restaurants, and this is a small town."

"I've spent plenty of time in bars," Cassie said.

"We don't have to drink."

"I don't plan to."

"Good. Then let's meet at the Club Moderne. They've got good cheeseburgers and good soup. It's right on a main street and easy to find. There are private booths in the back room where we can talk. Where you can ask me all of your questions and I'll attempt to answer them."

"I've seen it."

"Wonderful. Call when you get to town and I can be there in five minutes."

"I'll do that."

"I look forward to seeing you again, Cassie."

The use of her name got her nearly as badly as it had the first time. But she fought it.

"I look forward to seeing you, Matthew."

It took fifteen miles of interstate before Cassie's heartbeat returned to normal. When it did, she punched up her phone again and said, "Call Agent Tom Wright."

A bored female voice responded with, "Division of Criminal Investigation, Montana Department of Justice."

"Agent Tom Wright, please," Cassie said. "This is Cassie Dewell."

"Hold please."

Cassie had worked closely with Wright several years before when she'd alerted DCI about the goings-on in the Lochsa County sheriff's department. DCI was the agency that investigated other law enforcement agencies within the state. Wright proved to be a straight-shooting if do-everything-by-the-book bureaucrat. And unlike most bureaucrats Cassie had worked with over the years, Wright followed through.

Wright was a family man with a passel of kids who spent his vacations doing good works in Third World countries. Cassie suspected he was LDS, but she'd never asked and he'd never said. It made no difference to her because they seemed to share the same amount of outrage when it came to dealing with corrupt cops.

He picked up and said, "Well, this is a voice from the past. Please don't tell me you're blowing the whistle on another local sheriff's department."

She laughed and said, "Well, maybe not *everyone* in the department. But the undersheriff and his deputies, for sure. The sheriff himself is mysteriously missing, and so is a private investigator out of Florida."

Wright moaned. He said, "What kind of PI are you? I thought PIs spied on cheating husbands and that kind of thing."

"I do as little of that as possible, believe me. Do you have a few minutes?" Cassie asked.

He sighed and said, "For you, sure."

twenty-one

—=◦=—

J. D. Spengler chose the Flint Creek Motor Court in Anaconda for its location as well as its physical attributes. He figured if
he *had* to stay in a Podunk town like this that didn't feature the kind
of four-star properties he preferred, he'd go with what he always
chose—an older motel with doors that opened up to the parking lot
and no central hallway or lobby to pass through. This way, he could
come and go as he pleased without anyone knowing. And, if he
could indeed find a working girl while he was there, she could enter
his room from the outside without attracting attention.

When he tried to check in there was no one in the small lobby.
Spengler had to ring the bell on the counter to get someone's
attention. An older bald man in flannel entered via a door behind
the counter while dabbing barbecue sauce from the corners of his
mouth.

"The old lady made ribs tonight," the man said while he looked
Spengler over with a practiced eye.

"Ribs are great," Spengler said. "I'd like a room on the end of
the row for two nights."

"You're in luck. That one's open."

"Good."

"You seem to know what you want," the man said. "What
brings you here?"

"Business and pleasure," Spengler said. It was his standard line when asked by nosy locals. "Is there any action around here?"

The clerk looked at him suspiciously after he ran Spengler's credit card. "Where are you from?"

"South Florida."

"Well, there might be a lot of action down in South Florida, I wouldn't know. But there isn't much around here. Try Butte, maybe."

"Maybe I will."

His room was clean but unremarkable. There were cowboy prints on the walls and plastic cups in the bathroom. The television was bolted to its stand. Spengler put his bag on the bed and turned on the air conditioner. It moaned to life and vibrated as if possessed by a demon wanting out.

While it rattled, Spengler changed into all black clothing and pulled on a dark blazer. Black, he felt, made him look slimmer and it helped hide sweat stains.

He turned off the air conditioner and went back outside to the lobby.

He rang the bell and the man appeared, once again dabbing his lips with a napkin. When he saw it was Spengler again, he didn't hide his disdain.

"What now?" he asked.

"The air conditioner works like shit. It sounds like a buzz saw in there."

"That's because nobody ever uses it," the man said. "I'll take a look at it when I can. In the meantime, just open a window. It'll cool down tonight. This is Montana."

Spengler contemplated asking for another room but decided to try it at least for one night.

"Can you recommend a good place for dinner?" he asked.

The man squinted as if he'd never encountered the question before. Then: "Do you like hot pastrami sandwiches?"

"I do."

"Try Haufbrau's down the street. It's popular with the locals. They make a good pastrami and sauerkraut sandwich."

"What about breakfast?"

The man's eyes settled on Spengler's large belly.

"Tillie's. They've only got six tables and they don't take credit cards. But they make a chicken-fried steak the size of a baseball mitt."

"Thanks. Enjoy your ribs."

"I'd like to," the man said before he turned around.

Spengler sat at the counter at Haufbrau's and ate two hot pastrami sandwiches and a double order of fries. He washed it all down with two draft beers.

The place *was* full of working-stiff locals who all knew one another. Large families filled booths and let their children run wild. There didn't seem to be any prohibition about kids in bars in Montana, he thought. At least not in Anaconda.

He kept his eye on the waitress who wore denim jean shorts and a Haufbrau's T-shirt knotted at the waist. She was blond, in her late twenties, and she had a good figure. Nice legs. Maybe an athlete in high school, he guessed. Spengler tried to engage her in conversation when she brought him his second orders and second beers, and she was pleasant but disinterested in him. He lost interest in *her* when a rough-dressed man who was obviously in construction came in and kissed her hello and sat down. The man was covered with sawdust and his steel-toed work boots were the size of small dogs.

Still, when she brought Spengler his third beer, he asked her, "Are you from around here?"

"I've lived here all my life."

"Look, I'm trying to find an old friend of mine. Do you know Marc Daly?"

She laughed and rolled her eyes. "Marcus Daly founded this town. He died a million years ago."

Interesting. "What about Matthew Annan? Do you know him?"

"Sure. Everybody knows Matthew. He does a lot of good in this community."

He felt an electrical jolt shoot through him. "Do you know where I can find him?"

She looked at him askance. "Seriously?"

"Seriously."

She gestured behind the restaurant somewhere and said, "Seventh Street. He just moved a big old mansion there from Butte. Believe me when I tell you that you can't miss it."

"Thank you."

"What do you want with Matthew?" she asked. She seemed protective of Annan.

"Like I said, he's an old friend."

"I thought you said Marcus Daly was your old friend."

"I got confused," Spengler said while lifting up his mug. "Too many of these, I guess."

The home on Seventh Street was magnificent, Spengler thought. The waitress was right.

He parked on the street across from it and observed. The lights were on inside and there were no window coverings. After a few minutes, he saw a figure pass in front of the huge great room window. The man stopped there as if posing and he looked out over the unfinished front lawn with his hands on his hips. He didn't look up to see Spengler.

It was him, Spengler thought. He knew it from the poor photos he'd received from Candyce Fly and the physical descriptions he'd gotten from his other new clients. Spengler knew how Annan had been able to afford the small castle in front of him.

Spengler grunted from his full belly as he leaned to the side and popped open the center console. He grasped the handle of his .38 snub-nosed revolver and slipped it into the right pocket of his jacket. Then he grabbed his notebook from the passenger seat and got out.

He walked up to the house on large flagstones that had been placed but not yet secured into the soil. One rocked as he stepped on it and he nearly lost his balance. He felt more than saw that the man inside was watching his progress from where he stood at the front window.

The door had a heavy bronze knocker and Spengler was reaching for it as the door opened.

There he was. The man he'd been chasing for three months.

"Are you Matthew Annan?" he asked.

"Yes. Who are you?"

"J. D. Spengler. I'm a private detective from Tampa, Florida."

"I know where Tampa is. What can I help you with?"

Annan was pleasant and seemed genuinely curious, Spengler thought. He looked at Annan's face carefully when he said, "I'm here on behalf of Candyce Fly of Boca Grande as well as three other clients. Their names are Monica Weatherby, RuthAnne Sommers, and Brooke Alexander. Do you have a few minutes to talk?"

Annan didn't flinch. There was no tell at all. Either Annan was genuinely clueless or he was an accomplished actor. Or a sociopath.

"Okay," Annan said. "What do those women have to do with me?"

"You really don't know?"

"I really don't know."

Annan closed the door a few inches. "As you can see here, we just moved this house to this location. It's not yet finished and I'm running behind. I've got a lot to do to get it up to snuff. So if you don't mind . . ."

The door closed farther. Spengler stepped up on the threshold so that Annan would have to hit him in the belly with the door if he closed it all the way.

"Look, I've come a long way," Spengler said. The alcohol in his system gave him courage. "I really only need a few minutes of your time. I'm not on any kind of schedule now that I've found you. If you don't let me in now I'll just keep coming back, day after day. And I'll ask plenty of people in town about you. I'll ask them what it is you did to be able to afford this place. I look forward to hearing their answers. So, like I said, I need just a few minutes of your time."

Annan glared at him without moving. Then, with a sigh, he said, "A few minutes and that's it. But I warn you, the inside is a wreck."

Annan stepped aside and Spengler went in. As he passed Annan the man said, "I'd offer you a beer but it smells like you've had plenty."

He gestured toward a huge dining room table that was covered with blueprints and building plans.

"This is the best I can do," Annan said.

He gracefully slid into a chair on one side of the table and Spengler brushed the sawdust off a chair and sat on the other. There was at least ten feet between them.

Annan dug his phone out of his back pocket and placed it face-down within reach.

Spengler said, "You're a hard guy to find."

Annan shrugged. "I don't know why you say that. I've lived here all my life."

"But you do get around. Boca Grande, Chicago, Santa Monica, New York City. And those are just the places I know about."

"Business travel," Annan said. Then he looked at his watch to indicate that time was racing by and Spengler didn't have long.

"Oh, what business are you in?" Spengler asked.

"Finance."

The PI swept his hand to take in the interior of the house. "Business must be good, judging by this place."

"I've been fortunate."

Spengler leaned forward and clasped his hands together on the top of the table. He stared hard at Annan. "You're probably curious how I found you since you're pretty good at covering your tracks."

Annan shrugged and said, "I'm just curious about how much more of my time you plan to waste."

"What kind of business took you to the Gasparilla Inn in Boca Grande?"

Annan frowned but didn't reply. A tell, Spengler thought.

"My client told me all about it," he said. "So I was able to get a look at the guest list from February fifth through February twenty-seventh this year. It cost me a couple of hundred to a night clerk but it was worth it. That's the time line from when Candyce Fly did a meet-cute with a man claiming to be Marc Daly on the Lemon Bay golf course until he vanished like the wind with a ton of her money. I was disappointed at first to find out that 'Marc Daly' wasn't on the guest list for any of those days. But who was, I asked myself?

"So I dug further into the guest list," Spengler said. "Most of the guests during that period were couples who stayed only a night or two. After all, the hotel is pretty expensive and it's more of a vacation destination than a long-term stay kind of place. Snowbirds might rent a cottage for the winter, but likely not a hotel room for three weeks.

"It turns out there were only two guests who stayed that entire length. One of them was a ninety-year-old geezer. The other one was named Matthew Annan, and he checked in using his American Express gold card. Lucky for me and unlucky for you, the inn won't take cash for an extended stay."

"There's nothing wrong with staying in a hotel for three weeks," Annan said.

"I'm not finished," Spengler said, cutting him off. "So I employed a hacker. It's absolutely amazing what a good hacker can find about a person—especially if they know their name and their credit card number."

"Isn't that illegal?" Annan asked.

"Yes. But so is fraud. Anyway, please allow me to finish."

Annan reached up and tugged at his chin. Spengler surmised it was a tic Annan had when he got nervous.

"So my hacker did a nationwide search," he continued. "We found where Matthew Annan booked rooms all over the United States. We were especially interested in long stays, and we found them in the cities I mentioned earlier.

"Now, someone might think that a private investigator works alone, and I usually do," Spengler said. "But in this instance—knowing what I knew from my client Candyce Fly—I engaged the services of the top PIs located in Chicago, Santa Monica, and New York. Those cities all had long-term hotel stays under your name. I told each of those local PIs to identify prominent local women who fit a profile: extremely wealthy, of a certain age, lonely, and between relationships. Frankly, there were hundreds of names."

"I would think so," Annan said with a smirk.

"Anyway, I took those lists and gave them to my hacker. Which of these ladies, I asked him, experienced big unexplained hits to their assets over the last two years? Not depletions in the hundreds of thousands, Matthew, but hits in the millions. That narrowed down the list considerably. It didn't take long for my researcher in my firm to identify eight women who fit the criteria. So I contacted them all. Five of the women had other reasons why they lost a lot of their money suddenly. I won't burden you with the reasons.

"But three of the women told me stories very similar to the MO you used on Candyce Fly. You showed up at the right time, you charmed their pants off—literally—and they 'invested' in your made-up business or scheme. Then you vanished like the wind. The four women I mentioned to you earlier are now my clients. In all, you bilked them for $18.5 million. No wonder you've been so 'fortunate.'"

Annan said, "Assuming what you say is correct—which it isn't—you couldn't use that information in court. You admitted already it was obtained illegally."

"I won't need to use it," Spengler said. "I envision a situation where Candyce Fly, RuthAnne Sommers, Monica Weatherby, and Brooke Alexander are in the witness stand and one by one they point at you in the docket and say, 'That's him, Your Honor. That's the man who broke my heart and stole my money.' Man, the tabloids would be all over that trial.

"And these are just the women we know of right now," Spengler said. "Only you know how many others you defrauded. How many, Matthew? How many more are out there who would come forward if they found out you'd been caught?"

It irked Spengler that Annan didn't seem disturbed. The man was just as cool as when he'd arrived at his house.

"Excuse me," Annan said. He picked up his phone and tapped out a message, then put the device facedown where it had been before. A few seconds later, it chimed with an incoming message.

Annan didn't even seem to note the return message. He said, "Assuming any of this is true, which it certainly isn't, what is the point of you coming here today? Why haven't you just turned over all of this information to law enforcement and let them deal with it?"

Spengler sat back in his chair and smiled. He said, "You've got quite the scheme going, Matthew. You do your research, you build fake websites and fake online histories for whatever character you plan to play: Marc Daly, Bill Clark, Auggie Heinze, Marcus Daly. There are probably more I don't know about yet. Then you target these women and move in. I suppose it hasn't worked every single time. Maybe there are a few rich women out there who don't fall for your act. But it's worked well enough. And no one has been able to put it all together until now. You've had a pretty good thing going."

"You're wasting my time," Annan said. "This is all smoke and mirrors. What is it that you want from me? A confession?"

"No," Spengler said. "I want a cut."

Annan raised his eyebrows. "A cut?"

"Ten percent of the money you took from my clients," Spengler said. "And twenty percent going forward for any new cons."

"You've given this a lot of thought," Annan said through a grin. "Would your clients be happy with ten percent of their money? Theoretically, of course."

"It's not for them," Spengler said. "I've had months to think it through. While I was flying around the country spending my clients' money, I thought: *I'm* the one eating fast food and staying at the Flint Creek Motor Court, for Christ's sake. Isn't it about time *I* was able to cash in on my hard work?"

"Ten percent of $18.5 million is $1.85 million," Annan said. "It sounds like extortion to me."

"It's not extortion. It's my bonus for figuring it all out. Then I go away and tell my clients you just slipped through my fingers as I closed in."

"And they continue to pay you," Annan said. "Boy, you do have it all figured out."

"I spend a lot of windshield time in the car," Spengler said. "I have plenty of time to think."

"How would you know, theoretically of course, that another woman lost a chunk of her money?" Annan asked. "How would you know to demand twenty percent?"

"I'd know," Spengler said. "I've got my feelers out and I've got your methods down cold."

"The credit card," Annan said. "But credit cards can be replaced."

"With other credit cards," Spengler said, trying to sound bored. "We know how to track you and what to look for. You really can't risk using a fake card. Credit card security is just too good these days. So you have to check in using your real ID and a real credit card. You can pay cash for everything else, but that initial transaction needs to be clean or you'll be found out. If you don't believe me, you're playing with fire. I don't think you want to do that. Twenty percent is a small price to pay when you think about it. You can just bilk the next woman out of ten million dollars instead of nine million. That way, you're money ahead and everyone is happy."

Annan laughed and pushed his chair back to stand up. He said, "Mr. Spengler, this has all been an interesting mental exercise and a nice break from putting this house back together. But I think we're done."

Spengler was confused. He said, "So do we have a deal or don't we?"

"Of course not," Annan said. "Can I offer you another beer for the road?"

He walked across the room to a cooler and opened it. "I've got Coors, Coors Light, and Miller. I've also got water."

"What is happening here?" Spengler asked. "Are you insane enough not to make the deal? Do you really want to have your reputation destroyed and go to prison?"

Annan looked up. "Not gonna happen," he said almost cheerfully. Then: "I hate to tell you that you're not as smart as you think you are."

At that moment Spengler lunged across the table for Annan's phone.

"*Put that down*," Annan commanded. But not before Spengler saw a text thread with someone named "Deputy Doug."

Annan had typed: Need your help. My house.

Deputy Doug had replied: Rolling.

"That's right," Annan said to Spengler. "I called the police. They should be here any minute."

As he said it, Spengler looked out of the huge picture window to see a police cruiser screech to a stop on the street. The side door panel read, ANACONDA–DEER LODGE COUNTY SHERIFF'S DEPARTMENT. A big man in a uniform launched himself out of the vehicle and jammed his hat on his head while he approached the front door of the house.

"You've got to be kidding me," Spengler said. He hauled himself up. "You don't want the cops involved in this. What are you thinking?"

"I'm thinking," Annan said to Spengler while he opened a can of Coors, "that you should have stayed in Florida."

"Look—call him off," Spengler said in a panic. "You don't want me telling him what I've learned, do you?"

"Go ahead. He knows all about it."

Spengler felt a wave of sweat break through his scalp. He got it now.

"Call him off," he said again. "I'll leave. You'll never hear from me again."

"After all your hard work? I doubt that."

"I've got a gun," Spengler shouted.

"Are you threatening me?"

"No, Jesus. I'm not. I'm just letting you know so this cowboy doesn't get the wrong idea and start shooting."

"Then put it on the table," Annan said as the front door flew open. The cop entered in a crouched shooting stance. Spengler looked straight into the gaping muzzle of his service weapon.

"Mr. Spengler here has a gun," Annan said to the deputy.

"Good to know," the deputy said before firing four rapid shots.

twenty-two

◆—◎◜◞—◆

Cassie found a place called Esther's Country Kitchen on the south side of Butte across the interstate. She could see the close-packed city sprawled across the distant hillside through the front window of the restaurant.

She ordered an omelet and texted the address to Kyle. She wanted to eat a big breakfast so she wouldn't be hungry when she met Matthew Annan for lunch at the Club Moderne in Anaconda. It had always been a thing with her: feeling guilty for eating too much in front of men she didn't know well. This way, she thought, she could order a salad and skip the judgment.

Esther's was kitschy and homey and moderately busy with retirees who lingered over cups of coffee while they read the newspaper. She sat at a booth in the back corner. While she waited for her food and for Kyle to show up, she checked messages on her phone and was pleased to see there wasn't anything urgent she needed to respond to. The only news from her office was unsurprising: Isabel had called in sick for a "mental health day."

Her breakfast and Kyle showed up at the same time. He looked hollow eyed and disheveled.

Cassie removed her readers and placed her phone on the table. "Have a seat," she said to him. "Order breakfast if you'd like."

He nodded and squinted at the laminated menu while the waitress hovered patiently. He said, "Three eggs over easy, country ham, hash browns, and pancakes." Then: "Do you have Mountain Dew?"

"Yes."

"I'd like a large one, please."

To Cassie, Kyle said, "I'm a Mountain Dew man."

"I remember."

He looked happy with himself, she thought.

"Kyle, when is the last time you slept in a bed or took a shower?"

He thought it over. "North Dakota," he said.

"It's something you should think about."

He waved the idea away. "I'm outside all day," he said. "I sleep in my truck. I don't bother anyone."

"You can get a shower at most truck stops," she said. "I was reminded of that just today."

He shrugged and she let it go.

"I hope you'll get right to the point because I don't have much time this morning, Kyle," she said.

"Okay."

"What is it you wanted to ask me?"

He nodded and said, "Yesterday, I was in Deer Lodge. I spent the morning checking out a river for the treasure and I was starving, so I stopped to get something to eat. While I was sitting there, two guys came in. They were correctional officers from the prison, but it took me a few minutes to figure that out. They had uniforms that made them look like cops."

"Go on."

"They were talking to each other but I think they didn't know that I could hear them. One guy told the other guy he was going to buy a new F-150 and they argued about the best truck to buy for a while."

"Kyle, can you speed this up?"

Kyle said, "The one CO said he could afford a new truck *thanks to Sir Scott's.*"

Cassie shook her head. "What does that mean? From the poem or the treasure itself?"

"Well, at first I thought maybe they'd found the treasure, but I'm pretty sure they didn't. No, I would have heard about it and that news would be all over the place. So I think it had something to do with the poem, but I don't get it. It doesn't make sense to me."

"Me, either," Cassie said.

Kyle recounted verbatim the conversation between the two COs. Cassie trusted Kyle to recall everything in detail, even if it didn't shed any more light on what Kyle was seeking.

It was interesting, however, that the COs seemed to have shared information about Sir Scott's on a previous occasion. And the lines:

"What do you think? Will anybody ever find it?"

"The treasure?"

"Fuck yes, the treasure."

"Who knows? I couldn't care less. All I care about is that it helped me buy a new truck."

When he was done, Kyle asked, "Don't you have ways of finding things out about people?"

"I do."

"Can you do that for me? Can you look up this CO and find out about him? I know where he lives because I followed him home, but that's all I know. I think it'll help me find the treasure."

"You followed him home?"

"Don't worry. He never saw me."

Cassie finished her omelet and covered the plate with a napkin and sat back. She didn't mind eating a lot of food in front of Kyle.

"Kyle, you know how I feel about your treasure hunt. I think you're wasting your time."

He nodded and said, "Yeah. But I think this might mean something."

"Do you have a name?" she asked reluctantly.

Kyle pulled his wallet out and found the scrap of paper he'd written on. "The CO's name is Tracy Swanson. It was on his name badge. I think he knows something about the treasure but for some reason he's keeping it a secret."

"There might be another explanation," she said.

"Maybe. But why would he be talking about Sir Scott's that way? New Fords cost thirty to fifty thousand dollars. That's a lot of money. He must know something."

Cassie said, "Maybe I can check on him, but I can't get to it today. The databases we use are back in my office. When I get back, I'll plug in the name and see what we can find."

She thought that she *could* ask April to do the search in her absence. But she didn't want to give Kyle any false hope that he'd get an immediate answer.

"How long will you be around?" she asked Kyle.

"Maybe another day. I've got to get back to work."

"I'll do what I can," she said. "I've got your number. But it probably won't amount to anything."

"I have this feeling that it will," he said while he waited for his breakfast to arrive. "I just have a feeling about it," he repeated.

"How many times have you had a feeling you'd find the treasure?" she asked.

"All the time," he said with a crooked grin. "And I will."

"But what if you don't, Kyle? Then what?"

He looked up and tears filled his eyes. He said, "Then I can't help Grandma Lottie. I told you that. Look at me, Cassie. You know me. I ain't ever going to come into big money and I ain't ever gonna win the lottery, either. I've hit my ceiling. Finding Sir Scott's Treasure means everything to me."

His tears affected her and she looked away before she produced her own. "I just wish you wouldn't put so much stock into something that may not even exist," she said.

"Finding that treasure is all I've got. I feel like I'm getting real close, too. I've just got a couple more places to check."

Cassie reached out and squeezed his hand. "Oh, Kyle . . ." she said.

The waitress delivered Kyle's breakfast and Cassie let go of her grip so the plates could be set down in front of him.

"I'll find it," Kyle said. "But if you could help me with this CO I might be able to find it sooner."

"I'll do what I can."

"Thank you, Cassie."

"Take care, Kyle," she said as she slid out of the booth and went to the counter to pay.

Just as Kyle had a feeling about the treasure, Cassie felt pulled back into downtown Butte for reasons she couldn't quite explain.

She took the underpass beneath the interstate and cruised Butte's throwback urban streets and was once again transported into the 1920s.

As before, Cassie climbed the hillside to the imposing row of old mansions on the side of the hill. She parked at the gaping hole where Matthew Annan had bought and excavated the mansion that he later moved to Anaconda. It was as if looking at the empty space would somehow tell her more about him.

Why buy the old home in the first place? she wondered. For what it cost to buy, move, and renovate, Annan could have built a massive new house anywhere he wanted to. And why move the home ten miles away where it would stick out like a sore thumb? Annan could have purchased twenty houses in Anaconda for what this one cost.

She planned to get those answers soon.

She engaged the emergency brake so her Jeep wouldn't roll down the steep street and she climbed out. As she closed her door she was met by a young woman in period dress. The woman wore a long skirt and had a bonnet on her head. Freckles covered her nose and cheeks.

"Are you here for the tour?" she asked merrily.

"I'm sorry. What tour?"

"A tour of the Copper King mansions," the woman said with obvious disappointment. "Isn't that why you're here?"

"Not really."

The tour guide grinned and tried again. "We gather at ten and the tour takes ninety minutes. We'll get to visit all of the old mansions when Butte was the richest city in the West."

The guide listed all of the mansions they would visit that day.

As she named them and listed the onetime owners, Cassie felt a chill run through her.

"Could you please repeat those names?" she asked the guide.

"Sure." And she named the owners once again.

"Thank you," Cassie said. "You've been a huge help."

"Help with what?" the guide asked. She was confused.

"Something I'm working on," Cassie said.

Although she didn't sign up for the tour, Cassie fished into her purse and gave the guide a fifty-dollar tip.

"What's this for?" the young woman asked.

"Clarity," Cassie responded.

twenty-three

Undersheriff Duplisea scowled and cursed aloud when he passed the sign that indicated he'd now entered the Crow Indian Reservation east of Hardin. The mountains were behind him now and so was the City of Billings. The country around him was rough and flat and vast and he couldn't figure out just where in the hell she was headed.

He glanced repeatedly at the iPad that was propped on the passenger seat. He'd followed it all morning as the tracking device he'd installed on her Jeep left Bozeman and stayed on I-90 East along the Yellowstone River. It remained on the interstate while it turned south.

Wyoming? Why in the hell was she going to *Wyoming*?

He needed to get back to Anaconda and this Dewell woman was leading him farther and farther away. It was ridiculous. He'd need to locate her soon and find out what she was up to and get the hell back to town, which was now more than four hours away.

Duplisea had unfinished business. He'd promised he'd deliver Jillian Westphal's prescription from the pharmacy to her. She'd be getting antsy if he didn't show up with it soon, he knew.

Although he'd taken the cable off of her car battery so it wouldn't start, she might try to enlist a friend or acquaintance to go get the order for her. Duplisea didn't want that to happen. He wanted to deliver it himself. He *had* to deliver it himself.

To make sure she didn't get a wild hair, he called her as he drove. Jillian picked up on her landline.

"Jillian, it's Doug. How are you doing?"

"I'm tired and incontinent, but I'm getting along."

Never ask a sick person how they're doing, Duplisea thought, because they were likely to tell you.

He said, "I just wanted to let you know I didn't forget about you. I was headed to the pharmacy last afternoon when I had to go out on a call. Some idiot flipped his SUV on the access road and I was on-site there for three hours. By the time I got done the pharmacy was closed."

"I understand," she said. "Nothing ever works out as planned in law enforcement. You forget that I'm the wife of a cop."

"I didn't forget," he faux-laughed. "But hang tight. I'll get your prescriptions to you later this afternoon."

"Good, because I need them. Especially the hydrocodone for the pain. I'm just about out."

"Like I said, let me handle everything, Jillian. I'll see you later this afternoon."

"Thank you, Doug."

"You bet."

"Have you heard anything at all from Phil?"

"Not yet. But I'm guessing it'll be soon," he said and punched off.

The night before, he'd actually gone to the pharmacy and picked up her medications after accompanying her to her house. He sat in his cruiser and carefully inspected each bottle of pills. He chose the bottle of hydrocodone and slipped it into his pocket.

He waited until his office was all but empty before returning there. The dispatcher was in the building, of course, but she was in a different room than the duty room, where he worked. She was easily avoided if he entered through the back door. He made sure that his two graveyard shift deputies were out on patrol. They were. Their cars were gone from the lot.

He sat down at his desk and put on his readers, then carefully cut the prescription label off the hydrocodone container with an X-Acto knife. After making a color copy of it on the duplication machine and trimming the copy to size, he taped the original back on to the hydrocodone container.

Duplisea had an extra key for the evidence room most of his professional career, so there was no need to break in. The closed circuit in the hallway had been nonfunctional for a month, so there was no worry about that.

Inside, he rifled through a cardboard box of prescription medications that had belonged to a local addict until he found a plastic pill bottle the exact size of the hydrocodone container. He removed the label and flushed it and the contents away in the toilet used by the evidence room staffer.

The undersheriff easily located the large quart-sized baggie of fentanyl tablets that had been seized in a raid the month before. They were similar in size and shape to the hydrocodone tablets in her prescription.

After taping the copied prescription label on the new container, he carefully counted out and refilled it with the correct number of fentanyl tabs. He saw from the label that she was to take two of them twice a day. He doubted she'd make it to the second dose.

Then he pocketed the hydrocodone and placed the fentanyl into the paper bag with the other medications he'd picked up at the pharmacy. Duplisea carefully stapled the receipt to the bag so it looked like it hadn't been opened.

Annan had blown up when he heard what Duplisea was going to do. They'd had it out at his house the night before while Annan's day laborers stood around outside and waited for it to be over. In the end, Matthew didn't exactly come up with an alternative scenario but he could satisfy himself that he could act all righteously indignant about it. Matthew liked being in that position.

Duplisea, however, knew how it really was. These things were messy and mean. They were also *practical*. Matthew had a blind spot when it came to the practical part of what they did.

Some people, he knew, simply had to go away. Unlike Matthew, he knew there were people and situations that couldn't be charmed away. His job was to step in when the situation was dire and dirty work needed to be performed. That was his part of the arrangement.

It was hard, and Annan rarely gave him credit for it.

There couldn't be any evidence left when it happened, and the bodies had to be disposed of. It was the only way to keep the arrangement working. Annan wanted the arrangement to proceed but he didn't like hearing about the details. This was frustrating to Duplisea, and it was getting worse.

Like this Cassie Dewell character, Duplisea thought. Because she was female, single, and of a certain age, Matthew was convinced he could turn on his animal charisma and steer her off the case. He'd told the undersheriff as much, and perhaps he was correct. But Duplisea wasn't so sure.

After all, he'd observed Dewell in person working her investigation like a dog with a bone. Not only that, but he'd heard what she'd done up in Lochsa County as well as her involvement in locating and bringing down a corrupt Montana state trooper and a highway serial killer.

She had a steel will, Duplisea thought. She could be as dangerous to them as anyone ever had been. Matthew couldn't see it, but he could. That's why he needed to keep her close and watch her actions. She'd thrown him off the day before with her odd jaunt to Livingston. But he couldn't let her throw him further off in the future.

★ ★ ★

Annan liked to play the community savior and philanthropist. Every-body loved Matthew Annan, the local boy who made good and stuck around. He treasured making large donations to causes and organizations and receiving credit and awards. He loved how the people of his town protected and defended him against outsiders—people like Cassie Dewell and that Florida PI. But Matthew kept his hands clean and looked the other way when Duplisea had to step in and deal with outside threats and the possibility of exposure. It was getting old.

Duplisea had explained to Annan that switching out Jillian's drugs was the only way they could proceed. She was getting too vocal about the disappearance of Sheriff Phil, and she was threat-ening to bring in outside law enforcement. Violence wasn't the solution in a situation like this, Duplisea had explained. She was too old and too frail and too well liked. Everybody knew she had terminal cancer and could go at any time. In his role as undersheriff, he could easily persuade the county coroner not to do an autopsy. Switching out the fentanyl with the original hydrocodone would be easily done before the EMTs arrived to retrieve her body.

It could be done without any questions being asked.

In the end, Matthew had agreed with him. He waved his hand and turned away, but he agreed.

Just north of the Little Bighorn Battlefield National Monument—or, as Duplisea still thought of it, Custer's Last Stand—he started to wonder if the tracking device had failed or if the app on his iPad had malfunctioned. It made no sense that Dewell was heading out of state in such a determined fashion.

Maybe she was working another case that required going to Wyoming or beyond, but he doubted it.

He slowed his pickup and eased off the highway and rebooted the iPad.

As it powered back up, he expected the app to show that there had been an electronic glitch and that her Jeep was actually back in Bozeman—but it didn't. What it showed was that she had left the highway en route to the national monument itself. And then it stopped.

He checked for oncoming vehicles behind him and when it was clear, Duplisea floored the accelerator and roared back onto the highway. He planned to find out where she'd stopped and why. If the situation was right, he might deal with her right there and then.

If it wasn't, he'd turn around and get back to town to deliver Jillian's prescription.

Next to the hotel and casino owned by the Crow tribe was an exit and road that led east toward the battlefield itself. There were a half-dozen semitrucks fueling up at a facility up on the hill and ten or more private vehicles either gassing up or parked outside the building.

Duplisea had been there before and he knew that the business had a restaurant inside as well as a large souvenir trade: feathered headdresses, arrowheads, cavalry caps, things like that. It was the last commercial facility up the road and it was directly across from the gates of the national monument itself.

There were no trees anywhere to obscure his view, so Duplisea drove up the road slowly toward the gas station lot and he tried to put eyes on her vehicle there. At the same time, he didn't want to turn in and have her see him.

He took the entrance to the "truck" side of the facility instead of the "car" side. His eyes flashed back and forth between his iPad and the vehicles he could see out the windows of his pickup. The tracker app definitely showed that she was here—somewhere.

Duplisea reached over and toggled a button that changed the screen from a large-scale map to the smallest and most magnified view possible.

The red tracker orb showed that his device was located not on the car side, but on the truck side of the facility. And if it was accurate, it was less than fifty feet away.

It made no sense.

He hit his brakes and looked around. From his vantage point he could see the back of the station building and a trucker entrance to his right. But when he turned his head to the left he looked at the grilles of three big tractor-trailers fueling up side by side at the diesel pumps.

There was no Jeep.

"What the fuck?" he said aloud.

Duplisea parked his pickup next to the building. He climbed out with the iPad in his left hand and approached the semitrucks. The app guided him to a red Peterbilt with Washington plates and a refrigerated trailer behind it. The driver was nowhere to be seen.

He walked around the front of the truck and along its side. The tracker orb showed that he was in the right place. He could feel his anger swell up as he moved along the long vehicle. He'd been humiliated and he thought he wanted to kill someone with his bare hands. That someone was Cassie Dewell.

Duplisea reached under the hitch unit separating the tractor from the trailer and felt his hand grip around the familiar casing of the magnetic tracking device. With a tug, he pulled it free.

She must have switched . . .

"Hey, what in the hell are you doing?"

Duplisea looked up to see a squarish fat man with a backward baseball cap and stained T-shirt. He'd come out of the restaurant. He was the driver of the Peterbilt, and he was red-faced and angry.

"I said, what in the hell are you doing messing with my truck?"

The driver was big but soft, Duplisea thought as he assessed him. He'd measured up a lot of guys in his career. He and the trucker were probably about the same weight, he thought, but he knew he was taller and stronger. And angrier.

Duplisea reached back and pulled out his wallet badge from the back pocket of his jeans. He held it up and dropped the leather flap so the driver could see the star. Then he closed it before his name could be read.

He said, "I'm a Montana state trooper. We got a tip that a red Peterbilt with Washington plates was headed south hauling contraband. Do you have a CDL and paperwork for your load?"

The driver took a step back. "Are you nuts? I've got apples in that reefer."

Duplisea grinned. "Apples?"

"You want to see them?"

"I want to see your CDL and papers first. Do you have them?"

"Yes sir, I do."

Instant respect, Duplisea noted. It usually happened this way.

"Let's see 'em."

The trucker sighed and climbed up and opened the passenger door of his cab. He handed down a folder containing his shipping order and then his commercial driver's license. Duplisea was dealing with a trucker named Derrick Zeiss from Bremerton, Washington. And yes, the shipping order was for Washington apples to be delivered to grocery store warehouses in Denver and Colorado Springs.

"Happy?" Zeiss said. "Everything check out like I told you?"

Duplisea handed back the documents and said, "Open it up."

"Jesus," the driver said. He climbed down and mumbled under his breath as he walked toward Duplisea. The deputy let him pass and then followed him to the back of the trailer.

The driver used his key to unlock a padlock and then threw the locker arm. The door slid up on tracks with the sound of muffled thunder. Duplisea could immediately smell the sweet odor of fruit. Crates of apples were stacked on pallets and were nearly as high as the ceiling of the trailer.

"See?" the driver said.

"I can see crates of apples," Duplisea said. "What I can't see is what's behind 'em."

"Oh, come on. Are you asking me to unload them? Where am I going find a forklift out here in the middle of nowhere?"

"That's not my problem."

The driver glared at Duplisea and the deputy glared back.

"Look, I'm on a schedule," the driver said. "We're so damned regulated that if I take four or five hours out of my trip today it'll throw off my whole route. You can see there's just apples in here. Come on, Officer. Can't you be reasonable?"

"I am being reasonable."

The trucker said, "Isn't there some way we can work this out? I haven't done nothin' wrong."

The trucker was groveling now. Duplisea always enjoyed the high that came with getting the upper hand. So he milked it.

"Are you refusing to comply with my request?" Duplisea asked softly. He knew he had the dead-eye cop stare down cold. And it was working.

"Jesus, look around us," the driver pleaded. "There ain't nothing around here. Do you expect me to find a forklift in the middle of an Indian reservation? Or borrow one from one of those dead cavalry soldiers buried over there on the hill?"

"Watch your tone with me, mister," Duplisea said.

The driver shook his head and then fixed his eyes on the un-dersheriff. He also balled his fists. He said, "You know, now that I think about it, I ain't gonna do a damn thing here."

He looked hard at Duplisea. "Why ain't you wearing a uniform? Where is your cruiser? Where's your probable cause? You need prob-able cause to stop me and search my outfit. I haven't given you any—other than I have a red truck with Washington plates. You've got to show me something. What did you say your name was? You snapped that badge closed so quick I couldn't see it."

The driver's tone had completely changed. Now it was defiant. Duplisea hated that attitude.

"Okay, I'll show it to you again," he said.

Duplisea reached back but instead of grasping the wallet badge he gripped his revolver in its holster on his hip. With lightning speed, he swung it up so the front blade of its barrel caught the driver beneath his chin. It snapped the man's head back.

Duplisea stepped forward and hit the man hard on the right side of his temple with the heavy revolver and the driver dropped to his knees. Blood gushed from the wound beneath his chin and spattered the asphalt.

With an arcing backhand, he crashed the weapon against the trucker's left temple, then stood aside so the man could crash face-down on the ground. It was like felling a tree.

The trucker moaned, and Duplisea silenced him with another blow to the back of his head. The man's Seattle Seahawks cap detached and rocked upside down next to his head.

Duplisea lowered his revolver and looked around while he breathed in hard and deep. There were no witnesses.

The undersheriff looked at his watch and cursed. It would take more than four hours to get back and he'd already burned the entire morning. He wiped the blood, scalp, and hair off his weapon with a handkerchief and then holstered it. He smoothed back his black hair as he walked to his pickup.

Inside, he peeled out of the parking lot and squealed his tires on the access road back to the highway.

He said, "That bitch."

twenty-four

⋈

Two hours later, Cassie arrived in Anaconda with thirty min-utes to spare before her lunch meeting with Matthew Annan. She wanted to use the extra time to her advantage.

She cruised slowly by the Club Moderne and turned at the corner so she could surveil the side and back of it from the alley. It didn't appear that Annan had arrived. The BMW sedan she'd seen at his house wasn't on the street or parked in the small lot behind the building.

Aside from the heavy front door, there was a dock in the back for receiving shipments and parcels and a side door that opened to a picnic table apparently for the benefit of employees on break. The windows of the building were all shaded and barred, and apart from the glass wrap-around façade, she could see the rest was constructed of cinder block.

What she took from that was that if anything happened inside, it was unlikely that it could be seen or heard from outside. It was a mini-fortress of a bar.

Cassie parked a few blocks away and punched up Tom Wright of the Montana DCI.

"Me again," she said as a greeting.

"Yes, Cassie?"

"I'm about to meet with the subject I was telling you about. The location is Club Moderne in Anaconda. It's right on Park Avenue."

"I'm familiar with it," he said.

"You've been to a bar?" she asked with a smile.

"Very funny. Of course I've been to a bar."

"I've always wondered about that."

"Do you wonder because I'm Mormon?"

"Well . . ."

She could envision him rolling his eyes. Then: "I've got a favor to ask."

"After that insult you've got a favor to ask?"

"I do. I was wondering if you have any agents in the vicinity. If I get into trouble I might need some help."

"Let me look," Wright said. She could hear him tapping on a keyboard. Then: "No. Not today. As you know we don't have anyone permanently assigned in Butte and our guys on assignment are in other parts of the state. I'm sorry."

"Me, too," she said.

"Why not call local law enforcement?" he asked.

"Believe me, that's the last thing I'd want to do."

"Oh, that's right. Sorry."

"Well, I appreciate you checking on it anyway," she said. But she could feel a knot in her stomach forming.

"There is a state trooper I know," Wright said. "He's Ron Palmer and he's out of Butte. He's probably within shouting distance of where you're at."

"My history with state troopers isn't very good," she said.

"Just don't shoot him. No, Ron's a good guy and I can vouch for him. I've been to church with him and his family."

"Great," Cassie said. "He sounds great. Please send me his cell number. Then call him and tell him if I text him in the next few hours that I'm in an emergency situation and I need his help fast."

"What will you text him?"

"It doesn't matter," she said. "Something innocuous. But tell him if he receives *anything* from my number it means I'm in mortal danger and I need him to respond. He might want to call for backup as well from Butte or Deer Lodge or even Missoula. Anywhere but the local sheriff's department. Can you do that?"

"That's quite an ask," Wright said. "But yes, I can do that."

"Thank you, Tom. I really appreciate it."

"Take care of yourself. I hope you don't have to send Ron a text."

"Me, too."

Cassie decided not to carry her primary weapon on her person because she didn't want it to be seen. Plus, if she was sitting down as she supposed she would be, a handgun was difficult to draw in a hurry from that position. Instead, she removed enough items from her handbag that she could place her Glock inside it as well as a small canister of pepper spray and a couple of zip ties. Her secondary five-shot hammerless .38 snub-nose Smith & Wesson revolver went snugly into the outside shaft of her right cowboy boot. She fitted a small voice-activated digital recorder into an outside pocket of her purse as well and made sure it couldn't be easily seen.

Then, as she watched, Matthew Annan's BMW appeared and he parked his car behind the Club Moderne. From her viewing angle she couldn't see him get out.

Cassie parked her Jeep on the street in front of the bar. She wanted it to be obvious to anyone who looked for it.

Before climbing out, she checked her watch. How far had Duplisea chased the Peterbilt, she wondered? How much time did she have before he came back?

Cassie entered the Club Moderne through the front door and paused for a moment to get her bearings. It was dark in the way only bars could be in the daytime. There were no day drinkers present—yet.

A female bartender in her forties with full sleeve tattoos and a nose ring smiled and asked, "Eating or drinking today? Or both?"

"Eating only, I think," Cassie said. "Is Matthew Annan in the back?"

The bartender smiled with familiarity. "I heard the door open back there a few minutes ago, so I'm guessing it's Matthew. He always parks in the alley and uses that door. Would you like to look at a menu?"

"Please."

Cassie approached the opening to the back room and hesitated. She closed her eyes and took a deep breath. Her nerves were jangling and she hoped she didn't look as nervous with tension as she felt.

Like the bar area, there was no one in the back room—except Matthew Annan. He was seated facing her in the last booth staring down at his phone and texting something with both thumbs. When he looked up and saw her he quickly put the phone facedown on the table and got up. He seemed genuinely pleased that she was there.

Annan wore a long-sleeved yellow shirt with a button-down collar, tight jeans, and worn ostrich-skin cowboy boots. He looked perfectly fit and attractive, damn him.

He grasped her hand in both of his and said, "I'm happy to see you, Cassie."

"You are?"

"Of course," he said. "But your hand is freezing. Are you nervous?"

"A little."

"Don't be," he said with a gentle smile. "We're all friendlies here."

He stepped aside and swept his arm out and waited for her to slide into the booth opposite him. "After you," he said.

Cassie took her seat and scooted across it to the middle. She wished she'd done it with a little more grace. She placed her purse on the table next to the wall with the recorder on the outside facing the space between them.

He took his seat, shook his head, and said, "I'm a little disappointed in the youth of America right now."

"How so?"

"Well, a very nice young man and a hardworking girl responded to my ad and showed up at my house yesterday. They were really great and we got a lot done and I was expecting them to come back this morning. Suffice it to say they didn't."

He gestured to his phone. "Just now, I was trying to reach them to find out what the problem is when you came in."

Which one, Cassie asked herself, *had given Annan their number?* She was furious but did her best not to show it.

It was good timing when the bartender showed up with a single menu and handed it to Cassie.

"Matthew doesn't need one," she explained.

"Alas," he said.

Cassie looked it over and ordered an iced tea and a Cobb salad.

"They make great cheeseburgers here," Annan said. "They're famous for them."

"I'm fine," Cassie said, proud of herself.

He ordered a cheeseburger cooked rare and a draft beer. The bartender simply nodded and turned on her heel.

"So," Annan said, "have you been able to locate the gentleman you were looking for the other day?"

"No, but I've learned a lot more about him."

"Tell me," he said. "I find your job fascinating."

He sounded sincerely curious, she thought. She watched his face carefully as she spoke.

"He was working on a very interesting case with multiple clients. Each of those clients were defrauded out of millions of dollars. His investigation led him here." Cassie paused and said: "To you."

Annan seemed puzzled. He shook his head with a faint grin. "*Moi?*" he asked.

"You. Whether you're going by Marc Daly, Auggie Heinze, Bill Clark, Marcus Daly, or Matthew Annan."

Annan sat back. His eyes were locked into Cassie's. He said, "Well, you caught me."

She was speechless for a second.

"Yes," he said, "I'm probably the only man on earth to ever give a woman a false name while dating her. I'm guilty as charged, Officer."

He held out his hands upside down to her. "Slap the cuffs on me and take me to lover's prison," he said. Then he laughed.

"This isn't funny," she said. "Are you admitting to knowing Candyce Fly, Monica Weatherby, Brooke Alexander, and RuthAnne Sommers? Are you admitting to conning them all out of millions?"

"Yes to the first part and no to the second," he said. "I certainly knew all of those lovely ladies at one time or another. But I never conned them, as you put it. Why would I do something like that?"

"Oh, I don't know," Cassie said. "So you could buy a multimillion-dollar mansion and move it to your hometown?"

He tapped the table and turned serious. "*This* is where that house belongs. This little town. This is where the money came from that built that house. It's a long story and I guess I wouldn't expect you to understand it all."

He was suddenly filled with passion.

"Try me," Cassie said as their lunches arrived, and she had to admit that the cheeseburger looked great. But she was shaken and confused by his convincing words. And more than a little attracted to him as hard as she tried not to be.

"In order to understand what I'm wrongly accused of," he said, "you need to know more about me and this little town I live in. Once you hear about it you may find yourself looking at this allegation in an entirely different light. You've heard one side of the story, but I'm about to tell you another that, I pray, Cassie, will lead you to realize that you're barking up the wrong tree. You and that PI from Florida as well, I'd add."

"So now you admit you met him?" she asked. "Before you said you hadn't."

"I shouldn't have misled you," Annan said. "Yes, I met him. He stopped by my house and tried to extort me. When I called the police he got in his car and drove away. I haven't seen nor heard from him since."

"Why did you lie to me?" she asked. She was very aware of the recorder and she hoped she didn't signal it.

"He was a very unpleasant man," Annan said. "He was oily and filled with conspiracy theories based on nothing. I guess I didn't want to be associated with him in your eyes. I admit now that I shouldn't have lied to you and I'm sorry I did."

She speared lettuce on her plate and bobbed it at him to go on.

"Thank you," he said. "Thank you for giving me the opportunity to clear the air.

"First, about this place. Anaconda is a company town, Cassie. It didn't come to be in a natural way like other towns. That's the first thing to understand. Back at the turn of the last century, the Copper Kings in Butte didn't like the toxic waste their mines produced. They didn't like breathing the noxious air or seeing how the groundwater killed their precious gardens and lawns. So, Marcus Daly—that name again—came up with the idea to build a massive copper smelter far enough away from Butte that they didn't have to see it or smell it. Out of sight, out of mind. It's a theme to those of us who grew up here in the West, right? Big corporations move in, rape the land, exploit the workers, and eventually just pull out and leave the damage. It started when Marcus Daly founded Anaconda and built a railroad to ship the copper ore here."

Cassie interrupted. "When you say Copper Kings, you mean the millionaires who built that row of mansions in Butte, correct?"

"Yes."

Cassie withdrew her spiral notebook and read from it. "William Andrews Clark, Marcus Daly, F. Augustus Heinze. The names you adopted when you targeted our victims. I realized that today when I stopped there."

Annan grinned and flushed a little. "You figured that out," he said. "Not to mention William Rockefeller and Henry H. Rogers. The PI from Florida didn't get that far."

"I'm from Montana," she said. "The names were familiar. Why did you assume those names in particular?"

"Just an in-joke," he said. "It felt right."

"How so?"

"I'll get to that, Cassie. I was telling you about Anaconda."

"Go on."

"So Marcus Daly established the town and started building the smelter in 1900. He worked hard to lure immigrants here from the East and West. Irish, Chinese, Poles, Swedes, Serbians—dozens of nationalities. The only common theme was they were dirt-poor and desperate. He built houses for them and paid them in company scrip. He and his partners *owned* these people, Cassie. They controlled their lives like slaveholders. Workers weren't free to come and go, or to bargain collectively for better wages. Meanwhile, the copper kings dined on lobster and caviar in Butte, San Francisco, and New York City.

"My great-grandfather, Frank Annan, was a smelter worker who thought this was wrong. Have you heard of him?"

"I think I saw a plaque at the courthouse," Cassie said.

"Right, good. I paid for it," Annan said with a nod. "It was the least I could do for a great man I never met."

"Tell me about him," Cassie said.

"In 1917 there was the Granite Mountain Mine Disaster. It was the worst mining disaster in US history and it happened right here. One hundred and sixty-eight miners died in it, most from smoke inhalation. A hundred and sixty-eight men, Cassie. A hundred and sixty-eight families without husbands, fathers, brothers . . . it was terrible. Fortunately, Frank escaped or I wouldn't be here today."

Annan's eyes moistened as he told the story, Cassie noted. She didn't think they were fake tears.

"And the owners," he continued, "the owners who had chosen not to build in safety procedures or adequate ventilation in the mines—did next to nothing. They just hired more workers to replace the men who had died and went on with their business.

"Frank Annan said 'enough.' He organized the workers here to protest and strike for living wages and safety improvements. He struck for the workers to receive five dollars a day in pay, up from three dollars and eighty-five cents.

"So how did the mine owners respond?" Annan asked rhetorically. "They went to their favorite politicians and got federal troops sent here. There were actual camps and garrisons of the US Army right here in Montana to supposedly keep the peace. But they were actually government-sanctioned strikebreakers.

"During that time, seven masked men arrested my great-grandfather and lynched him for a trumped-up crime. Nobody was ever arrested or tried for it. Frank's great legacy was that he helped establish the labor movement here. Anaconda was once known as the 'Gibraltar of the American labor movement,' thanks to my great-grandfather and others who risked their lives for worker's rights."

"That's a good story," Cassie said. "I'm not sure what it has to do with fleecing women out of their fortunes."

"I love the people here," Annan said as if he hadn't heard her. "Those old ethnic neighborhoods still exist in one form or other. The people here are tight and they take care of each other. They've all been betrayed by the big corporations who brought them out here and abandoned them, but they stick together. They fight for each other, just like Frank. I owe them everything I am, and everything I can do for them until I die.

"For all of my life," he said, "I stared at those Copper King mansions in Butte and I thought about the men who built them and how they looked down on the people here. The people they poisoned and exploited for generations. I always thought if I could that I'd buy one of those mansions and uproot it and move it back to the place it always belonged. I did it for the people."

As he said it, Annan flushed red. He was embarrassed, she thought.

"You stole money from wealthy single women for the people?" Cassie said. "Really?"

"I'm sorry, but it's the truth," Annan said, looking away. "And I didn't *steal* a penny."

"You're telling a part of the story," Cassie said. "There's plenty you left out. Like Anaconda was the first city in the nation to elect an entirely socialist local government. Or that many of the early labor leaders—maybe even your great-grandfather—were card-carrying members of the Communist Party. Nobody held a gun to their heads and made them move to Montana. They came here for work to feed their families. Some might say the workers bit the hand that fed them."

"Of course I disagree. It was a different time," he said. "A different world."

"But you act as if it happened yesterday," Cassie said. "As if you're getting revenge for something that just took place."

"You don't understand," Annan said while leaning forward across the table. "Roots here run very deep. Family is everything. People here don't forget. The blood of Frank Annan still runs through my veins."

Cassie recalled the cemetery in town. She'd never seen such reverence for the departed.

"So what?" Cassie asked. As she posed the question she swept her hand and accidentally spilled the iced tea across the table and into her lap.

"Oh dear," Annan said, sopping up what he could on the table with his napkin.

"I'm fine," she lied. Her legs and lap were soaked.

The waitress appeared instantly with dry bar towels. Annan must have signaled her somehow, Cassie thought. Cassie dried out the spilled tea on her seat and soaked up the worst of it on her thighs.

"That was embarrassing," she said.

"I never saw a thing," Annan assured her.

"Back to our topic at hand," she said after surreptitiously checking her wristwatch. They'd been there for more than an hour. She needed to speed things up.

Cassie looked up and took in his eyes. "You targeted those women," she said.

"Correct. But not for the reasons you think."

For the second time, she had no real response.

"I never conned any of them out of money," he said. "You've got that all wrong."

"Matthew, you took nearly twenty million dollars from them. And those are just the women I know about."

He shook his head vigorously. "No, no, you've got that wrong. Like I said, you only know one side of the story. I never, ever asked for money from any of them. If anything, they begged to give it to me despite my strong objections."

"Come on," she said. But his strong reaction threw her off a little.

"Here, let me show you," he said. For the first time, she thought, he seemed anxious.

Annan dug into his back pocket and produced a second phone. It was a cheap burner. Cassie recognized it as the type described to her by Candyce Fly.

He activated it and scrolled through a thread of text messages. Then he handed it to her. "See for yourself," he said.

Cassie took the phone from him and their fingers touched

again. She felt a mild warm jolt that coursed completely through her.

> Candy: Please tell me what I can do to help you out. I want to help.
>
> Daly (Annan): Lord, no. I can handle this on my own. I don't want that kind of obligation, not to mention that it could affect our relationship.
>
> Candy: I INSIST on it. Send me your bank details.

She scrolled down further and it was more of the same. Candyce literally throwing money at his venture and Daly (Annan) refusing to take it.

She looked up at him.

"They're all like that," he said. "If you have the time I could show you four separate threads from the four women you mentioned. Not once did I ask for money. Not once."

"But you took it," she said.

"Eventually, yes. That's true. But not before warning each of them off repeatedly. I told them all that no investment is a sure thing, that most new businesses fail. And that's the absolute truth. Look, Cassie, I want to tell you something but I don't want you to take it wrong."

"What is it?" she asked suspiciously.

"These women feel scorned," he said. "Maybe rightly so—I'll grant them that. No one ever likes to be rejected. But really, what we're talking about is scorned women who want revenge on me for leaving them. I'm not saying all women are like that, not at all. I'm sure you aren't. But you aren't a wealthy woman who has lived her life getting everything she wants, either, I'd suspect."

Cassie felt her neck get hot. "You're saying that all four of these women are just crazy ex-girlfriends?"

He paused. "Well, yes. I guess that's what I'm saying. But there's something else. There's another reason I reached out to them."

Cassie started to say, "Because they were rich and single," but she held her tongue.

"How deeply did you dig into these women?"

"I've read profiles of them done by a researcher," she said.

"How far back did this researcher of yours go?"

"I'm not sure what you mean."

"Then I'll tell you," he said. "How far did your researcher go back to see where they got their money in the first place? None of these ladies just became rich, you know."

She had no idea where he was going. She said, "Candyce Fly and her husband were prominent Realtors in Boca Grande. RuthAnne Sommers married a Chicago tycoon. Is that what you mean?"

"No. You need to go back further. There's something that connects them. Remember the Copper Kings."

Cassie looked at him with a skeptical side-eye. "Are you telling me . . ."

"Yes, I am," he said. "Each of those women came from fortunes generated by *their* great-grandfathers. Candyce Fly came from Clark money. Monica Weatherby came from Daly money. Brooke Alexander came from Rockefeller money. And RuthAnne Sommers came from Heinze money even though her parents squandered most of it when she was a teenager. They all started their lives with silver spoons in their mouths. I should say 'copper spoons' because they were mined and smelted here in Anaconda by laborers who smothered to death in the mines or lived lives of indentured servitude. No, these women had blood on their hands."

"That's insane," Cassie said. "Great-grandchildren shouldn't have to pay for the sins of their long-gone relations."

"Why not? My people here continue to pay." Annan gestured toward the wall of the bar but intended to take in all of Anaconda beyond. "Many of them still live in poverty. Alcoholism and sub-stance abuse is through the roof and unemployment is high. We've lost population in every census and we're headed in a direction that will result in my town becoming a modern-day ghost town."

"I'm not buying that this was all innocent payback," Cassie said. "What about the websites you created that went dormant after the money was paid? What about the fake bios?"

"Most businesses *fail*, Cassie," Annan said. "Especially in the economy of the last few years. I've won some and I've lost some. That's how it goes. Just because a business fails it doesn't mean I'm a criminal for launching it."

"I see," Cassie said to placate him while she scooted out of the booth and stood up. "You'll have to excuse me for a minute. I drank too much coffee this morning, I'm afraid."

"It's in the hallway," he said helpfully.

In the restroom she closed and locked the door and sent a text to Trooper Ron Palmer.

Club Moderne
801 E. Park Ave.
Anaconda

She slipped her phone into her jacket pocket and went back to the booth. As she approached Annan she noticed that he, too, had been on his phone. Again, he set it aside facedown on the table.

Had he checked in with Duplisea to find out how far he was out? If so, the race was on.

She sat down and he surprised her by reaching across the table to hold both of her hands in his. Softly. Warmly. And she didn't pull away.

"Thank you for being so willing to listen," he said. "It means a lot."

She said, "What about the so-called movie about RuthAnne Sommers?"

He smiled and said, "Have you ever dealt with Hollywood types, Cassie? They promise you the moon and you end up with nothing more than a vapor trail. The reason so many of them are rich is because so many projects get financed but never get made. It goes with the territory, I'm afraid."

Then: "Are you wet right now?"

The question came out of the blue. Was he asking about the spilled tea on her lap or . . .

"Candyce Fly committed suicide this week," Cassie said.

Annan blinked and for a moment his grip released on her hands. "I didn't know that. What a tragedy. Do you know the reason?"

"She went broke."

"I'm so sorry if her investment in my firm contributed to that. I really am. But wasn't she also paying the PI from Florida exorbitant fees?"

Cassie pulled away and sat back. She said, "How would you possibly know that unless he told you?"

For the first time since they'd sat down together at the booth, Annan didn't have a quick counterargument. Instead, his face went slack.

"You almost had me going there for a while," she said. "But it's not me you need to convince, Matthew. You'll need to convince a judge and jury when the three ladies you conned testify against you in court."

Cassie checked her watch again, then glanced at the back door.

She said to him, "I think we're done here for now." She gathered her purse close and patted the outside of it while she stood up and faced him. "Everything we discussed is on tape. I'd caution you about trying to flee. Running is a bad look right now."

"You taped me?" he said sadly.

"Yes."

"Is that legal?"

"Yes."

Annan reached out and picked up his primary phone and checked the screen. He was no doubt checking to see if there was a reply from Duplisea, Cassie guessed.

"He was out chasing a Peterbilt truck," she said. "Maybe he's still chasing it."

When Annan looked up he simply looked depressed, she thought. It pulled at her heartstrings even though she knew better.

"It doesn't have to end this way," he said.

"Matthew, I'm single but I'm not rich. So it never really started."

"I'm not who you think I am."

"No," Cassie said, "you're actually worse. We need to have a conversation about what happened to Spengler. And your county sheriff, for that matter."

He looked up at her sharply. "Those aren't on me," he said.

"Until this second I wasn't sure they were linked. But thanks for clearing that up."

Annan slumped back in the booth and rubbed his face with both hands. When he moaned he sounded pathetic, she thought. Also not a good look.

He said, "It's not too late to stop this before it gets much worse."

Cassie was confused. "Stop what?"

He tapped the back of his phone with his fingertips. "You must think I'm stupid," he said. "Don't you think I got the plates run on those two kids who showed up yesterday to work for me?"

Cassie was chilled to the bone and couldn't speak.

"April Pickett and Ben Dewell," Annan said. "They gave me

false names but it took a single phone call to a law enforcement friend to find out who they really are."

He paused and looked up at her before he added: "And where they live."

"No," she whispered. Had Annan diverted Duplisea's return to go to Bozeman instead? Were Ben and April being targeted as they spoke?

"No," she said again. "Leave them out of this . . ."

At that moment the back door was shoved open so hard it struck the wall with a bang.

Undersheriff Doug Duplisea had arrived. His bulk filled the doorway. He gripped the top of his service revolver in its holster.

"It looks like you're coming with me, Miss Dool," he said. He looked angry and no doubt humiliated from his fruitless pursuit of her that morning.

She turned and glanced over her shoulder to see the waitress slip down behind the bar. Cassie knew he had the drop on her and there was no place to run. She was terrified but she was also glad Duplisea was in Anaconda and not Bozeman. Better her than those kids . . .

Then, from outside: "Hey, mister."

She recognized the slurred voice.

"Kyle, *no!*" she cried.

"Hey, mister," Kyle repeated.

Duplisea rolled his eyes and turned around in the doorway. His revolver cleared the holster . . .

BOOM!

The undersheriff staggered back a few steps. He glanced over at Annan. He was confused.

Outside, Cassie saw Kyle eject a spent shell from his 20-gauge shotgun and pump a new one into the receiver. He did it duti-fully with his tongue out. Her readers poked out of his front breast pocket. She'd apparently left them at the diner in Butte and Kyle, being Kyle, had followed her in order to return them.

Bless you, Kyle . . .

Cassie ducked to the side near the booth to both block an exit attempt from Annan and to avoid getting hit from cross fire. At the same time, Duplisea regained his footing and raised his weapon again and pointed it toward Kyle.

There was another *BOOM*. The undersheriff spun a half-turn and crashed to the floor. His chest was a ragged floral bloom of red.

Cassie quickly recovered from her shock and kicked Duplisea's gun away from his twitching hand. She turned on Annan and commanded, "Stay right where you are."

"Cassie," he pleaded, using her name just one more time, "let's be reasonable here."

She pulled the Glock from her purse and trained it on him. "I've shot better men than you before," she said, knowing it probably wasn't true.

A distant siren increased in volume. It was coming from the direction of the interstate.

Then to Kyle: "Put the shotgun down and step away from it. I don't want anyone to think you're an active shooter."

"A what?" Kyle asked.

"Just do it please, Kyle."

Kyle shrugged and lowered his gun to the gravel of the parking lot. He did it gingerly so as not to scratch the stock. The siren got louder. It was just a couple of blocks away.

To Kyle, Cassie mouthed the words, "Thank you."

He smiled awkwardly and gave her two thumbs-up.

twenty-five

✦✦⊙☰✦

"So Kyle is completely cleared?" Cassie asked Tom Wright.

"He's completely cleared," Wright said. "Turns out we not only had your testimony but the bar had a CC camera for the back parking lot. The footage is crappy but there's no doubt Westergaard didn't pull the trigger until Duplisea drew on him. It was self-defense all the way, so we cleared him and sent him back to North Dakota."

"Wonderful," Cassie said, "especially since self-defense is a controversial topic these days."

"Not in Montana, it isn't."

Cassie was a little hurt that Kyle had not stopped by on his way home, but she figured he needed to get back as soon as he could to check on Grandma Lottie. Additionally, she guessed Kyle had been spooked by being questioned. His past experiences with some law enforcement personnel hadn't been good.

They were in Wright's office within the DCI wing of the Montana Department of Justice in the state capital of Helena. Cassie had just arrived, having driven from Bozeman that morning. It was one of her favorite short drives in the state, especially in early June. To her, a "short drive" in Montana was anything under two hours.

The journey had included views of snowcapped mountains of the Bridger, Elkhorn, and Big Belt ranges surrounding her, the banks of the Missouri River bulging with runoff, and the hundreds of newborn calves in the painfully green meadows.

Wright's office itself was the complete opposite of that. It was institutional light blue, claustrophobic, and cheerless—despite the cluster of family photos behind him on his credenza. He had a large family of cherubic children and an attractive wife, she noted.

He swiveled toward her in his chair and said, "You might have heard that Annan is fully cooperating."

"I heard."

"He's blaming everything on Doug Duplisea. And I mean everything."

"Not a surprise. Do you believe him?"

Wright shrugged. "So far, I guess. I'm afraid we don't have any hard evidence otherwise. Annan led my officers to an abandoned mine outside of Butte. That's where we found Spengler's body in the trunk of his car, plus poor Sheriff Westphal's remains. There was also the body of a local named Tim White. Duplisea's prints were on the lock of the mineshaft gate and we found the key in the glove box of his pickup.

"Annan claimed he knew about the mineshaft location because he used to go drinking there with his friends in high school, including Doug Duplisea. Duplisea used to say that if he ever had a body to get rid of he would use that old mine, according to Annan."

Tim, Cassie thought. Tim White.

Tim, Doug, and Matty.

She recalled Lyla's warning: *Watch out for them! If anybody goes missing around this town it's because of one of them or all three of them. Watch out!*

Lyla pretty much had it correct all along, Cassie thought.

"You know," Wright said, "if I were to have to dump a body in Montana I think I'd do it in Butte. There are hundreds of old mines on that hill. Who knows what we'd find if we started digging into all of them?"

"Were all of the victims killed with Duplisea's weapon?" Cassie asked.

"It's too early to say because we don't have the forensics back yet. But I'd bet on it. Except for White. He didn't appear to have any injuries. He likely drowned in the mineshaft, according to the local coroner."

"He was a buddy of Annan's and Duplisea's, from what I understand," Cassie said. "The three of them grew up together."

Wright nodded. "I've heard that, too. White must have gotten crossways with them somehow. Or at least Duplisea."

Wright leaned forward across his desk and clasped his hands. He said to Cassie, "You know I don't have much use for PIs, but you may have saved a life back there in the Club Moderne."

"You mean my own?" she asked.

"Besides your own." He smiled. "We found a prescription bottle in Duplisea's truck for Jillian Westphal, the sheriff's wife. Inside were capsules of pure fentanyl. We think he replaced the contents and that she was next. What a scum he was."

"Why?" Cassie asked. "What did she do to him?"

"She probably asked too many questions about her husband, is my guess. But like a lot of the details of this case, we may never know the whole truth. The only guy who could tell us is dead."

"I can live with that, I think," Cassie said. "What does Annan say about his relationship with Duplisea?"

"Oh, quite a lot as it turns out," Wright said. "He claims Duplisea took twenty percent of everything Annan earned out in the world. Annan said it was protection money and he was forced to pay it."

Wright raised his eyebrows and said, "Another thing. Annan claims that it was Duplisea who researched and targeted the fraud victims using law enforcement resources. We're running diagnostics on the computers in the sheriff's department to see if we can corroborate that. So far, we can't."

"What about Annan's devices?" Cassie asked.

"Annan's phone and home computer were both completely clean. We found nothing on either to prove that he researched the victims on his own. Or, I should say, he was careful to delete any records from them."

Cassie said, "Annan is really smart. I think he kept Duplisea at arm's length so if things went bad he could blame everything on him and walk away. Like he's trying to do now."

"Yeah, I hear you," Wright said. "But there's no doubt the undersheriff was getting paid. We found receipts and deposits. The timing and amounts correspond to what Annan got from each of your women victims.

"So far," Wright said, "we can't connect Annan to the murders. There are no witnesses who are still alive, and his phones—all five of them, I think—show some texting between Annan and Duplisea but nothing incriminating. There are no smoking gun communications. Everything is pretty innocuous and could be explained away. Duplisea was law enforcement, after all. He knew better than to spell things out that could get him in trouble."

Cassie nodded. "I think when they communicated they did it in person. My son and intern saw them together at one point doing exactly that. They knew better than to leave a digital trail of any kind."

"Makes sense."

Cassie said, "I think they were in it together from the jump. It was a criminal racket. Annan was the charmer and Duplisea was the muscle. They worked it all out together and played their parts. They've been doing this kind of thing since they grew up together as pals in Anaconda. They shared the same grudges."

"I suspect you're right," he said. "But we don't have anything to prove that at this point. Annan is good at playing the victim. He comes across as *very* sympathetic."

Cassie smiled. "Let's hope when he goes to trial it's an all-male jury. And believe me, you'll never hear me say that ever again for the rest of my life."

"He got to you a little, then?"

"A little," Cassie said. She hoped she didn't blush.

"Well, you're not the only one," Wright said. "The town is rallying behind him. Since we were able to freeze all of his assets they're doing a big fundraiser to help pay for his legal effort. Apparently, he's a huge philanthropist in Anaconda. He built their new football stadium, he buys equipment for the clinic, he funds the homeless shelter . . . they love him."

"And he loves them," she said. "No one claims he's all bad. That's how he justified what he did. But he's bad *enough*."

"We think so," Wright said. "We think as this investigation continues we'll find more on him. I'll keep you posted."

"Thank you," she said. Then: "What will become of that Copper King mansion he relocated?"

Wright shrugged. "Who knows? It's in legal limbo. Maybe they'll make a museum out of it or something. Or more likely a shrine to Matthew Annan, savior of Anaconda."

Cassie said, "I was wondering if it could be sold with the proceeds going back to the fraud victims."

"Maybe the judge will go for that, but I kind of doubt it."

"He'll become a martyr," Cassie said. "Just like his great-grandfather. I kind of think he'll be okay with that."

After signing her affidavit and attaching the report she'd written about her investigation into Matthew Annan on behalf of Candyce Fly, Cassie looked up and said, "I have another favor to ask you."

Wright moaned. He said, "Can't I wrap this all up first?"

She smiled. Meaning, *no*.

"What?" he asked.

"Do you have friends within the administration of the Montana State Prison? Someone you trust?"

"Do you mean a fellow Mormon?"

"Yes."

"Sure—why?"

"I need to get some unofficial background on a particular CO there," she said. "I need someone to grant me access."

twenty-six

↻➤

SEVEN DAYS AFTER

Cassie occupied a round table with a steel-mesh top in the corner of the visiting area of the Montana State Prison in Deer Lodge. Both the table itself and the bench seats surrounding it were bolted to the polished concrete floor. She was nervous and fidgety.

They'd taken and stored her purse, phone, wristwatch, jewelry, and dignity in one of the battered lockers in the intake lobby that morning. Cassie felt vulnerable and exposed, which she knew was their aim.

The walls were painted off-white and a television with its sound muted showed an afternoon game show. In the corner were small chairs and a box of toys for visiting children. The toys looked dated and dirty, Cassie thought.

A short-sleeved correctional officer sat behind a steel desk against the north wall. He was there to keep an eye on inmate interactions with visitors and to enforce the list of rules printed on a laminated poster taped to the cinder-block wall behind him.

KEEP CONVERSATIONS CIVIL
NO PHYSICAL INTERACTION
NO MORE THAN ONE INMATE PER TABLE UNIT
NO ITEM EXCHANGE
NO EXCEEDING TIME LIMIT

No, no, no, no. Cassie was certain she wouldn't do well in prison, either as a CO or an inmate

The room was largely empty except for two prisoners in identical orange jumpsuits and blue slip-on boat shoes. She observed them furtively because she didn't want to be caught staring.

One inmate was a wiry Causcasian with stringy black hair and a neck tattoo of a fist emerging from his collar gripping a double-bladed knife. He was missing most of his teeth. Across from him was a mousy woman in glasses who seemed painfully shy and needy for him to touch her and hold her hand. They whispered their conversation to each other and when the woman reached across the table to cup his jaw, the CO behind the desk said, "Break it off." Her hand shot back as if she'd touched an electric circuit.

The second inmate was a bulky American Indian with a black braid halfway down his back. His visitors—she guessed—were his parents. The three of them sat wordlessly at his table and stared at their hands. The only time they looked up was when the CO barked at the other man. Then they returned to staring at their hands.

There was a hum and a click and the electronic lock opened on the east door. Cassie looked up to see an inmate enter with a CO a step behind him.

She sized up the inmate as he approached. He looked to be in his mid-sixties. He had longish swept-back ginger hair streaked with silver, a neatly trimmed goatee, and green eyes that sparkled with wry pleasure, as if he was amused by her. His orange jumpsuit was a size too large but the man wore it as if it were a badge of honor. The CO treated the inmate with deference, despite his apparent haughtiness.

The man had a strong resemblance to his younger portrait on the back of his book jackets.

After delivering the inmate to Cassie's table, the CO nodded to her and left to join the CO at the table in an apparent effort to give her and the inmate their privacy.

Cassie stood and extended her hand. "As you probably know, my name is Cassie Dewell."

The inmate reached out and shook. His grip was warm. "Regis Stanhope."

"It's nice to meet you, Mr. Stanhope," she said. "I believe you owe me twenty-five thousand dollars."

Stanhope threw his head back and laughed. He attracted the attention of everyone in the room and the CO behind the desk threw him a scowl.

"I suppose congratulations are in order, Cassie Buzz-Buzz," he said "How, pray tell, did you find me?"

"Sit down and I'll tell you," she said.

Cassie kept her voice low. "I came here today with Agent Tom Wright of the Montana DCI. We've just had a long and very productive conversation with a CO by the name of Tracy Swanson," she said.

"That rat," Stanhope said with a chuckle. "We hate rats in prison, you know."

"Well, he's very intent on keeping his job here," she said. "We made him a deal that we wouldn't inform his supervisor in regard to what he did for you on the outside if he told us everything."

"How did you even get on to him?"

"I'm good at my job," she said. "Isn't that why you hired me in the first place? To try and find you? To find the man who actually wrote the 'Sir Scott's Treasure' poem that started this stupid treasure hunt?"

"It's not stupid," Stanhope said, revealing his incisors. "It's delightful. The treasure hunt has been a source of delight not only for me, but for the world at large."

"I got that right, didn't I?" Cassie asked. "I didn't say you wrote the poem on the menu board in Manhattan. You actually wrote it in here and gave the job to Tracy Swanson to take it and copy it inside the restaurant. Then you sent him to Billings to post the photo of the treasure chest. And you paid Swanson to deliver my retainer so I'd assume you were on the outside all along."

"Is that what Swanson told you?"

"Yes."

"Well, he certainly turned out not to be trustworthy," Stanhope said with regret.

Cassie continued. "The call you made to me came from his cell phone, which you borrowed from him against regulations. Swanson isn't too swift: it was still there on his call register when we looked at it."

"Perhaps I hired the dumbest guard in prison," Stanhope said. "I'm starting to believe that. But I'm not discouraged, not in the least."

"What do you mean?"

"*You* found me," he said. "There can be no denying that. I owe you your bonus fair and square. But based on what you know and how you found me, can your investigation possibly be replicated by one of the treasure hunters? I think not. How likely is it that a treasure hunter will run into the likes of Tracy Swanson? That ship has sailed."

Cassie smiled and said, "One did."

Stanhope's eyebrows shot up in alarm. He wasn't expecting that.

"One did what?" he asked.

"One of the treasure hunters overheard Swanson bragging about what he was going to spend his Sir Scott's money on."

"Who is this person?" he asked.

"That's privileged information."

"I'll pay you for the name. I'll double your bonus."

"No deal," Cassie said.

"There are things you aren't telling me," he said.

"Correct. I'm under no obligation to do so. Now tell me, did you have someone other than Swanson hide the so-called treasure? He swears he didn't do it."

"He didn't," Stanhope said.

"So who did?"

"That's privileged information," he said, mocking her.

"There isn't any treasure, is there? It was all a scam."

"How dare you," he spat. His face was instantly red. "You have no idea what you're talking about. Of *course* there's a hidden treasure. I hid it myself."

Cassie gave him the side-eye. "Sure you did. Where? In the prison yard?"

Stanhope leaned across the table and glared at her. "I hid it myself. It was a week before my unfortunate ... incident. I had planned to post the poem myself but I had to get help later to complete the setup. I assure you there is a treasure and that someday it will be found by clues within the poem itself. And that's the important thing," he said. "It needs to be found based on the clues within the poem—not by discovering my identity."

"I understand," she said. "I heard you the first time you told me that. But I've got questions."

"Go ahead."

"Your three novels did okay but they weren't bestsellers. I may get this wrong from memory but their titles were *The Ides of Ipswich*, *Chronicles of Suffolk*, and *Stories of East Anglia* ..."

"*Tales of East Anglia*," he corrected.

"Fine. Anyway, they got some good reviews and sold modestly here and in the UK. Given that, how did you amass the fortune you supposedly hid?"

"Did you come here to insult me?" he asked. "My books did fine."

"Not three million dollars in gold fine," she said. "I looked them up."

He said, "My fortune, alas, didn't come from my work. You may not know this, but very few authors make fortunes from their work. That's not why we write."

"I've come to understand that," Cassie said, recalling her recent interviews. "So where did the money and treasure come from? How can you prove that it even exists?"

He crossed his arms over his chest. "I don't have to prove anything to you."

"You do if you expect me to stay quiet about finding you."

"That's blackmail."

She nodded. "You could say that. And promising a nonexistent three-million-dollar treasure to innocent dupes could be construed as fraud. I've about had it with men committing fraud lately."

Stanhope stayed still but his eyes shifted to check out the two COs. For the moment, the man at the desk was showing the other something on his phone and neither were looking their direction.

Carefully, without making any sudden movements, Stanhope undid the top button of his jumpsuit and reached inside beneath his left armpit. He came out with a small paper square. He slipped it to Cassie across the table and mouthed, "Don't let them see it."

He looked away while she unfolded the damp square. She really didn't want to touch it but her curiosity got the best of her.

It was faded photo of an open treasure chest leaned against the base of a thick pine tree. Inside the chest were what looked like gold coins, one-ounce bars of gold, and jewels. She wished it hadn't come from his armpit.

"I keep it on my person for inspiration," he said quietly. Then he took it from her, folded it again, and slipped it back.

Swanson sighed. "My second wife was heir to a San Francisco frozen seafood conglomerate. When she died her rather large inheritance went to me. I write to keep my sanity and my curiosity intact, not for profit. But wait until I publish my memoirs. I'm working on them now. *Then* you'll see a bestseller, my dear." His eyes twinkled.

It took her a moment, then she said, "You're going to write a memoir from the point of view of the man who started the treasure hunt."

"A treasure hunt that captivated a nation," he said with a wolfish grin.

"A treasure hunt where five people died trying to find it, and more might add to the body count," Cassie said. "I know personally of a young man who has given up all of his vacation time and weekends trying in vain to find your treasure. He's a very good person who has been through a lot in his life. Now he's wasting the rest of it on your stupid treasure hunt."

"You've got it all wrong," Stanhope said. "I've given him hope. I've given many people something they couldn't find elsewhere: hope and a reason to seek adventure in a staid, increasingly totalitarian society."

"I want you to call it off," Cassie said.

Stanhope laughed and rolled his eyes theatrically. "How could I possibly do that, even if I was so inclined? Look around us. *I'm in prison.* If I 'call it off' the treasure will still be out there and people will still try to find it. I can't exactly rush out there and recover it at the moment."

"Maybe you could send Terry Swanson," Cassie said. "He's done other things for you."

"And it appears he can't keep his mouth shut," Stanhope said sourly. "I'm through with that blabbermouth."

Cassie said, "Send someone else you can trust."

"There's no one I can trust. Not with millions in gold."

"You'll get out in a year or two. How many more people will have died by then?"

"That's not my problem. The world is filled with losers and reprobates and people who just aren't very smart. I can't make people be safe, and I can't save them if they're bound and determined to hurt themselves. I keep saying, over and over, that no one needs to risk their lives finding the treasure. I mean—look at me, Mrs. Dewell.

I'm not exactly a specimen of physical fitness, so therefore I hid the treasure where I could easily access it. I didn't climb into a canyon on ropes or ford a raging river with an eighty-pound box of gold. I put it in a place I easily walked to.

"*It's all in the poem,*" he nearly shouted. "The location is glaringly obvious! And it'll all make for a richer read when I complete my memoirs."

She studied his face as he talked. Cassie could tell that Stanhope was adamant about letting the hunt go on.

She asked, "What is it about discovering your identity that will give away the location of the treasure? Is it something in your novels? Your books are historical fiction and set in England."

"Yes. So what?"

"You told me you didn't want to be discovered because of your writings."

"I said that?"

"You did."

"Well, that was certainly a slip. I shall be more careful in the future."

"So what is it?" she asked again.

He smirked. "That's privileged information."

"Damn you," she said as she smacked the table with the heel of her hand. The action brought the attention of both COs.

"No acting out, miss," the CO behind the desk cautioned.

She motioned to him that she was under control. As she did a thought suddenly hit her. She wished she had her phone to confirm it.

Stanhope apparently noticed her quick change in demeanor and it worried him. He looked around as if preparing to get up and leave. She couldn't stop him. Wright had used up all of his favors, especially getting the interview with Stanhope in the first place. She doubted Stanhope would now be inclined to add her name to his visitor list.

She would never see or talk to the man again. And she'd be shocked if he actually paid her the money he owed her without a fight.

"You owe me twenty-five thousand dollars," she said. "A deal is a deal and my attorney friend assured me it would be considered a legal contract in a court. But I'm sure you don't want to go to court and be exposed, correct?"

Something passed over his eyes. After a beat, he said, "I'll ask my lawyer to send you a check."

"Thank you."

Stanhope placed both of his hands on the table and pushed himself up. "Well," he said, "this has been a nice diversion. You can't imagine how tedious each and every day is in here. The only things that keep me going are hearing news from the treasure hunt and working on my memoir. But this has been nice."

Cassie looked up. "Besides Swanson, am I the only person who knows it was you?" Cassie asked.

"Yes," he said. Then: "Why do you ask?"

Wright was waiting for her in the intake lobby when Cassie emerged from the visitation room. He looked up and said, "You look wrung out."

"Thank you," she said.

"Get anything?"

"Maybe," she said. "I'll tell you about it on the way back."

"I was talking to a couple of the COs," Wright said. "Stanhope is pretty slippery."

"He is," she said as she retrieved her personal items from the locker.

"Is he the poet?"

"I'll get back to you on that," Cassie said as she gestured toward the door to the women's restroom. "Give me a minute."

Inside, she powered up her phone and opened up the web browser. She quickly found the bookseller bibliography site she'd used earlier to find out about Stanhope's published novels that were still available for purchase. But this time she scrolled further down.

"Bingo," she said with triumph.

In the parking lot on the way to Wright's DCI cruiser, Cassie said, "Can you give me a minute to make a call?"

"Sure." He sighed. "We're late as it is to get back to Helena. Might as well be even later."

"Thank you."

Cassie walked toward a brick structure that enclosed Dumpsters. It was far enough away that Wright couldn't overhear.

She called Kyle, who answered on the third ring. He sounded out of breath.

"Hey, Kyle."

"Hey, Cassie. Sorry, I'm working and I stopped to get a Mountain Dew. I left my phone in my truck and I had to run to get to it."

"Kyle, stop everything you're doing and listen to me carefully."

"Wow—okay. I'm listening."

"I'm going to send a web page to your phone. It's a page about a Montana author named Regis Stanhope. When you read it, ignore all the stuff about Ispwich, Suffolk, and East Anglia. Just keep scrolling down."

Cassie recalled the page on her phone and texted it to Kyle.

"Got it?" she asked.

"Yeah. It looks kind of boring."

"It is. But keep scrolling."

She waited. Finally, he said, "Okay, I got to the bottom."

"What does it say?"

"Hmm. It says *Barefoot Wanderer*, 1987—out of print."

"It was his first book when he was barely in his twenties. Now read the subtitle."

Kyle read, "*Barefoot Wanderer: Fly-fishing and Coming of Age on the Waters of Grand Teton National Park*."

"Kyle," Cassie said, "the man who hid the treasure and wrote Sir Scott's poem is Regis Stanhope. *Barefoot Wanderer* is his first book. He didn't want anyone to ever find it."

"How did you ever find him?" Kyle asked.

"You found him, Kyle," she said. "You found him. I just followed up."

After an inordinately long time, Kyle said, "You're telling me I've been looking in the wrong state?"

"That's what I'm telling you."

"My God, Cassie. There aren't that many rivers in the park."

"Find the book, Kyle," she said. "Go to your library and ask for help, or look for it online. There has to be a copy for sale out there somewhere. Then go find that treasure, my friend."

His voice caught when he said, "I'm going to find it, Cassie."

"Call me if you do," she said. "Be careful and give my best to Lottie. And don't tell a soul about this call."

"Are you kidding me?"

twenty-seven

The mid-June morning sun was burning the sequins of dew off the grass as Cassie Dewell merged into traffic on the interstate toward Butte. She wore her best dark suit and polished red cowboy boots and she was prepared to testify at the preliminary hearing for Matthew Annan.

As usual with prosecutors, Cassie thought, the local DA in Butte had overcharged Annan in the hope that at least a few of the counts would stick. The charges included multiple counts of wire fraud, "fraudulent conveyance" in regard to the purchase of property with stolen cash, "instrument made with intent to defraud in the transfer of real property," and other obscure statutes Cassie had never heard of.

Basically, the local DA was on a mission on behalf of the city fathers of Butte to exact revenge on Annan for buying one of the most iconic mansions in the city and moving it to Anaconda and leaving a gaping hole in Copper King Row. It was Butte sticking it to Anaconda one last time, she thought.

Extradition requests for Annan had come from the states of Illinois, New York, California, and Florida on behalf of RuthAnne Sommers, Monica Weatherby, Brooke Alexander, and Daney Tanner. All four victims were scheduled to fly into Montana and testify at the trial as well. Cassie looked forward to meeting them although she wasn't really sure she'd like them personally. Or they, her.

That's when her phone chirped and the screen on the dash said she'd received a text message via Bluetooth. She pressed "*Hear it,*" but there was no audio.

Cassie eased to the shoulder and retrieved her phone.

There was no text message, but there was a photo.

Kyle was smeared with mud and grime but he was grinning almost manically. He was in a dense pine forest with sun-dappled boughs behind him. In his hands he hefted a small open metal chest discolored by weather. Inside, gold coins gleamed in the early morning sun.

Cassie thumped the dashboard with the heel of her hand and cried, *"Yes!"*

Acknowledgments

I'd like to thank those who helped in the creation and completion of this novel. First, the locals in Anaconda and Butte, Montana, who unbeknownst to them were my hosts and tour guides of these two unique locations.

Second, my invaluable first readers: Laurie Box, Becky Reif, Molly Box, and Roxanne Woods. Thanks again.

Kudos to Molly and Prairie Sage Creative of cjbox.net for social media expertise.

It's a sincere pleasure to work with the professionals at St. Martin's Minotaur, including Kelley Ragland, Jennifer Enderlin, Andy Martin, and Hector DeJean.

Ann Rittenberg—thanks for always being in our corner.

C. J. Box
Wyoming, 2021

Dave Neligh Photography, Inc.

C. J. Box is the author of more than thirty books, including the Joe Pickett series and the Cassie Dewell series, and a story collection. His books have been translated into twenty-seven languages. He has won the Edgar, Anthony, Macavity, Gumshoe, and Barry Awards, as well as the French Prix Calibre .38, and has been a Los Angeles Times Book Prize finalist. A Wyoming native, Box has also worked on a ranch and as a small-town newspaper reporter and editor. He's an executive producer of ABC's *Big Sky,* which is based on his Cody Hoyt/Cassie Dewell novels, as well as an executive producer of the Joe Pickett television series for Spectrum Originals. He lives with his wife on their ranch in Wyoming.

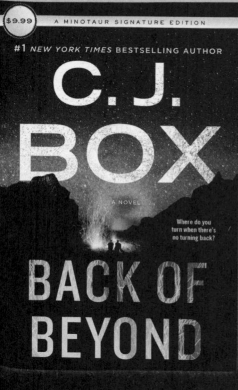